MW01124859

Rogue Wolves

Rogue Wolves

The Redaction Chronicles Book 3

James Quinn

Copyright (C) 2018 James Quinn

Layout design and Copyright (C) 2019 by Next Chapter

Published 2019 by Terminal Velocity – A Next Chapter Imprint

Edited by Lorna Read

Cover art by http://www.thecovercollection.com/

This book is a work of fiction. Names, characters, places, and incidents are the product of the author's imagination or are used fictitiously. Any resemblance to actual events, locales, or persons, living or dead, is purely coincidental.

All rights reserved. No part of this book may be reproduced or transmitted in any form or by any means, electronic or mechanical, including photocopying, recording, or by any information storage and retrieval system, without the author's permission.

Also by James Quinn

For Niki,
Without whom the brave and beautiful Eunice 'Nikita' Brown would
not exist.
xxx

"We penetrated deeper and deeper into the heart of darkness"
Joseph Conrad, Heart of Darkness

CLASSIFIED: TOP SECRET

OPERATIONAL/INTELLIGENCE/SOURCE – INTERNAL TERMI-
NOLOGY PROTOCOLS/2846457

Rogue Wolf: an operative, agent or source that has violated orders
and is classed as out of control by their parent intelligence network.
Redaction: terminology used to describe the assassination and state-
sanctioned killing of enemy operatives, extremists and rogue agents.

———

Prologue

Antigua, Caribbean – September 1965

The diver had spent the past week swimming along the same stretch of the Antiguan coastline. It was a beautiful stretch; clear waters, perfect vacation brochure beaches, quiet atmosphere. It was the perfect place to relax and maybe even to retire to. One day...

And why not? he was older now, with the free time and resources to be able to do that. Maybe he would retire here completely, leave the USA behind once and for all. Maybe write a novel here? Be like that Fleming guy and write spy stories. Well, they did say write what you know about. Didn't they?

Richard Higgins had once been one of the CIA's shining stars — in fact, he had risen to the lofty heights of Assistant to the Deputy Director of Operations. He had been a Cold Warrior of the old school. A spy's spy.

Until the fall....

To him, the fall was born out of duty and the desire to do the right thing. Some people, he was sure, viewed it as an act of revenge. And while many may have secretly sympathised with him, as professionals, they would cast a disapproving eye.

Richard Higgins lifted his body out of the warm water and looked around at the coastline. There was nothing for miles, only tranquillity and peace. The only other 'neighbour' was a small sailing boat, bobbing about, anchored a mile away in the distance. It was seemingly empty.

Should he go for another swim? Perhaps a bit further this time, maybe out towards the edge of the reef. Why not? Swimming was part of his daily exercise regime while he vacationed here. He jumped in the water again, feeling it swirl around his body and began to swim away from the shore with powerful strokes.

The 'fall' had been forced upon him. The illegal operation that he had been a part of had come unstuck, the sources blown and the operation had come to the attention of the CIA. Higgins was left between a rock and a hard place.

He had been called in and grilled by the interrogators from the Agency's Office of Security. He had held out as long as he could but it was a wasted effort. They already knew everything, anyway. It was a cluster-fuck.

Then, while sitting in his interrogation room, at the 'Farm', the CIA's secure compound in Virginia, the door had opened and in had walked his erstwhile boss, the Deputy Director of Central Intelligence, Roy Webster. Webster was the second in command of the entire Agency, answering only to the Director of Central Intelligence himself.

He had hated Webster on sight.

Higgins had been given a choice. Tell us what you know and we let you retire gracefully and with full pension. Fuck us about and you'll spend the rest of your life in the Penitentiary.

So of course he did as he was told. Really, he had no choice. His accomplices were dead and the illegal operation was blown sky-high. Better to retire with a few dollars to spend and try to rebuild his life post-Agency than to fight for a losing cause. He signed the usual confidentiality agreement stating that if he ever spoke out and embarrassed the CIA or the American government, he would be buried in the deepest and darkest hole they could find.

So his life over the past four months had consisted of long walks, vacations and very little else. But he was okay, he could adapt... eventually.

He had made it out to the farthest part from the beach; any further and he would be hitting the open ocean. For a man in his sixties, Higgins was wise enough to know his physical limitations and he decided to turn back, satisfied that for today, at least, his physical exercise was complete. Besides, it was nearly lunchtime and all this exercise had made him ravenous.

It was when he was halfway back that he suddenly felt a huge tug on his leg, causing him to be pulled beneath the waves. His first thought was shark attack! But even in the shock of the moment, his mind was aware enough to know that there was no pain in his leg from a shark bite, no blood, nothing. It was as if he had been grabbed by a giant octopus.

The shock of suddenly being pulled beneath the waves by this strong force made him gasp involuntarily and, as a consequence, he pulled a large amount of water into his lungs. He started to panic, his arms flailing, and his legs desperately trying to kick out as he was sucked down into the depths.

But he couldn't kick out. Whatever it was that had him was incredibly strong and was pulling him further and further down. He looked around, letting his eyes acclimatise to being underwater, trying to see what kind of beast was determined to drag him down to a watery grave. He blinked and saw, not a monster of the ocean, but a human form wearing goggles, breathing apparatus and flippers.

A frogman!

The eyes behind the mask were invisible and the panicked reflection of Richard Higgins was the only thing that shone in them. The frogman was huge, strong, and powerful. He took a hold further up Higgins's legs, so that he had both of them wrapped up in one strong arm, restricting the panicking man's attempts to swim back to the surface.

The only thing that Higgins could do now was to flail his arms to try to give himself some power. But his strength was ebbing, he was worn out, the last trickles of adrenaline had left his system and his body's oxygen reserves were almost zero.

The frogman, aware of Higgins's situation, jerked on his body once more and began to pull him down towards the ocean floor. Once they had reached the bottom, and with Higgins exhausted, the huge frogman clamped one powerful hand around Higgins's throat and pushed him down on his back, onto the ocean floor.

Higgins tried to gather up a last ounce of strength to fight back, but he knew it was useless. The frogman's hand was holding him in place, choking him, knowing that it would be mere seconds before death would come for his victim.

The frogman continued to press down, putting his full weight onto the man's body. Higgins bucked and kicked a few more times, then, as his body went limp, the frogman began to relax the pressure. He knew that as soon as he released his grip on the dead man's throat, the body would start to rise to the surface. The frogman estimated that the dead man would be found washed up on the beach further down the coast at the next turning of the tide.

And then it was done. The frogman let go and simply swam away in a different direction, leaving the drowned corpse to its own devices.

Almost a mile away, the frogman climbed out of the water and into his little rowing boat that he had anchored up the coast. He stood to his full height of just over six foot five and stripped off his diving gear, wetsuit and goggles. Then he dried himself off and put on shorts, deck shoes, short-sleeved shirt and sunglasses. He had transformed himself into just another vacationer.

His task, as requested by the CIA, was complete. It was the easiest million dollars that he had earned in a long time. He had been given the contract and had almost smiled at how easy it would be. No need for weapons, ammunition or any of the other tools of covert assassination. No, not this time. All that was needed was timing and pure brute strength. And he had that in spades.

His other great skill was that he was able to make organised murder look like either an accident or natural causes. In this case, the body of the dead man would be found and it would be assumed that he had simply swum out too far and drowned, or had a heart attack.

He cared not.

But what he did care about was *who* he had killed today.

The Agency had informed him that his target was a low-level agent who had blown an operation in Europe and needed to be removed. The name had been Phillip John, an American black market dealer in Berlin. But the moment that he had seen the photograph of his target, he knew instantly who the man really was. He knew because it was his job to know and that was why he was the best in the business.

The target had been the Assistant to the DDO, Richard Higgins. The CIA had ordered the murder of one of its own senior officers. Now, that was a useful piece of intelligence that he had acquired... very useful indeed. Who knew, maybe one day he would be able to use that snippet of information for his own gain.

But for now, he would store it in his vast memory, along with all the other useable intelligence that he had of the assassinations, espionage and general skulduggery that he had performed for the great and the good of the secret intelligence war.

Chapter One

Palais de la Méditerranée Casino, Nice – March 1973

The casino at 3 a.m. was a subdued bustle of activity, tension and devil-may-care opportunity for the rich and powerful of Nice. It was half empty, the frivolous players having long ago retired to their hotels, suites and villas and only the most steadfast gamblers still remained.

It was a world that Jack 'Gorilla' Grant had skirted around the edges of many times in his life, but had never belonged to and probably never would. In truth, he had no desire to, either. To him, being here dressed in dinner jacket and black tie in the early hours of the morning was just a job, nothing more. It was certainly not a place he would want to frequent by choice. In many ways, he regarded himself as something of an inverted snob.

And what a job it was! He sipped at his glass of heavily watered down Black Label and turned his attention to the centre roulette table, one of six ornate tables that made up the main room. There was the usual assortment of old gamblers and losers, once-rich aristocrats now hoping to reclaim their former fortunes by luck and chance. But it was the man at the head of the centre table that drew the eye.

He was of Hungarian descent, corpulent and middle-aged. His tie had been loosened and, even at this distance, it was obvious that he was sweating beneath the fine cut of his expensive suit. And while his face smiled openly, his eyes had the dead look of a midnight torturer.

Scattered about at various points in the vicinity were the Hungarian's bodyguard team. They did nothing to blend in and, in Gorilla's not so humble opinion, a blind man could have spotted them a mile away. Gorilla thought the protection team were flagging. He knew that they had been on the go for several days now on their entertainment jaunt to the South of France. For them, it had been a whirlwind of excursions, lunch dates followed by hours of hanging around the hotel of the 'Principal', and then off out again for dinner at one of the most exclusive restaurants in Nice, before finally spending the last three nights at the casino. Add in the odd French hooker and the Hungarian kept his security detail on pretty much a full-time itinerary.

Up until recently, the Hungarian had been a colonel in his country's security apparatus, but a recent defection to the French Secret Service, along with a host of intelligence 'product' that he had brought with him, had turned him into the SDECE's new best friend.

Gorilla had been assigned this job several days early, presumably after the Hungarian had spent weeks locked away with his case officers, being de-briefed somewhere. This was the Hungarian's treat for being a good boy. Grant wasn't part of the 'official' protection team. The Hungarian's bodyguards had been supplied by the DST, the French internal Security Service. Gorilla thought that they looked sloppy and off their game, too busy chatting, preening themselves and being distracted by every woman that walked across the casino floor. Well, they were French after all.

Gorilla was there as the eyes and ears of the French Secret Service, the SDECE. They needed a good man on point, able to keep an eye out should things get a bit violent and he was the contract man that people came to when things got unpleasant. He was also deniable if anything went wrong.

The bodyguards and the Hungarian didn't even know of his existence. He was doing what he was good at, keeping out of sight, staying hidden and watching the scene with his gunman's eyes. In the trade, Gorilla's role was known as protective surveillance. If anything went down, the bodyguards would be there to whisk their VIP away to safety and protect him – or take a bullet for him.

Gorilla, on the other hand, was there to run interference and do the killing of the assassin, quietly and unofficially, then disappear into the shadows once more. Beneath his jacket he had an official SDECE identification card in a false name and a 9mm Heckler & Koch P9 semi-automatic pistol.

He had a perfect vantage point on the upper balcony, with a clear view of the gaming tables and the patrons of the casino. He could see the winners, the losers, the grifters and the hookers, all keen to latch onto the gentleman who had just had a big win. From a professional point of view, it was unparalleled. He had his back to the wall, perfect vision on the access and entry points, and if, God forbid, he should have to draw and fire, he had a perfect sniper point to take anyone down.

But for now, everything looked normal. The gamblers were gambling, the bodyguards were pretty much switched off and the Principal looked happy, especially now that his 'date' for the evening, a tall, lithe blonde woman in her thirties, was snaking her arms around his waist in a seductive way.

Gorilla took one more sip of his drink. It was good, but it would be the only one he would have tonight. Alcohol slowed you down, made your reactions foggy and, in Gorilla's line of work, seconds counted. Gorilla's mantra had always been that seconds could be the difference between a bullet in your head, or in the enemy's head.

He glanced down as the cheer from the main table filled the subdued atmosphere of the room. Evidently the Hungarian had just won big! He was clapping his hands together like a fat child about to be let loose on a cake. The blonde hooker had slithered her way around to his front and was kissing him while his hands were running over her ass.

He took a last sip at his drink and reflected on his working career. Over the past few years, things had gone well for Jack 'Gorilla' Grant. He had been recruited by the French several years earlier, after a series of prolonged meetings over many months, to work for them as a contract agent. He wasn't a full-time staffer, there was no way that the SDECE hierarchy would allow that, but for an experienced field agent and Redactor like Gorilla Grant, there were always rules that could be bent, if not broken, to ensure that he was on board.

His reputation as an expert small arms specialist had preceded him and the French were always involved in some kind of skulduggery where an experienced assassin was needed. So far, it had been an interesting three years for him. He had an apartment in Paris, the pay was good and the 'jobs' were interesting, to say the least.

He returned to his chore of scanning the crowd once more and observing his VIP for the night. It was then that it happened. And later, when his senses had returned to him and he was able to analyse the events clearly, he remembered that it was when the Hungarian threw his cards down on the gaming table that the event happened.

Because, at that exact moment, the explosives beneath the gaming tables in the casino all detonated at the same time. There was the deafening *crump* of the explosion, then the numerous blast waves, a brief smell of airborne chemicals from the *plastique...* and then the screaming started.

Up on the balcony, the blast had shattered the cocktail bar and had thrown Gorilla backwards, knocking a nearby table over onto him. But even in the fugue from the blast, he was still professional enough to roll with the shockwave and have his weapon drawn and up, looking for targets.

He rolled onto the flat of his stomach, the upturned table offering cover and concealment for now. He flicked off the safety and kept his finger off the trigger until he saw a possible target. His ears were ringing still and the smell of smoke and burning flesh was nauseating. He could just make out the brutalised remains of the cocktail waiter and barman who had served him only moments before.

Ignoring the scene of horror mere feet away, he forced himself to snake forward on his belly to peer down at the charnel house that lay beneath him. It was a maelstrom of bodies and blood. The explosives, while not large, had done enough damage in a small space to decimate the majority of the patrons of the casino. A woman in a blue cocktail dress had lost most of her lower limbs and was screaming, a tall black man was spread-eagled across a chair, clearly dead, his face peppered with metal. Elsewhere, bodies were strewn at unnatural and ugly angles.

Then, at the far end of the room, the main doors to the gaming room slowly opened, causing the smoke to billow upwards in the draught. It was a dramatic entrance, almost biblical in its grandeur, thought Gorilla. He watched as three killers, armed with stubby-looking machine-pistols, moved in formation, spreading out across what was left of the large gaming room. Gorilla noted with a professional eye that they looked alert and precise. One man was guarding the exit door, ready to move or kill, while the others scattered around the room, looking for any survivors, fingers off their triggers but barrels pointed and ready.

Then, through the black smoke of the fire, another figure emerged. One that was tall, slender and masculine and, like his cohorts, dressed in an expensive business suit. His face was covered in a black balaclava which completely hid his identity and in his hand he held a Russian-made Tokarev pistol.

He gave a murmured order to his tame gunmen and they set about moving among the dying and the wounded – executing them one by one. Single bangs reverberated around the room, followed by screams, followed by more shots.

The tall figure carefully made his way through the abattoir of bodies until he reached what was left of the centre gaming table. He reached down with one leather-gloved hand and lifted back a quarter of the wooden frame. Beneath it, disfigured but still very much alive, was the body of the Hungarian. The man was panting deeply; his body was hyperventilating and his clothes were covered in the blood and fleshy remains of his blonde escort. The hooker had taken the brunt of the blast.

The tall figure crouched down and carefully, almost lovingly, wiped away with a gloved finger a smear of blood that had coagulated in the Hungarian's eye.

"I... I told them nothing. I swear..." said the Hungarian, through blood-encrusted lips.

The assassin gazed down at the burnt and broken man and said clearly, "Colonel, you did well to survive our little booby-traps. However, it is of no consequence. To betray me is to court death... and death has found you."

There was a moment of understanding on the Hungarian's face. The massacre in the casino had been carried out purely in order to get near to him and kill him. The assassin took a small, match-box-sized device from his jacket pocket and carefully placed it onto the Hungarian's forehead. He then squeezed the side of the box to activate the device and stood well back. The amount of explosives inside the box was small, minimal; it wouldn't even have blasted open a lock on a door.

But against a human head it was devastating. One moment the Hungarian was staring back at his killer in horror, the next, there was a *pop* and the Hungarian's head had blown apart, leaving a bloody pulp from the neck up.

Game on, thought Gorilla, as he raised his weapon, took a bead on the nearest gunman below him and fired, taking him out with a single, clean head shot. The killer dropped. Gorilla quickly turned his aim to the man nearest to the doors. The H&K barked three more times as he put rounds into the killer's chest.

The final gunman was in position behind a marble pillar, but, with the execution of his team members, he had quickly sprung into action, darting for cover. It was only the tall assassin who remained stock still. He simply raised his weapon and pointed it in the direction of where the shots from the balcony had been fired from. He held his fire as, from that position, he wouldn't have been able to see the person shooting down on him anyway. Instead, he simply held the weapon in place, finger ready on the trigger in case a target presented itself.

He looks like he doesn't care if he could be killed or not. That's some control, reflected Gorilla. Seconds later, he heard the heavy pounding of footsteps on the staircase that led to the upper balcony.

Gorilla knew what was coming. He was ready. He simply rolled onto his back, braced his feet against the floor, knees bent, and punched out the H&K two-handed along the length of his body, between the 'V' made by his thighs. His trigger finger was ready.

A figure wearing sunglasses and business suit emerged at speed towards the top of the staircase. Gorilla just had enough time to make out the shape of an unidentified machine-pistol before he fired, taking out the front of the gunman's cranium. The killer slithered to the floor and Gorilla heard the sickening thuds of his body rolling slowly back down the staircase.

With the last gunman down, Gorilla rolled onto his stomach, then nimbly jerked his body up so that he was kneeling, protected behind the stone balustrade. He risked a glance and just in time caught the back of the tall assassin moving out through the service exit. As an afterthought, the man discarded the balaclava over his shoulder and went on his way, out into the night.

Gorilla Grant was up and running, hitting the staircase, taking the steps three at a time, one hand guiding him on the handrail and one hand holding the H&K out front as a precaution. He hit the lower floor running, dodging in and out of the bodies and heading for the same service exit that the assassin had used. He shoulder-barged the exterior door open, his weapon up and searching for targets.

The service exit led out into a side street at the rear of the Casino. He led with his pistol up and ready, scanning the dark street ahead of him. Nothing. Gorilla moved quickly, expertly, knowing that time was of the essence here. He searched the corners of the adjacent doorways, but again, nothing.

He had a simple choice – left or right? The right led into a warren of side streets that made up the bulk of the buildings in the centre of Nice. The left led to the seafront and the beach. His reasoning told him that it should be to the right. After all, the assassin could get lost in the mazelike streets relatively easily, especially in the dark. But... there was something nagging at him. Call it a gut instinct, and Gorilla Grant liked gut instincts; they had kept him alive on many occasions.

He paused for a second, slowed his breathing and listened calmly. Nothing... nothing.... nothing... and then there it was – footsteps moving at speed. In the distance for sure, faint, but heading off to his left, to the beach, to an escape route.

His instincts took over immediately. He removed the old magazine from the H&K and slammed in a full one. A quick check to ensure that the weapon had a round in the chamber and he was off, running as fast as he could, determined to catch his quarry.

The speedboat that was waiting for the assassin was a Phantom Venom 4-seater. It was small and it was fast and Gorilla knew that if the tall assassin reached his escape vessel, he would be gone within seconds.

Gorilla had made it to the end of the dark side street and he burst onto the brightly lit main seafront. The first thing that he was aware of was the small number of passers-by coming to look at the smoke drifting up from the casino windows and, in the distance, the blare of sirens. The second thing was the dead DST bodyguards strewn over the official vehicles. Then his eyes sought out his target, the tall assassin. The man, his features still hidden to Gorilla, was walking calmly and purposefully down onto the beach and towards the waiting speedboat that was bobbing in the surf.

No fucking way, sunshine, thought Gorilla. *You may think you have control of this, but I'm here to spoil your day.*

Gorilla sprinted across the road, ignoring the late-night revellers who gawped at the sight of an armed man running at night, and jumped down onto the sand no more than twenty feet away from the assassin. Gorilla had the H&K P9 up and aimed. He had the back of the unknown assassin in his sights. He was lined up and ready when suddenly, the assassin did the strangest thing. It was almost as if he knew that Gorilla was there – almost as if he was expecting him. The assassin turned and threw what Gorilla thought was a grenade.

Gorilla instinctively flinched and dived off to the side, landing hard on the sand, trying to avoid the inevitable shrapnel from the explosion. But this was no grenade that could kill and maim. At the last minute, Gorilla was aware of a small black object, the size of a soup can, landing mere feet away from him. Then instantly, there was a loud bang and a flash of blinding white light and, for the second time that night, Gorilla Grant's hearing and senses were temporarily knocked out. It was a stun grenade; non-lethal but effective, designed to disorientate, nothing more.

Seconds later, the tall figure was standing over him, a silhouette against the white of the moon. The voice, when it spoke, was surprisingly deep, cultured and accented, like that of a European gentleman addressing an underling. Its tone was kind but authoritative.

"I understand that *you* are the new *me*?" said the assassin.

Gorilla, his hearing starting to return but still fading in and out, managed to make out the words, "the new me". What did that mean? He flicked his head around and saw his H&K P9 lying on the sand next to him. If he was fast, he could reach it. He felt sure he could. He could end this now!

"I don't take too kindly to people trying to take my crown. It has been earned over many years and it is not for you to take, Gorilla Grant," said the assassin. Gorilla inched his hand along in the sand… inches away from the pistol… within reach, really… but his eyes never left the outline of the tall man standing above him.

"Young upstarts must be taught a lesson. So here, let me be your teacher for tonight."

The shot was fast and literally came out of nowhere. Gorilla had been aware of the flicking of the elbows, a single flash as the gun barked, and then the pain in his hand. The pain was searing and he lost his mind and howled – whether in fury or agony, even he did not know. His *hand*! The bastard had put a 9mm sized hole in the back of his hand! Gorilla knew instantly what that meant. Small arms specialists like him with mangled hands were done, over, retired. Dead.

Through tear-filled eyes, he glared at the assassin above him. "Come on, you bastard, just finish it. You've taken my hand so finish me off for good. Bullet to the head. Just get on with it," said Gorilla, snarling.

The assassin stared for a moment longer, as if unsure what to do, then lowered the gun and slipped it beneath his jacket. He remained staring down at his prey, considering the bloodstained man before him. The moment of calm was broken by the inevitable blare of police and ambulance sirens in the streets above, heading to the carnage at the casino. The assassin picked up the discarded H&K P9 and threw it wildly behind him, out into the surf.

"Try to follow me and you die, Grant. You have my word on that," he warned.

Then slowly, calmly, he began to walk out into the surf, the water lapping around his waist as he reached the boat. A second figure rose and held out a hand, hoisting the assassin over the side and into the body of the vessel. There was a gunning of the engines as it started to move away from the shore. The figure of the assassin stood proud, unafraid and in silhouette against the dark moonlit night.

Why didn't he kill me? wondered Gorilla. He had no answers. All he had was agonising pain and the realisation that he had been bested. He could do no more than watch as the speedboat began to gather pace and within seconds, it had disappeared into the night.

Chapter Two

LeGrand Clinic, Switzerland – July, 1973

The LeGrand Clinic was ideally nestled amidst the breathtaking mountains and basked in the clean air of the Swiss Alps. It was a private clinic that offered in its literature, 'the best in top musculoskeletal rehabilitation, healthy aging and holistic repair'. It was one of the finest private hospitals on the planet and its clientele were composed of the rich and the privileged who paid for exclusivity and cutting-edge medical treatment.

The fifty room private clinic (complete with state-of-the-art hospital facilities) boasted a Five Star restaurant, well equipped fitness room and a movie theatre and was set amid well-manicured lawns complete with heated swimming pools. In the background, the magnificent snow-crested Alps stood like a guardian to protect the recovering patients. It was a relaxing haven in an otherwise turbulent world and all serviced by an attentive and professional staff.

Jack Grant sat on the open-air terrace, wrapped in a quilted winter ski jacket. LeGrand staff had provided all of these (for a fee) to ensure the safety and comfort of the clinic's clients. A half drunk cup of dark roasted coffee sat on the table before him. His mirrored sunglasses reflected the vista of the nearby mountains and his stillness could have appeared unnerving to the casual observer. He looked like a wealthy businessman taking a moment to reflect upon his recent medical misfortunes, but glad in the knowledge that he had found sanctuary at the LeGrand.

In truth, he was bored. Jesus, this place was numbing his brain!

The past four months had been an exercise in frustration for him. Since his last mission that had ended with the shootout on the beach in Nice, Jack Grant had been mothballed by the SDECE. As far as the French were concerned, he was a busted contract agent – literally and figuratively. His gun hand was shot to hell, hence the series of operations and subsequent physical therapy here at the LeGrand, and he suspected that the reason that they had kept him 'out of the way', here in the clinic in the Alps, was because they were seeing if he had lost his nerve. They wanted to see if the Gorilla was a man who could still offer them something.

The only good thing was that the French had agreed to pick up the tab and get him fixed up with the best surgeons in Europe. They obviously still rated the Gorilla's worth in that sense. After all, every agent has a fuck-up from time to time. It's normal; it's part of the game. The most important thing is that they can come back from it. After all, a gunman and intelligence agent who can't do the job any more would quickly find himself out of work... or worse.

There was no retirement plan in this game, no later life benefits. You worked and worked and retired under your own steam, or you ended up dead. Not that he was planning on retiring any time soon; he had too many good years left in him, busted gun hand or not. And he certainly wasn't planning on leaving the business in a wooden box, either.

He drained the last of his coffee and got to his feet. He had had enough of staring at fucking mountains for one day, so he decided to walk across the gardens and back to his suite. He took his time and ambled. He was in no hurry to return to his luxury room overlooking a stream. In a very real sense, it had become his cell. He felt trapped here and wanted to get back to his own life, his own apartment in Paris… to get back to the work he did best.

He spoke to his daughter twice a week, calling her private boarding school in Hampshire. Since his sister had passed away two years ago, Katy had been even more determined to have her father, her family, around her as much as she could. Grant had stepped up to the mark and between them, they had reached a happy medium. It wasn't perfect, and it wasn't the life that he truly wanted for her but, for the moment, it worked.

Katy still thought that her father was an executive for one of the big oil companies, travelling all over the world, and he was happy to let her carry on believing that. They had the odd weekend away at the end of term, sometimes at his apartment in Paris, sometimes over to the USA, occasionally to Spain for a beach break.

He was extremely proud of her and always enquired after how she was doing at school, what she liked, who her friends were. So far, her big things were science, David Bowie and horse-riding, but not necessarily in that order of importance. They had formed a bond over recent years that he never thought would have been possible; the gruff, world-weary dad and the pretty thirteen-year-old. God, he missed her.

He walked past the reception, nodded to the receptionist and glanced over several brochures in the card holder. Apparently, a Card Club was being held that night – jeez! He was seriously thinking about organising an escape club to see if they could make it over the border!

A few more nods to the 'inmates' and then he climbed the immaculately vacuumed staircase to his room. It was that time of the day when guests were out walking in the hills, strolling in the grounds or visiting their medical practitioners in the clinic, so, for Grant, it was a peaceful time when he didn't have to communicate with people for communication's sake.

As he approached the door to his suite, his sharp, trained eyes noticed that something was amiss. He stood in front of the classically furnished white door and inspected its edges. His eyes stopped upon the corner by the hinge. The small piece of tape that he had fixed to the edge of the door was snapped. It was his own private version of an intruder alarm. He would always fix it in place after the housekeeping staff had completed the daily round of laundry, making the bed and cleaning. So, by 8.30 a.m., the 'intruder alarm' was always in place. And so far, in all of his time here, it had never been broken. Until today.

His hand instinctively reached for the pistol that wasn't there, either on his hip or in the shoulder holster underneath his arm. He scolded himself and clenched his fist in anger. He knew that something wasn't right. Was it an old operation that had come back to haunt him? Was the SDECE's security leaky and the enemy had finally penetrated it to eliminate one of their best operatives? Whoever it was, they had made a clumsy attempt at entering and had been found wanting. Well, bad news for them!

He placed the key in the lock and readied himself to take down whatever was waiting for him in the room. As the key turned, his hand grabbed the handle as he simultaneously pulled and pushed. He burst in, key in his hand, ready to flail and slash and stab.

The room was as he had left it that morning; neat, tidy and with the panoramic vista of the mountains that always amazed him. Except... except for the seated figure outlined against this dramatic backdrop, who said, with just a touch of mischief in his tone, "Ah. I've been expecting you, Gorilla Grant."

Chapter Three

"You know, we wouldn't do this for just anyone."

Jack Grant always thought that the man had the look of a French Dean Martin about him, that smooth and easygoing manner wrapped up in an urbane and charming persona. No wonder the women fell at this guy's feet. He was the epitome of the cultured French intelligence officer.

Paul Sassi was anything but ordinary. A former Major in the 3rd Foreign Parachute Battalion, he had fought against the OAS in Algeria and was now a senior officer of the SDECE's Action Service. His department's responsibility was running a series of contract 'action agents' for the French Service – all at arm's length. You wanted a deniable job doing, Sassi's unit could get you the man or the woman. Sassi was the man who had personally recruited Gorilla Grant and had run him as an agent for the past three years.

Sassi was sat waiting, his back to the window and the Alps framed in the background. He causally tossed a glossy magazine that he had been flicking through onto the glass coffee table in front of him. "Almost four month's convalescence, all expenses paid, the best surgeons in

Europe… It shows you how much we value you, Jack. How's the hand mending?" said Sassi, his voice smooth and welcoming.

For an answer, Grant opened and closed his hand slowly, wincing as he did so, his discomfort evident. Even after all these months of surgery and physical therapy, he still couldn't bring all the fingers together at the same time. It was like watching a windup toy slowing down. It was slow and clumsy.

The assassin's bullet had entered the back of his hand just below his index finger, close to the web space of the thumb, severely damaging the radial nerve. It had only been by a miracle of a few millimetres that it hadn't severed it completely. A centimetre to the left and the damage would have been beyond repair. The surgeon had told him that a direct hit to the radial would have resulted in loss of feeling and loss of grip strength, and in that statement Grant knew that would mean he would never be able to hold a gun or a blade with that hand ever again.

Following the surgery on his hand, he had been immobilized in a cast-type splint for a further eight weeks. That had been the easy part. What had come next was torture. Rehab had taken a further five weeks.

Three times a week, his rehabilitation had consisted of working with the physical therapy staff, who would move the joints to help him make a fist and straighten it out again, as well as opening and closing the fingers. He worked on grip strength, squeezing a ball, putty, and then moved onto fine motor skills, picking up specific objects with finger and thumb. His current forte was using chopsticks, something that he had never been able to do effectively in the past.

His regular Physical Therapist, a pretty blonde girl with a West Virginia drawl, called Courtney, told him that PT didn't stand for Physical Therapy – "It really stands, Mr Grant, for Pain and Torture." Judging by the regular sharp intakes of breath as she manipulated his hand, he could agree with that.

Sassi looked over at him and nodded, concern etched upon his face. No case officer likes to see one of his best men incapacitated. Grant sat down on the leather sofa in the middle of his suite and sighed. "They tell me that I will be able to use it in time, but that it will never have the fine motor skills that it had before the bullet tore it up."

"You need anything?" asked Sassi.

Grant nodded. He knew what he had to do. Jack Grant had quickly come to the shattering realisation that he would never be able to shoot with his right hand, his natural hand, competently ever again. For a man of his skills and reputation, it was the same as an opera singer being struck dumb. "I need to retrain, Paul."

Sassi looked confused and swung an arm out expansively, gesticulating at the luxury location around them. "*Merde*, Jack, you have the best of everything here. We've given you top rate surgeons and the best physical therapists…"

"I don't mean that."

Sassi paused and let Grant's serious tone sink in. "Okay. Explain."

"I need to be operational again. It's who I am, what I do. What I'm good at. But even I know that *this*…" he held up his hand, "is beyond hope."

Sassi had to admit that while Gorilla Grant had been an exceptional intelligence operative while he had been under SDECE control, it was his skills as a paid assassin that he was valued for the most. Sassi had been coming under increasing pressure from his senior command at the French Secret Service to cut the little Englishman loose. "What is one Englishman who can fire a pistol?" they argued. "Any bloody fool can pull a trigger, damn it, Sassi!"

But Paul Sassi had stood his ground and fought for his agent. The trouble was, the voices were getting louder and more vehement and he was not sure how much longer he could keep his top gunman safely tucked away in this mountain retreat before matters were taken out of his hands. He needed Gorilla Grant back working or he would be 'retired'.

"Okay, I'll ask again. What do you have in mind and what do you need?"

So Gorilla told him.

Sassi looked at him, wide-eyed and not a little sceptically. "And you think that you can do this?"

"I'll have to. I don't have any other options," said Grant. "What about getting operational again?"

Sassi stood and smiled. "One thing at a time, *mon ami!* Let's not try to run before we can walk. I'll get you what you want. You just be ready and waiting."

A week later, a parcel arrived by special courier and was delivered to his suite. Grant had been expecting it for days. He knew what it contained and was eager to get to work.

In the seven days since he had last seen Sassi, Grant had upped his training regime. He still kept his PT work for his injured hand, Courtney was as strict as always so he had no choice, but he also began to introduce a private regime to strengthen his left hand.

But subterfuge came naturally to Jack Grant. He needed to be strong again and, in order to do that, he needed to feel a modicum of pain. Over the past week he had carefully, and out of the vision of Miss Courtney, flushed away the painkillers that he had been taking for the past few months. He needed them out of his system, needed to wean himself off them. He would rather have the pain than the numbness that the drugs provided. Drugs slowed your reactions down and made you sloppy. He wanted to be his own man again.

Inside the parcel from Sassi was a Beretta 1923 which had never been one of Grant's favourite guns, even with a good shooting hand. But that in itself was no problem. He reasoned that if he could make his new shooting method work with a gun he hated, he could more than make it work with a gun he was comfortable with.

Along with the pistol came two spare magazines, a cleaning kit, plastic holster and a dozen boxes of 9mm ammunition. There was also a little private gift from Sassi; a box of Cohiba Cuban cigars.

Over the past few years, they had become Gorilla Grant's secret vice. Sassi knew that Gorilla liked to savour them and would smoke one to relax and unwind, and it had been their little tradition that at the end of every successful operation, a fresh box of cigars would be delivered to Grant's apartment.

The final thing the parcel contained was a note which said: *I'll be back in three weeks. I'll send a courier every week with a fresh batch of ammo. For your sake, get practising. Enjoy the Cohibas. Sassi.*

He started slow, started small. For the first day, he did nothing but hold the empty gun in his left hand, getting used to its grip and how it sat in his palm. There was no other word for it but weird. It was the equivalent of learning how to write with your non-natural writing hand. Then, when he felt as comfortable as he could, he stood in front of the bedroom mirror in his suite. Dry-firing was the poor gunman's bread and butter training drill. It was free and gave you the opportunity to instil muscle memory.

The pistol was in a cheap holster attached to his left hip and, in slow motion, he moved his left arm in a fluid action. When he had a good grip on the butt of the weapon, he carefully pulled the gun up and out and then, when it had reached a point parallel to his pectoral muscle, he extended it out in a straight line. He needed the motion of a perfect right-angle; straight up the side of his body and punched out in front.

Then he re-holstered. Then he did it again and again… and again… slowly at first, but then getting more confident. *Baby steps, Jack*, he thought.

It took him a full week's work to get comfortable with those baby steps and, by the end of the first week, he was fast and smooth to the draw. The second week was his literal trial by fire. Dry-firing was all well and good, but it was hits on targets that counted. So every day Grant took the long walk out of the clinic and out into a private patch of land nearly a mile away. He never passed a soul on these illicit forays, the location was that remote.

He had set up a basic shooting range at the edge of a forest consisting of a cardboard target nailed to a large tree. He began at close range, no more than a few feet and slowly, over the next few hours, he gradually began to back up until finally he had reached the thirty feet mark, the extreme of effective close-quarter shooting.

To an observer, it would have looked as if this crazy man who was shooting out in the forest had never held a gun before in his life, he was that slow. But Grant knew the wisdom of this; slow and steady wins the race. He had to undo everything that he had known about drawing and firing and start again. What had once been an almost instinctive and natural way of shooting without thinking, had been replaced by a conscious thought process. It was the brain's way of over-compensating, re-wiring itself and working that much harder in order to accurately hit the target. At the end of the day, he packed up the target and the kit, cleaned the gun and trekked off back to the clinic.

On the second day, he jogged down to the 'shooting range' and spent the day working on quick draws. Then he sprinted back to the clinic. On the third day, he once again went for his now routine run and spent the day working on situational shooting – moving and firing, stepping off-line and shooting at multiple targets and then the obligatory run back to the clinic for a shower and some fresh food. By the end of that week, not only was his shooting more accurate, but he felt fitter and more confident in the role of a left-handed gunman.

He had worked out a system of drawing the weapon, dealing with stoppages, two-handed shooting, one-handed shooting, reloads – in fact, the whole gamut of techniques that he expected to use in the future. Once he was satisfied that he had an effective shooting system, Gorilla stood in the calm of the forest and, for the first time, lit up one of the Cuban cigars that Sassi had bought him. It was his reward for all his hard work. He savoured its flavour and sucked in its aroma.

Then he stuck it in the corner of his mouth, chomped down on it and reloaded the gun. "Once more," he said out loud, standing square onto the target, ready to draw. "Just for fun."

At the end of the month, Sassi came to visit him to see how his agent was recovering. They took a walk down to the shooting range and Grant had Sassi sit on a log in the centre of a half circle of trees, six in all. On each tree, he had nailed a cutout cardboard target.

Grant walked away from the target area, twenty paces, then stopped and faced Sassi. Grant's face was set in a grim mask of determination and concentration. He saw nothing but the targets. The Frenchman was an irrelevance.

Sassi, to his credit, remained impassive. He had been under fire in combat before and he knew the level of skill of the 'Gorilla', but it still gave him pause, even if he didn't outwardly show it.

"Give me the word when you're ready," called Grant.

Sassi nodded, swallowed once and then said, "*Aller!*"

Gorilla moved, walking at a steady pace, hands by his side. He was calm. And then, in his mind's eye, he was in the middle of a scenario, armed attackers coming at him, an innocent bystander at their centre. The draw was smooth and confident, his left hand snaking around his body to the left hip of his jeans, guiding the hem of his shirt out of the way, and then the weapon was up and out, pointing straight ahead at the nearest target. His right arm acted as a rest, to steady his aim. His thumb flicked off the safety, his finger was off the trigger, ready and waiting.

In the old days, his first close-quarter battle instructor had always instilled in the students the CQB rule of 3: "*When entering a kill zone, always shoot the first one that moves: he's engaged his brain and is now a threat!*"

Gorilla shot the first target; a double tap to the head. A target to the side got the same treatment. Then another. He dropped out the empty magazine and slammed in another with his right hand and then the Beretta was up and on target again.

"Next," said the instructor in his memory," *shoot the men nearest to you. They are close enough to attack you! They must be eliminated.*"

Gorilla was ten feet away when he shot out the targets either side of Sassi. The Frenchman felt the whisper of the bullets as they passed him by, heard the *crack/whump* as they hit the targets. He was almost upon Sassi, they were nearly touching.

"*Finally,*" said the instructor in his memory, "*shoot everyone else that is left! We don't want them to get into the fight; we want to take them OUT of the fight!*"

Gorilla pivoted left and fired at the last remaining target. The two holes appeared as expected, in the head.

Grant stood with the weapon pointed down. He stripped out the magazine, cleared the chamber and placed it gently on the log next to Sassi.

Sassi looked down at his watch. "Impressive, twenty seconds. Not bad for a 'lefty'."

Grant grinned. "I could probably get that faster. Problem is, you gave me a garbage piece of hardware to work with, Paul."

"Okay, okay," conceded Sassi, smiling. "You've proved that you've still got it."

Grant frowned and shook his head angrily. "I've proved nothing, except that I can make it work in a controlled environment. Going out into the field and doing it against a live opponent is another matter. For that, I need new weapons, ones I'm used to, not this hunk of junk you've given me here," he said, flicking a look at the old Beretta.

"Okay. Leave it with me. I have something in mind that I'll think you'll like, something a bit special."

Grant cocked his head quizzically. He knew better than to try to push Sassi; the intelligence officer enjoyed being enigmatic. It was what made him such a good spy.

Chapter Four

SDECE – Action Service Headquarters, Paris – August 1973

La Piscine was the informal name for the Service de Documentation Extérieure et de Contre-Espionnage, France's external intelligence gathering and covert operations organisation. Nicknamed 'the pool' because of its close proximity to the swimming pool belonging to the French Swimming Federation, its actual address is on the Boulevard Mortier, on the 20th Arrondissement in Paris.

But even within this most secret of establishments in the French capital, there is another address that is even more covert. This belongs to the Action Service of the French intelligence agency and is based out of an old Fort at Noisy-le-Sec, a fifteen minute drive away from SDECE headquarters.

From here, the spies, agents and 'hard men' of the Action Service are sent out to infiltrate, sabotage and assassinate enemies of the state. Everyone from OAS terrorists to Communist agents had been placed under the intelligence microscope. And it was here, on a sunny spring morning, that Paul Sassi climbed into his standard black government issue Citroen and drove into the centre of Paris.

That morning, he had been summoned to the office of Colonel Delgarde, the current head of the Action Service. As usual, the Colonel had been in a bullish mood, something that didn't usually bode well for his officers for the rest of the day.

"An operation is in the offing, Sassi. It's all highly classified. This one comes all the way from the top, way above the DG of the Service. This one came from the Minister himself. I want you to lead this operation," the Colonel had boomed across the office, as Sassi watched him pace like a clockwork soldier. And that had been it. Sassi, with his usual focused mind, had set about reading the intelligence packet that the Colonel had given him.

However, he wasn't quite sure why this new operation had put the Colonel in such a foul mood. It was only later, when he sat in his small office surrounded by the trophies of wars gone by – unit photos, medals in frames, a knife that he now used as a letter opener – and then read the documents enclosed, that he understood.

He skimmed them once, and then read them through in detail twice. At the end of it, he whistled in surprise. The Colonel was a serious man, loyal to his department and Sassi knew that he didn't like his operatives being used for someone else's political agenda. Sassi had been involved with politicians long enough to know that when someone high up wanted a 'dirty job' doing, they didn't care about the professionals doing the work or any collateral damage, they only wanted results that would save their own necks.

It had been the final line in the intelligence packet that had really hit home and had also been quite revealing: *this operation should be handled by third party agents at 'arm's length' and should be 100% deniable. No SDECE officer should have a direct involvement in the field.*

It was clear that the operation called for a deniable operator, someone professional, covert, but good enough to get results quickly. For Sassi, there had been no need to think about who he would choose.

Judging by the intelligence in the files, it seemed that fate had decided who it was to be. The coincidence was staggering, especially to an intelligence officer like Sassi who didn't believe in coincidences. He knew instantly that he would bring his best freelance agent back into harness. He would call back Gorilla Grant.

Sassi met with his agent later that day at a café on the fashionable *Rue du Château d'Eau.* Gorilla was already waiting, had been for the past thirty minutes before Sassi arrived. Both men looked like successful businessmen enjoying an afternoon *café noir* to discuss a potential business deal. It was relaxed but professional, ties loosened but jackets still on and unbuttoned.

"Here, I have a gift for you. Something to complement your new left-handed gun skills," said Sassi, pushing over a small black attaché case across the table. "Have a brief look now. You can have a more detailed look when you get back to your apartment."

Grant took the attaché case, popped the locks and opened it just enough so that he could make out its contents. He raised an approving eyebrow, nodded, and then resealed the case. He would inspect it in detail when he was back in his apartment.

"I think this piece of 'equipment' will be perfect for you. I ordered three, all configured for left-handed shooters. You have this one here. The others are secured in safety deposit boxes, one in Hong Kong and the other in New York, for when you find yourself in those parts of the world. For now, think of this one as your 'European' gun," said Sassi.

"Thank you," said Gorilla.

"For our best men, we always offer the best resources. That's how much we value you, Jack. Looking after you following that hit in Nice, the hospital, rehabilitation, the whole care package, getting you back into the field. We recognise your worth," replied Sassi, patting the other man gently on the arm.

Gorilla cocked a quizzical eye at the Frenchman and smiled. "Are you flattering me, Paul? Because normally, when a Frenchman starts down that path of flattery someone usually ends up getting fucked. And to be honest, you're just not my type!"

Sassi laughed despite himself. He had always liked this quiet, tough little Englishman. He was a good covert operator but, more than that, he was a man to be respected.

"I have a job for you, something that I think you would enjoy. We want you to track a man, find him, hunt him down. He's dangerous, the best in the business. But we think you'll be able to succeed where others might fail. We think you have an edge, a better motivation than some of our other agents."

"I think, old son, you'd better explain," said Gorilla cautiously. He sipped at his coffee, his eyes scanning around to make sure that they weren't being watched. Talking details out in public always made Gorilla wary.

"We think we've identified the assassin on your last job in Nice, the man who shot up your hand. We want him found and we think you're the man to do it."

"I'm in, tell me everything," said Gorilla without hesitation. His brow was already starting to furrow; he could feel the anger rising in himself.

"You may not feel that way when you find out who it is."

"I don't care who it –"

"It's Caravaggio."

"Fuck!" said Gorilla Grant. Talk about spoiling his good mood.

The man codenamed Caravaggio, and unofficially known among the intelligence networks as *The Master*, was a *crème de la crème* intelligence agent and assassin who had been involved in the covert operation business since before the war; a gentleman spy, a ruthless killer, a Cold War ghost. In the small milieu of the intelligence networks, he was the stuff of legends. It was said that he could get to even the most secure and hidden targets anywhere in the world – and he never failed to fulfil a contract.

And, like most legends, the stories of his exploits seemed to reach fantastical levels with every decade. Frequently, he was said to be operating in different parts of the world at the same time, usually against several opposing factions of the same conflict.

He had the ear of the Chairman of the KGB, he had assassinated several high ranking Nazis with his bare hands, and had kidnapped politicians and held them for ransom almost throughout every decade. There was also a rumour that he had been a double and triple agent so many times throughout the Cold War, that not even the intelligence agencies were sure *who* he was actually working for. He was successful enough to pick his own contracts and name his own price, which was always high. He was a most dangerous man.

And, despite all of these interconnecting strands, he was still now, some forty years later, unidentified. Nobody knew his real name and the people that had once seen his face had long since died – many in violent circumstances. His personal security was impeccable and his cut-out list was extensive. Unless you knew the right people and their people and their people, there was no way that you would even be considered for an audience with The Master.

CIA, KGB, SDECE, the Italians, Chinese… Caravaggio had contacts in almost every intelligence network. He had worked on every continent, had been at the top of his game… and then he had disappeared.

Grant thought back to the shootout on the beach all those months ago. What was it the assassin had said – "I understand that you are the new me"?

He decided to press the thought further with Sassi. "Why would he know about me? I assumed he had retired years ago, or was dead. I've never even operated against him, as far as I know!"

"Well, whatever the reason, he's evidently heard of you. It seems that you've been making a splash on the international circuit and among the intelligence networks and that you've caught his eye," said Sassi.

Grant nodded. It was certainly possible and, without blowing his own trumpet, he had acquired a reputation as an effective operator over the past few years. Probably, and to his own knowledge, there were only a handful of agents on the planet that could match Gorilla and his skills. It was a small pond that he operated in. He had been involved in everything from taking down agents and covert courier work, to good, old-fashioned 'redactions'.

"So why do they want him? Why now?" he asked.

Sassi shrugged, seemingly unconcerned about the reason, just how it was going to be completed. "He has acted against French targets, against the France national interest. The Elysée Palace has had enough. The most recent threat is that we have intelligence to believe that this man is plotting to assassinate the President."

"Of France?" laughed Grant.

"Of course!"

"Piss off! Why would he do that?"

Sassi shrugged in the way that bored Frenchmen do. "Who knows? Perhaps he's crazy, but I doubt it. Chances are he's working for a big payday to bring him out of retirement. Either way, it's irrelevant. It's a mission. It's your mission if you want it."

"Just me? A plot against the President of France and you're sending one solo British gunman after him? Really?"

"Don't be ridiculous, Jack. Of course we aren't. We have every resource in the French Secret Services looking at this, not to mention the anti-terror police, the military, all of them. But this is an agency-wide covert operation. Clandestine all the way. The operation is being run directly from the President's office. But you are my man, a contract agent for the Action Service, and I want you to start the hunt to track him down and terminate the threat independently of the police, military or the rest of the SDECE."

Grant nodded, but he didn't believe him. But that was okay. In Grant's opinion, there wasn't an intelligence officer alive who didn't lie to his agents at some point. It was expected, it was normal. But Sassi was usually a straight shooter as far as he knew, so whatever he had been told, he seemed to believe.

Besides, reasoned Gorilla, if he wanted honesty and fair treatment, he should have got a job in a convent. All Gorilla Grant wanted was to do what he did best and be operational again, and if that meant going up against one of the greatest assassins of the age, then that's exactly what he would do.

Chapter Five

When he had first decided to settle down in Paris, Grant had leased a three bedroom apartment in a quiet side street that was two blocks' walk from the Seine. He had spent money on it and had bought only the best to fit it out; décor, furniture, the latest TV and stereo entertainment systems. It was a subtle and tasteful bachelor pad that, as much as anywhere, he was happy to relax in and call home.

He let himself in, scanned the room, threw the keys into the little ashtray that he kept on a ledge by the door and sat down on the couch, placing the attaché case on the coffee table in front of him. He flicked open the locks and studied the equipment inside.

There was the pistol itself, which had a threaded barrel to take a silencer. The accessories consisted of a silencer, leather inside-the-waistband holster designed for covert carry, a shoulder holster, a spare magazine pouch, two magazines, a cleaning kit and two boxes of ammunition. There was also a complementary double-edged boot knife in case the operative wanted to go all old school and bloody.

Grant took out the pistol first and examined it.

The ASP 9 was a single stack, double action 9mm semi-automatic pistol. It had started life as a variant Smith & Wesson 39, Gorilla's old gun when he had been employed by the British in the 1960s, and had been the brainchild of a shadowy gunsmith from New York known within the intelligence milieu as 'Mr Theodore'.

Some said Mr Theodore had worked for the CIA before going freelance and producing high-end weaponry for professional and discerning clients. Mr Theodore had taken a number of S&W 39s and made up to two hundred modifications to them. He had narrowed it down and shortened the original frame, then he had removed the sights and re-fitted it with his own unique version, the Guttersnipe sight, which were specially designed for close quarter instinctive shooting.

The Guttersnipe sight consisted of a groove-like channel that ran along the top of the pistol and narrowed towards the muzzle. Inside the grooves on the three sides were triangular shapes that were designed to focus the eye to the channel's natural target. The principle was simply that the sight's 'choke point' would allow the shooter to direct his aim instinctively, without consciously looking at them.

Grant wasn't too sure about all that. He was very much an instinctive gunman of the old school, so to him, there was nothing new in the sighting principle. Besides, most of his targets were at bad breath distance, anyway and nine times out of ten they never even saw him coming.

Mr Theodore had also instigated a clear magazine and grip so that the gunman could see how many rounds were left. All in all, it was a unique weapon designed with covert carry and shooting in mind. Grant chamber-checked the ASP to make sure that it was safe and then spent ten minutes manipulating the actions on the pistol to get a feel for it, noting how the safety and magazine release were geared for the left-handed gunman.

Very nice, he thought. Whoever Mr Theodore was, in Grant's opinion the man certainly knew how to make a covert quality firearm. It was like his old 39 but more discreet and niche.

The final item inside the case was a brown manila folder that would contain an intelligence briefing pack, plus passports, IDs and cash and credit cards made out to a fictitious name. He pulled out the intelligence briefing pack and studied the papers inside.

Everyone in the trade knew the name of Caravaggio; he was the epitome of the fictional super-spy – part Sidney Reilly, part James Bond and part Scarlet Pimpernel. He had been a 'name' since before the war, and yet there was still very little actually known about him; at least as far as the French intelligence service was concerned.

He was reputed to be a freelance intelligence operative with no localised affiliations, responsible for numerous assassinations both sides of the Iron Curtain, one hundred percent ruthless and never known to have failed at a mission. One source described him as a 'playboy assassin'.

There was a list of the known operations that he was rumoured to have taken part in, some for wartime German intelligence and a couple of vague and blurry photographs that could have been Mickey Rooney or Babe Ruth, or anyone for that matter. He flipped a page and ran down a list of possible contacts, most of whom were dead.

The most interesting notation was from an unnamed source, which, in Grant's experience, usually meant that it had come from signals surveillance. There had been a partial transcript of a conversation between two men; one from a number registered in the Mediterranean and one in the United States, more specifically the state of Louisiana.

The voice of the male from the Mediterranean had been run through the voice analysis systems of whatever intelligence unit had captured it out of the ether. A hit had come back and correlated from a similar one that had been captured from a soviet telephone call in which the name 'Caravaggio' had been identified. The date of the call from the Mediterranean to the USA was listed as three months earlier.

Grant frowned. Voice analysis was something way outside of his knowledge, and he suspected that even now in the 1970s, it still wasn't one hundred percent accurate, no matter what the experts had said. But what seemed clear was that they had voice-analysed and confirmed that the male was Caravaggio and that he had some connection to an individual in Louisiana.

One of the intelligence monkeys at La Piscine had run a search on the USA number and had narrowed it down to a club in New Orleans called The Pink Lady. The club was owned by a man named Armand Guillame, a retired arms dealer with connections to several intelligence networks. It wasn't much to go on, but it was the only lead that he had at the moment and really the coincidence was just too much. There had to be a connection. Maybe this slim lead would be the first step in tracing Caravaggio.

Grant put in a call to SDECE operations and told them what he wanted. Once it had been confirmed, he put the phone down and decided to shower. Twenty minutes later, he was out and checking his watch. 5.30 p.m. He picked up the phone again and dialled the international number of the all-girls boarding school in Sussex, England, heard it ring and waited.

He got through to the school receptionist first and asked for his daughter by name. It was a spur-of-the-moment call, a family emergency. Could he speak to her for a few moments?

He was told to hold the line and then, five minutes later, he heard, "Hello... Daddy? Is everything okay?"

"Hi, love," he said. "Everything is fine. I knew they wouldn't let me talk to you if I just said I wanted a quick chat. You know I'm only supposed to call on the weekend or in an emergency, so..."

"Oh, *Daad*... They'll go mad here if they find out!"

"I know, I know, I'm terrible. But it will be me going to hell, not you, so don't worry," he laughed. "How's everything there?"

"Oh, fine. Latin is *soooo* boring, but I've decided to try out for choir practice so that's cheered me up this week."

"All the girls okay?" he asked. 'The girls' were Katy's little group of friends. They had a Hannah, a Neve, an Ella, a Phoebe and some other names that he couldn't remember off the top of his head.

"They're fine. Two of them had a row the other day and I had to sort it out," she said. That was Katy, thought Grant, always wanting to solve problems.

"Okay. Good. You need anything?"

She said that she didn't. "When can I come and visit again? I love France."

"Well… look, that's why I'm calling. The office wants me to go away on a work project for a few weeks, maybe as long as six weeks. I'll call in when I can but it might be a bit sporadic. But once that's done, maybe we can go on a little vacation, maybe Spain for a week in between terms?"

"Sure, okay… Spain sounds cool!" she said, giggling with excitement. "Where are you going, anyway?"

"Oh, somewhere boring and hot with terrible food," he said jokingly. "Remember that time when –" He heard a voice in the background; it was undoubtedly one of the Year Heads at the school trying to hurry Katy along.

"Oh Dad, I have to go. It's Miss Davies. She's a horror monster!"

"Oh. Okay, love. I'll talk to you soon. I miss you. I love you," he said, hating the fact that the call to his little girl was so brief.

"I love you too, Daddy. Oh and Dad?"

"Yes?"

"Don't forget to get me a present! Preferably two! 'Bye, love you!"
End of call. Kids! Typical!

Chapter Six

Hotel Alba, Via del Corso, Rome

The hooker rolled the black silk stocking carefully up her long, slim, tanned legs and attached it to the garter belt that would hold it in place. For the past thirty minutes, she had been naked as she cavorted around the luxury hotel suite with her 'client' for that night.

'Cavorted' was probably the wrong word; he had tried his best to grab and grope her. She, on the other hand, had tried her best to remain flirty whilst still keeping him at bay… at least until the sedative that she had slipped into his drink had taken effect.

She had hoped that a combination of the nakedness of her slim body, the freedom of being out from under the watchful eyes of his 'minders' and the potency of the champagne would distract him until the drug kicked in, which mercifully it had a few minutes before.

The client was, in fact, a Major in Iraqi intelligence whom she had seduced in the hotel bar. She had caught his eye, flirted, been invited for a drink and then dinner. The hotel room was a natural consequence of the chain of events.

The Iraqi had dismissed his two-man security detail for the evening, so that he could have this dalliance with this beautiful Italian woman. It had been easy to seduce him and slip the sedative into his drink – embarrassingly easy, in fact. She just wished all of her jobs were this easy.

In truth, she wasn't a hooker. She wasn't even Italian. Her cryptonym was 'Nikita' and she was one of the best bounty hunters and freelance intelligence agents in the business.

She continued dressing, slipped on a midnight blue cocktail dress and stepped into her high heels. She smoothed out the creases in the dress and admired herself in the mirror. What she saw was a medium-height woman, slim and athletic of build, and with the pale complexion of the redhead. Her red hair made the green eyes in the pale face stand out and many a man had fallen for those emerald eyes in her thirty-five years.

She reached into her purse and took out a standard pair of police handcuffs and fastened one end to the sleeping Iraqi's wrist and clicked the other end to the steel-frame headrest of the bed. The snoring Iraqi was going nowhere.

She counted that he was her thirtieth target over the past few years. His crime? He had been responsible for the assassination of a group of exiled Iraqis living in Paris. One of the men's brothers, an exiled Iraqi who had turned his knowledge of the Middle East oil industry into a successful consultancy business, had paid for the Iraqi intelligence officer to be tracked while he was visiting Europe.

And that was when the bounty hunter known on the international circuit as Nikita had been hired. Find him, track him, capture him, and don't ask questions to what happens to the target after the capture. Those were Nikita's four work rules, and so far in her career they had worked pretty well. Although she guessed that this particular target wouldn't be doing any prison time. Revenge usually involved body disposal, eventually.

She sat down on the end of the bed, picked up the suite's telephone, dialled 9 for an outside line and then keyed in the contact number she had been given. The phone rang the customary three tones before it was answered by a brusque voice.

"Yes."

"It's Nikita. The package is wrapped."

"Problems?"

"Never," she said.

"Of course," laughed the voice. "Can we collect now?"

"Absolutely. Room 324. I will be waiting," she replied.

"Good work, Nikita. Our people will be there soon."

The call ended and she replaced the handset. She reasoned that the clean-up crew would be knocking on her door within the next thirty minutes. She looked out at the lights that poured down onto the Via del Corso. Thirty minutes, just enough time to have a glass of champagne. After avoiding the Iraqi's efforts at groping her, and then shanghaiing him, she reckoned that she'd earned it. So that's where she sat waiting, sipping her drink, watching the traffic and listening to an Iraqi spy sawing logs in his sleep.

Eunice 'Nikita' Brown had been born thirty-five years earlier in Virginia, USA. Her father had been Captain Melvin Brown of US military Intelligence, G2, and her mother, Katya, had been a nurse at a local hospital that specialised in wound care treatment for US servicemen.

Her mother's family had escaped from the Bolsheviks in 1919. They had settled in America and, from an early age, her mother had taught Eunice the Russian language. Katya always referred to her little girl as 'my *pashtuka*', her little cowgirl.

Eunice had been a good girl, but there had always been a wild child element in her, even from early age. Once she hit her teenage years, she had become a fully-fledged rebel. Many a time, her father would travel into town and drag her away from the motorcycle gangs that she was hanging out with. There was no messing with his thirteen-year-old daughter, he wouldn't allow it. He loved her, but he would not tolerate her hanging out with what he considered 'James Dean wannabees'.

Not that Eunice couldn't handle herself. Hell no, her father had seen to that and made sure she could fight boys older than her. Many a boy had earned a busted nose from trying to get too fresh with Captain Brown's daughter behind the local liquor store. Eunice could certainly pack a punch. Her father said it was the flame-red hair that gave Eunice her temper.

Her greatest friend was her little brother and, even though she loved him with all her heart, Eunice knew that Stevie wasn't like other little brothers. The other kids called him a 'retard' but Eunice preferred to think of him as 'special'. He was sweet and loving and the two of them would spend endless hours lost in each other's company.

One day, Stevie had wandered off into the woods. Daddy was away and Momma had panicked when she had seen that his room was empty. Eunice had literally just stepped off the school bus when her mother had come rushing out.

"It's Stevie, its Stevie... he was in his room and now he's gone!" Her momma was frantic. The Sheriff was notified and a search party was hastily organised to find the special kid that had gone missing.

Two hours later, Eunice had had enough of sitting on her hands, waiting in her bedroom for news. She had set off in the dark with a torch and a pocket knife for emergencies, using the tracking skills that her father had taught her. She knew Stevie better than anyone, knew how he thought and how he moved. She knew his limitations – where he would go, where he wouldn't go. And, more importantly, where he liked to go when he was sad.

She had found Stevie two hours later, sitting down by the lake, rocking back and forth. He was scared and lost.

"I fell, Euney. I fell and lost my shoe," was all he said.

She slipped an arm around him and hugged him tight, then led him back home... back to a house full of Momma's friends, the neighbours and the odd policeman. It was Eunice Brown's first 'tracker operation'.

Daddy had been away a lot. She never knew where he went, only that whenever he returned after months away, he would have a cool suntan and bring her and her brother exotic presents. Papyrus paper from the Middle East, tribal masks from Africa and Buddhist beads from... hell, somewhere.

Then one day, she and Momma received the news that Daddy wouldn't be coming home. A mission, they had been told. Missing in action behind enemy lines. Daddy was gone. Momma had hugged her and Stevie to her chest and they had all cried.

Eunice remembered the funeral well; full military honours, but with a closed casket. Whatever had happened to Daddy had been bad enough not to let his family see him one last time. She remembered the words spoken by the soldiers and the men that Daddy had worked with. *War hero. Patriot. Brave man.* They meant nothing to her. He was just Daddy... her Daddy. The man she loved the most.

Momma hadn't coped well at all. In fact, she had been a mess. A widow, and looking after one teenage daughter and an eight-year-old who had special needs. It had all been too much. She had had to stay at home and live off her widow's pension and then the grieving and the pain had started, followed by the drinking and the long spiral downhill into depression.

Almost a year to the day of her husband's funeral, Katya Brown had hanged herself out on the hill. It had been the place where her husband had proposed to her all those years ago.

After her mother's death, things moved fast in the life of Eunice Brown. She and Stevie went to live with their paternal grandparents on their ranch in Bedford, Virginia. It had been a healing time for both of the Brown children, made that much easier by the love of Papa and Mama Brown.

There were long summer days and nights of playing, crying, mourning and learning to live again. Stevie would always stick close to home, to his grandma, but Eunice was more adventurous and would often go out in the woods with her grandpa, where she learned to hunt, track and shoot with the old man.

Financially, the children were well taken care of thanks to their father's army pension, and while Stevie was provided with a day facility at a care home for children, Eunice was enrolled in Randolph-Macon Women's College in Lynchburg, Virginia.

Papa Brown, a retired US Deputy Marshall, got her a summer job working for a local private investigator/bail bonds firm that an old buddy of his ran. Her work was mostly office-based; after all, Virginia was no place for a young gal to be messing with criminals and hoodlums. But even there, she was smart enough to see a pattern in an offender's modus operandi and run a detailed trace, gather information from surreptitious telephone calls or run a bit of camera surveillance on a suspect's car. Papa Brown declared her a natural.

She had thrived at Randolph and graduated with a Double Major in Psychology and Classics. Still unsure as to what she wanted to do in life, and with no real direction, she applied for and was accepted into a civilian position with the recently formed Defense Intelligence Agency, working as an intelligence analyst. Up until that point, the ratio of women employees compared to men was small within the DIA, but a language skill is always a great leveller in the intelligence world.

The remit of the DIA, unlike its civilian counterpart the Central Intelligence Agency, was to acquire useable military intelligence material for the American military.

Thanks to her fluent Russian, Eunice was soon fast-tracked to work in the US Embassy in West Berlin for the next three years. And, while much of her work was office-based translation and information analysis, it did provide Eunice Brown with two important things that would help her on her later career path. First, the DIA had enough trust in her to grant her top secret clearance, and second, it gave her a practical exercise in the working of intelligence operations. So it came as no surprise when, a year later, she moved from the military branch of government over to the civilian side of operations, namely the CIA.

After her training period at the 'Farm', the Agency's training facility in Virginia, Eunice Brown had spent the next two years on a series of European postings. In the late 1960s, the CIA was leading the way with the use of women as field agents and, while it was still frowned upon for female operatives to be at the cutting edge of things, there were still opportunities for women agents to assist with operations. But, on the whole, they were resigned to following their male counterparts around.

And then there were exceptions like Eunice Brown...

Eunice had always had that independent confidence that enabled her to handle stressful and high conflict situations; her experiences had made her one of a kind, unique.

It was in 1968 that she made her reputation within the Agency and it came in the form of one Colonel Sergei Lvov. Lvov was an old school KGB thug who had been the bane of both CIA and SIS network operations in Berlin at one time. He was a tough, no-nonsense operator whom the Agency both feared and respected. To gain the knowledge that he had would be gold dust for them.

It was inevitable, then, that the Agency would make a 'pitch' to try to recruit him. What was more remarkable was that Lvov accepted; in fact, he damned near snatched the hand off the CIA officer leading the recruitment.

"What took you so long to ask?" he grumbled. "Of course I will work for America. It is my dream."

The CIA man thought it was Lvov's greed and taste in Western prostitutes that motivated him, rather than the inner workings of democracy.

The double-agent operation lasted for a profitable two years, until it was feared that his cover was blown and his life was in danger. The radio traffic said that the KGB spy-hunters were on the trail of a traitor in the KGB Berlin Station and the net was closing in.

The CIA wasted no time and set about implementing its emergency escape plan for Lvov. But the station personnel were stretched and time was running out. The only man capable of extracting the Russian was a good twelve hours away by plane and it was feared that it would be too late by then.

It was the Berlin Operations Base Station Chief who received a knock on his office door late at night. He had been poring over options in the Lvov extraction and so far, it wasn't looking practical. His men would stick out like a sore thumb if they tried to bring out the Russian, and the CIA officer who had direct control of the op was stuck in an airport somewhere. Fuck!

So he was surprised to see his newest Station Officer, Miss Brown, standing over him with an operational plan in her hands. She placed it carefully down onto his desk and said, in her sweetest southern twang, "Sam, I think I would like to go and bring our boy home, if that's alright with you?"

Sam, the Station Chief, had almost flung her out. Then he read Eunice Brown's operational plan and changed his mind instantly. An hour later, he had approval and the operation was a 'GO'. Eunice Brown would be the officer bringing the agent out from behind the Iron Curtain.

She had been infiltrated in under cover of darkness in classic style, armed with only her wits and several sets of false papers. She had met her contact on the East German side and had been dropped off at the proposed rendezvous – and that was the last that the CIA heard of her until two days later, when she had safely delivered her agent to a CIA safe house in Helsinki.

How she had ended up in Helsinki after being dropped off in Germany was still a mystery, and how she had completed this seemingly impossible task was, to many in the CIA, still a highly classified secret. All that the Agency handlers knew was that a very happy former KGB officer had arrived in one piece in what must have been one of the most daring extractions in the Agency's history.

"That Nikita, I love her," cooed Sergei Lvov to his de-briefing team.

"Nikita who?" they had asked?

"The woman, the red-head. I don't know her true name but to me she will always be my Nikita," he had said. And the codename had stuck with the love-stricken KGB man; 'Nikita' Brown, the sassy Agency officer who had gone in behind the Iron Curtain to rescue one of the CIA's best intelligence sources. Her legend was created, and she became a specialist in the Clandestine Services for tracking and extracting people from dangerous situations and environments.

Several more successful extractions of High Value Targets later, and Nikita Brown decided her time as an Operations Officer was over. There was no angst, no soul-searching; she simply recognised that being one small part of a big, cumbersome organisation like the CIA was no longer the life she wanted. Her challenges lay in a new and different direction.

There were men in her life, of course – Eunice was a beautiful, attractive woman – but none of them stayed around for long, either because they couldn't cope with the challenge of her, or because they failed to keep her interest. Maybe it was a little of both.

She decided that her career, at least, lay in the direction of the US Marshal's Service based out of the Las Vegas Field Office. If she thought the work that she had completed so far with the DIA and the CIA was tough, it was nothing compared to what the Marshals had to deal with. Eunice Brown spent three happy years hunting down criminals, tracking killers and providing close protection to her principals as part of the US Witness Protection program. She excelled at the work and even her senior officers had to acknowledge that she had an uncanny affinity for this type of work. She was a natural born hunter.

Then came the shootout that ended her career. It was a raid for a wanted felon, nothing she hadn't done a hundred times before. Like most of these things, it was a dawn bust. The felon had burst out of the rear of the house just as Eunice had been about to enter. She had taken a .45 to the gut before a fellow US Marshal had killed the man.

She had spent a month in the hospital, having nearly bled out on the day of the shooting, but the surgeons and the nurses had brought her back. The surgeon who had operated on her had declared to his staff, "That's one tough broad!"

She made some big decisions while she was confined to the hospital bed. Papa Brown, now in his nineties, had come to visit her and brought with him a stack of his old western novels and magazines to read. "Come home, Euney. It's where you belong. Come back to Virginia," he had said, holding her hand.

She had said she would think about it. She knew that he had been on his own, rattling around on the ranch, since Mama had died several years before.

When Papa had gone, she had started to read through the old magazines and books. They were stories of the old West, of gunslingers, cowboys, bounty hunters. She read about a man named Tom Horn, who had apparently been a legend. Horn had been a soldier, cowboy, range detective and man-hunter. Eunice devoured the material over a period of two weeks. By the time she was due to be released from hospital, she knew what she was meant to do. She would do what she knew best and what she was good at. She would be the modern Tom Horn.

She resigned from the US Marshal's Service and moved back to Papa's ranch in Virginia so that they could look after each other. When Papa had passed on that summer, Eunice had moved her brother to an expensive private care facility where he would receive the best treatment. He would come and visit her during vacation time and they would spend time together at the ranch, like they had done when they were children.

But Eunice knew that she had to start getting her work life in order. She 'set out her shingle' and began working for herself, turning Papa's old study into a small office space for her business. A phone call here and there, and her reputation with senior CIA officers at the Agency soon ensured that 'Nikita' Brown was the go-to man-hunter and tracker in the freelance intelligence business.

She had spent six weeks tracking the Iraqi intelligence officer all over the planet. The man had obviously been on a whirlwind tour of 'friendly' spy networks, countries that were sympathetic to President Hussein's regime. So far, Eunice had spent a lot of time in the Middle

East and North Africa, tracking her target. So this brief visit to Rome was obviously part of the man's rest and recuperation period... his own treat for all his hard work.

That was what she had counted on. Snatching him would have been difficult in somewhere like Tunisia or Libya; not impossible, but difficult. But here in Rome, away from an array of Arab secret services, it was a walk in the park for someone with the skills of Nikita Brown. She gathered as much information about his personality and movements as she could, before she made her approach. She had seen the type of whores that he liked, tall and coquettish, and she altered her appearance to suit the role. After that, it had been the flirtatious approach, the subtle word and the seductive murmurings that had ensnared the Iraqi.

She took a final sip of her champagne and put down the glass.

There was a gentle knock at the door. She stood and walked across the suite to open it. She knew it would be the clean-up crew disguised as hotel room cleaners. They weren't her people, not the ones she would normally have sub-contracted, and they worked directly for the client who was paying for this whole operation. Once the Iraqi had been captured and removed, her part in the whole exercise was finished.

She opened the door and stood back, aware of several dark bodies moving into the gloom of the room, each carrying items to help move the sleeping body covertly out of the hotel and into a waiting van.

The final man who entered was pushing a large laundry trolley. The exit method. Nikita watched them as the crew went to work, unshackling the man and lifting him into a body bag.

"How long will he be out?" asked one of the clean-up crew

She shrugged. "About another hour or so, I would guess. Have fun."

The man started to say something else, ask another question, maybe. Whatever it was, she didn't hear it. She had already left the suite and was on her way down the elegant corridor to the elevator.

Two days later, Eunice Brown landed at John F. Kennedy International Airport after a direct flight from Rome. Despite the horrendous flight time, she still looked elegant, dressed in a dark trouser suit and open-necked white blouse, her high heels clicking along the concourse as she made her way to the internal flight terminal that would take her south to her home.

It would be another two hours before she touched down in Preston Glenn Field Regional Airport in Lynchburg. Then she would take the bus to the car park and pick up her red 1968 Ford Mustang Fastback with the souped-up V8 engine. In the trunk, as always, were the tools of her trade, secured in a locked box: a Remington pump action shotgun with pistol grip, a Smith & Wesson .38 revolver, a spring cosh, several boot knives and an electric stun gun. She never left home without them.

Even driving fast, it would be another hour before she reached the tiny backwater town of Bedford, Virginia and arrived at the ranch that was her home. And then, finally, she would sleep.

The telephone rang at exactly 8.30 a.m. the next morning. It was the start of her working day.

"Yes?" she said.

"Nikita?" A man's voice. She knew who it was instantly.

"Yes," she confirmed.

"This is Gibbs."

"Good morning, Mr Gibbs, how can I be of help today?" Her tone was businesslike, professional.

Gibbs paused. He knew that he had to get this right. He needed the skills of the contract agent Nikita. He also knew how independent she could be. That was the problem of having someone who was an expert in their chosen field, especially in a trade like Nikita's. They could accept your offer, but they could also refuse. "Something important has arisen. We have an assignment for you, if you are interested."

"What type of assignment, Mr Gibbs?"

"It's a Track and Recovery operation, a High-Value Target. We have made all the arrangements for you."

She frowned and her voice became curt. "Mr Gibbs. Nobody makes arrangements for me. I conduct my own planning."

"I understand, I merely assumed..."

"Then please don't assume. That would be a mistake."

Eunice had no time for Gibbs. He was the worst kind of shark in a suit, someone who had never been at the front line. In fact, most of his career had been spent pushing paper and climbing the greasy pole of power, but he still felt the need to tell people who did their jobs day in and day out, exactly *how* to do them.

Gibbs ran a company called Executive Information Services, or EXIS for short, which was housed in an anonymous office building in the centre of Washington. It portrayed itself as an independent corporate security consultancy with a range of high-end exclusive clients. In truth, it was a CIA front company that handled a range of 'dirty' off-the-books operations solely for the Agency. EXIS's mantra was 'plausible deniability'. Gibbs was its operations manager and head honcho.

"I apologise. We were just trying to stay ahead of the game. This operation is most urgent," said Gibbs, his fingers tightening around the telephone receiver in anger. *Goddamned freelance agents*, he thought.

"Courier over the information that you have and I will give you an assessment by the end of the working day," said Eunice. Her voice was that of a woman very much in control of the situation.

"Of course, I'll get right on it. And the price?"

"It will be my usual fee plus expenses. I'm not a carpetbagger, Mr Gibbs."

"No, of course not. I'm sorry if it came across that way. I will make sure that you receive the files by lunchtime," stuttered Gibbs.

"If it plays out and I think it is feasible, I will be on the road the next morning. Agreed?"

"Yes, of course, I –"

"Goodbye, Mr Gibbs."

He heard the phone click dead in his hand. In his office, Gibbs replaced the receiver in the cradle and sat for a few moments in silence, trying to calm himself and waiting for his anger to subside. He hated…
hated… being talked to like that by an agent, either freelance or one under control, it made no difference. It wasn't what he was used to.

The fact that Nikita was a woman, a good-looking woman to boot, made it all the more irritating. But at this point in time he needed her – or, more accurately, he needed her undisputed skills.

Chapter Seven

Gorilla Grant had flown into LaGuardia on a false Canadian passport and had stopped long enough in New York to refresh himself and to 'clear' the American ASP pistol from the safety deposit box in the bank in Manhattan.

After that, it had been a flight the following day, direct to New Orleans. He hadn't worried too much about the ASP in his checked luggage, as he had forged paperwork to prove that it was registered in his false name and that he was competing in a pistol shot tournament in Louisiana. Aside from that, as long as it was secreted safely away and out of reach during the flight, no one cared.

He had booked himself into an anonymous hotel in the French Quarter. Upon entering his room, he had immediately flung open his window and had been assaulted with a cacophony of aromas ranging from manure and fish, to diesel and jasmine. It had been a disconcerting experience for the first few hours. With the smattering of the French language, New Orleans patois and the architecture of the buildings, it was as if a little piece of a French or Spanish colony had been transported into the Deep South of America. Nevertheless, he had dumped his case and set out into the evening, determined to explore.

Gorilla could see why New Orleans was nicknamed 'The Big Easy'. There was a kind of carefree tempo to the place, a shedding of reality that was replaced with the sultriness of forbidden opportunities. It was his first time in the city and so far, he had blended into the atmosphere and the rhythm of the streets. He had taken his time getting used to the city, especially around Canal Street, with its bars and hidden corners. In another context, one not work-related, it would have been his chosen location to relax and unwind.

He'd even had a chance to watch the street people whilst sitting in the infamous Café du Monde, where he had indulged in the iconic beignets, *café au lait*, and a glass of straight bourbon. At this time of year, there was humidity in abundance. It was something that Gorilla had never had a problem with in the past, until he had spent a night here. Now, his skin felt saturated.

As Gorilla had walked through the French Quarter, down along Canal Street, he found that strangers kept coming up to him, wanting to talk to him. At first, he thought it was someone aiming to get 'physical'. After the third or fourth approach, when a young woman came up to him and asked him if he wanted a little hash and said there was a party going on and would he like to come and see the real "NEW-OR-LEENZ?" Gorilla reasoned that the people of New Orleans were just very friendly and liked to meet people who were new in town.

At least that seemed to be the case, which was just as well because Gorilla had his ASP hidden under his jacket and his cut-throat razor in his trouser pocket, in case the friendly ones faded away and were replaced by the type who underestimated him physically. So far, that hadn't been the case.

La Dame Rose, The Pink Lady club, was located just off the main strip of Bourbon Street and was actually three bars in one. The street level was the main bar for the tourists. The second level up was where the Latin music bands played and it was known for its rough clientele, for whom fighting in the middle of a set was the norm. The third level was the most shadowy. It was dark and sultry and was the place where the couples, hookers and their clients would go for privacy and intimacy. It was the norm to see half-dressed people and hear the moans of pleasure from the dark alcoves. Its walls seeped with lust.

The Pink Lady was owned by a man with a worrying reputation in New Orleans. Armand Guillame was a fifty-year-old Creole nightclub owner, gangster and arms dealer. He had a violent past and had spent five years doing prison time in Angola. Word had it that he had done bits for the CIA in the '60s and had made a name running arms to the anti-Castroists. It was also rumoured that he was one of Caravaggio's most trusted emissaries.

Guillame was the man who could contact the Master; the man who could set up contracts, make introductions and set the terms if need be. He knew where the bodies were buried. For all that, he took a cut of the final contract fee. If anyone knew how to find Caravaggio, it would be Armand Guillame. Not that he would just roll over and spill his guts easily, but Gorilla had a way of loosening tongues from even the most reticent of informants.

As it was early afternoon, the Pink Lady was closed and while the citizens of Bourbon Street were out and about at this time of day, it was quieter than it would be when the night came. Gorilla chose the wisest and most practical option for a covert entry – a window at the rear of the building that gained him access to the men's toilets on the ground floor. There was no subtlety going on here, no tools or Government Issue 'lock pick' guns. He simply smashed the glass open with a brick and flipped the latch. It had been embarrassingly simple.

The ground floor was a normal bar that had obviously seen a heavy night – glasses still uncollected, chairs at awkward angles. But aside from the smell of stale beer and whisky, things seemed pretty normal. Gorilla moved towards the stairs, taking a quick glance around. Nothing. Silence. He moved up cautiously, pulling out the ASP and holding it close to his body in a retention position in case things started to get 'noisy'.

It was when he reached the top of the stairs that he saw the body. Gorilla scanned the dimly lit and expansive room; the tables, chairs, bar and, of course, the stage. Splayed out on the stage where the band would play, and looking for all the world like a five-pointed star, was Armand Guillame. His head was hanging back over the lip of the stage, causing his throat to be raised prominently. Gorilla approached cautiously, the ASP leading the way, and then he bent down to take a closer look at the body of the dead man.

On the left side of Guillame's neck, just below his ear, Gorilla noted that there was a perfect puncture wound the size of a small button. A bead of blood had formed there and coagulated. It looked like a red full-stop. Whatever had killed him had to be long, thin and sharp, so as to be able to penetrate to the brain and cause an embolism, Gorilla guessed. A spike, maybe? The nearest thing that Gorilla could envision was a more murderous version of an old woman's knitting needle.

He was about to turn and straighten up when he heard the distinctive *click*. He knew what it was without even looking. It was the sound of the hammer of a revolver being cocked. He knew that sound from experiences past. Instinctively, he froze. He had learned that from past experiences, too.

"Don't move, Jack, I'd hate to have to spoil that pretty face of yours." It was a woman's voice, playful and teasing, and it came from behind him. The soft drawl put her birthplace as southern United States. North or South Carolina –he always got those two mixed up. Maybe Virginia.

He knew who it was immediately, without even looking. Apart from anything else, only one person in their profession called him by his Christian name, everybody else called him Gorilla. He lowered the ASP and slowly turned his head round, eager to confirm that the person who had gotten the better of him was who he thought it was.

He took in the weapon that she was holding first – a revolver, the aperture pointed directly at his forehead, one perfectly manicured, red-nailed finger curled around the trigger, ready to fire.

He looked beyond the gun and saw her clearly for the first time; the long red hair that even now she was brushing away from her face, the strong cheekbones, the bright green eyes, and the immaculate make-up. She was dressed in jeans and a black leather jacket.

She permitted herself a little smile and winked at him. He knew what she was saying – "You're good, Jack, but I'm better." It was the game that they played.

He smiled back at her... couldn't help himself. *We are well met, she and I,* he thought. *She's a bitch!*

"Now, lower that gun and kick it out of reach," she said. The playfulness had been replaced by a touch of steel in her tone.

Yeah, nothing has changed, thought Gorilla. *She's definitely still a bitch.*

They had first met over eighteen months ago in a restaurant in Asuncion, Paraguay. Gorilla had been there tracking a former Nazi counterespionage officer who had been responsible for the executions of several French resistance leaders during the war.

It was a nothing job for him, not real intelligence work, more the fact that someone in the French government wanted revenge. The SDECE had discovered the man's new identity, traced him and now they wanted one of their freelancers to terminate him. Gorilla had received the call and had been on the next plane out.

He had checked into the Gran Hotel Paraguay and had spent the first twenty-four hours getting together everything that he would need for the 'hit' on the German the next day. That night, he had dined in the hotel restaurant alone. Then she had entered... and what a bloody entrance, a tall, slender redhead in a figure-hugging green dress. She certainly turned heads. They had locked eyes briefly, almost as if they had met before, with that recognition of uncertainty.

"I can recommend the fish," she had said, sitting down at the adjacent table.

He had looked over and nodded. He saw her for the first time that night. The long, vibrant red hair cascading down over her bare shoulders, the aliveness of the green eyes. His gaze made it halfway down her slim body before he caught himself. She was quite the package, a film noir femme fatale come to life.

He noted the accent immediately. American. From the south, but with the softer tones of a woman who had travelled. "Thank you. I'll try it. Much appreciated," he replied.

"Not a problem," she said, never taking her eyes off him. And there it was, that teasing tone all wrapped up in a husky voice.

"Are you English?" she asked.

"Canadian."

"You don't sound Canadian?"

"Oh, I've spent a lot of time in Europe, mainly in London. The accent comes back when I'm back in Ontario," he said, trying to sound convincing.

She smiled sweetly and nodded. "I wonder if I could ask a favour? I know it's a terrible imposition, especially as we don't really know each other yet..."

Yet? he thought.

"....but could I join you for dinner? I've been getting a lot of hassle from some of our fellow guests of the male variety. Some are quite intimidating. I think it's my red hair – they seem to see it that I'm 'available'. I'm not. At least, not to them!" She giggled coyly.

And that had been it. They had dined together; the food had been good, and the company pleasant. She had done most of the talking and had introduced herself as Eunice, Eunice Gibson. She pronounced it *Yeww-Neece*, which Gorilla found endearing.

Eunice was in Paraguay to work with a client. Her job?

"Why, I'm an interior designer. I've been asked to consult on the foreign ministry's meeting rooms to make them more palatial," she had said.

He had introduced himself as Jack McKenna, an oil executive for one of the big oil giants; a dealmaker out to get the best deal for the clients as well as the consumers. Paraguay was his new stomping ground in the oil business.

"I wouldn't have put you as an oil executive. I'm quite good at reading people. I would have said that you had been some kind of soldier.... security or something like that. Just the way that you carry yourself."

"I'm afraid not," he said, his hands clasped tightly together in front of him.

"I'm just teasing you, Jack," she said, brushing a lock of red hair from her eyes. "I'm here for a few days more. Maybe we could meet up tomorrow?"

"I'm working all day tomorrow, unfortunately."

"Anywhere I know?"

"I'm not sure. I don't know which places you know in this country."

"Try me."

"Luque," he said. "I have to see a man up there. Business."

She paused for a moment. "No," she said. "I've never been up there. Maybe tomorrow night, for drinks?"

"Again, I can't. I'm sorry. I have a direct flight out tomorrow evening."

She ran one perfectly manicured red nail around the rim of her wine glass. "Now Jack, us Southern gals aren't used to having to work this hard to get a man to notice them. Maybe I'm losing my touch."

He smiled. "I can assure you that you're not, believe me!"

"I understand, Jack. Well, you can't blame a girl for trying." There was a certain shyness about her as she smiled at him, then stood and smoothed out her dress.

Gorilla placed down his napkin and stood also.

Eunice held out her hand. "Thank you for a wonderful dinner and for being a chivalrous protector this evening."

"My pleasure."

She leaned forward and kissed him on the cheek. He could smell the soft scent of her fragrance: vanilla and jasmine. It smelled of sultry sex to him. And that had been it, a nice dinner and a bit of flirting.

The next day, he had travelled to San Antonio for the hit on the Nazi war criminal. He had the man in his sights, weapon ready, just waiting for him to leave his work for the day in a pharmacy. Gorilla had watched the German close-up the small shop and had been across the street, ready to pounce on his target.

Just as Gorilla was ready to draw and fire, a van screeched to a halt and a woman jumped from the rear of the van. Whoever she was, she was agile and fit, dressed in black, with dark sunglasses and a woollen knit cap to hide her identity.

She sprayed the German directly in the face. The man screamed and instantly threw his hands up to his eyes. The female kidnapper wasted no time. She clubbed him around the head with a wooden cosh and bundled him into the rear of the van.

Gorilla stood there stock still, his gun still stuffed into the pocket of his jacket. The whole thing had taken twenty seconds and he hadn't even had a chance to move! He got a glimpse of the back of the female kidnapper before she turned around, and spotted the shock of red hair poking from underneath the knitted cap. He was still coming to terms with it when she looked at him directly from across the street and smiled that sweet, flirtatious smile of hers. Then she slammed the rear of the van doors before it drove off at speed into the night.

It was definitely Eunice. He stood there in the darkness, bathed in the amber glow of the streetlight and wondered if, for the first time in years, he hadn't been taken for a ride by a pretty face.

When he had returned to Paris, he had asked Sassi to find everything that he could on whoever 'Eunice' was.

Sassi had searched the SDECE files and then had checked with liaison services. It hadn't taken long. "She's got a hell of a reputation by all accounts, although our service has never used her. She seems to operate mostly on the American and Asian markets," he said.

"So who the hell is she? How did she get to my target?" growled Gorilla.

"She is a freelance bounty hunter with CIA connections. Name of Eunice Brown, her cryptonym is Nikita. She's one of the best hunters in the business, has a reputation for always tracking down and bringing in her quarry. Dead or alive."

"And what happened to Fritz the Nazi? Any ideas?"

Sassi had shrugged. "Who knows? He could be anywhere. The Israelis would be my best bet, or maybe the relatives of one of his victims. Nikita was just the contractor to deliver him. Either way, head office isn't too concerned, they saved us the job of taking him out."

Over the following months, Gorilla had come across her name once or twice, an operation here or a rumour there. On a trip to Colombia, he had missed her by a few hours, but she had been playful enough to discover which hotel he was staying at and get a note delivered to his room. He had ripped it open, blinked once, twice then read it again and again.

It had said, *Hey Jack, why do we keep missing each other? You still owe me a drink? Love, Eunice xxxx.* He could smell her perfume on the note, sultry, sensual hints of vanilla and sandalwood.

She was like a nagging pain in the back of his skull. That red hair, that sassy manner, the way her eyes flashed when she was teasing him. Just the thought of her would drive him crazy. He wasn't sure what was the worst, the fact that he regretted not taking her up on her offer to meet again, or the fact that she had the drop on him during the hit in Paraguay.

And now here she was again, once more in his life and once more having him exactly where she wanted him, with those green eyes teasing and the biggest revolver in the world pointing directly at his head.

She had taken his gun and patted him down, finding the cut-throat razor in his pocket, and now she had him backed against the wall. "You know they don't bury the dead in New Orleans. The bodies have a tendency to get pushed back up out of the ground," she whispered.

"Did you kill him?"

She shook her head and held a silent finger up to her lips. "Shhh.... No, I didn't. But I think whoever did is still here in the club."

Gorilla looked around. If the killer was still here, then he or she was still here for something else. The only thing that he could think of was something up in the manager's office, some piece of information – which seemed the most likely conclusion if this was connected to The Master.

"What are you doing here, Jack?" she asked, her brow furrowed in confusion.

Gorilla shrugged. "I'm a tourist, just seeing the sights."

"Bullshit!"

"Can I have my gun back?"

"No."

He sighed. "Okay, but we can't stay like this forever."

She considered this and reasoned that he was right. Time was ticking and they had a dead gangster in front of them and his killer somewhere nearby. "Okay. Work with me on this, Jack. I'll search down here, you take the upstairs level."

Gorilla looked up at the stairs leading up to the top floor. It looked dark and like a big old bear trap. He wasn't too enthusiastic about walking into it unarmed. "At least give me my razor?"

She kept the gun trained on him, gave his request a moment's consideration and then took the razor out of her rear jeans pocket and tossed it to him. He caught it with his left hand and flicked it open to inspect the blade. Then, satisfied, he closed it and put it back into his pocket.

"First one back wins," she said and he nodded in agreement.

They went their separate ways through the darkness of the club, he upwards and she heading towards the ground floor level. Before she disappeared out of sight, he cast an inquisitive eye over his shoulder to watch her – the graceful movements, the swaying of the hips, her jacket unzipped, the flash of her red hair over her shoulders, and the .38 revolver held professionally in her hand.

Gorilla took his time moving forward, remembering what he'd learned on a close quarter battle course years ago. "*When moving up wooden stairs, always tread on the edges nearer to the wall and not the middle. The middle creaks and can alert an enemy.*" It was advice that had never let him down all these years.

The stairs led up one flight and turned directly onto a small landing that held the manager's office – Guillame's, he guessed. The door was open and he could hear the faintest of noises from inside.

He silently removed the razor from his pocket and opened it one-handed, letting it rest easy in his palm in anticipation of the violence that was sure to come. At the top of the stairs, he craned his neck to peer around the corner. He saw a small office space; desk, chairs, telephone, filing cabinet. It was usual, normal.

What wasn't normal was the man who was kneeling down beside the desk in the small office and rummaging through a floor-mounted safe. Gorilla could hear the rustling of paper and assumed it was either money or documents.

The man – the killer, he assumed – was small and slight of build, his jet black hair cut short. He seemed to be concentrating intently on whatever he was looking for inside the safe and then, almost too late, he became aware of a presence behind him, and started to turn his head slowly so he could see whatever was behind him. And there, standing in the doorway, was Gorilla Grant, glaring down in fury at the back of a black-suited assassin who had just murdered his next lead.

The kick came out of nowhere and sent him reeling back down the stairs, landing on the stairwell handrail, sending the razor flying out of his hand. It was followed up with a punishing series of kicks to his hand and arm from the figure above him.

Gorilla howled in agony, his arm rendered temporarily useless, before looking up and briefly seeing a dark-suited Chinese man. The man was frail, small, and nondescript, his face bland and impassive. He was like a black shadow on the stairwell.

In the darkness, Gorilla was aware of the small, dark figure moving past him at speed and then turning and delivering a final open-hand strike. The strike shot into Gorilla's temple, and it was delivered with such power that he blacked out for a moment. He came out of the fog seconds later, but by that time he knew that the assassin was making his way out of the club. Maybe Nikita would be able to slow him down.

He climbed to his feet, his head swimming, then he stopped for a moment and looked down. Something lay at his feet. He picked it up, glanced at it and dismissed it for later. Then, after retrieving his cut-throat razor with his left hand, he bolted after the little bastard who had worked him over.

Chang, the assassin, ran.

Though he was a small man, almost frail-looking, he had excellent fitness and speed. Even if his pursuers had numbers and weapons against him, Chang was still agile enough to be able to outrun even the fittest of hunters. He had one block to run before he reached his vehicle parked in a side street.

Killing the Creole had been no problem for a man of Chang's skills. For that, he had used his assassin's needle. It lay in a thin sheath and was hidden inside his waistband, running down the seam of his trouser leg. When he pressed a small button and then retracted the handle, it separated from its main body to reveal a thin steel spike about thirty centimetres long. The head of the spike was razor-sharp and was designed to penetrate via a small puncture into the vulnerable spots on a victim's body, such as the brain and the heart. For Mr Tai Loong Chang, it was a weapon of subtlety that appealed to his fastidious mind.

The hardest part had been orchestrating getting into the victim's presence, but then again, his Control had taken care of that and had arranged the meeting. What had bothered him the most was the subsequent intrusion of the strangers. He had taken the Creole, had felt the life drain from him and no sooner had his body hit the floor than Chang had been aware of someone entering downstairs. He knew that it wasn't the cleaners or the employees; Guillame had been instructed to have nobody else present for the meeting.

Chang had made his way quickly to the top floor office to complete the last part of this mission: to find any documents that linked Armand Guillame to the rest of the Caravaggio network. And find them he had. Wire transfers, phone numbers, even the address of one of the network's safe houses in Montevideo. Then he had heard movement on the floor below him, and then whispered voices. The operation had been compromised in some way.

Chang was small and lithe enough to be able to virtually disappear into any environment. He had been taught well over the years, learning how to evade, how to be covert and how to kill silently. Silent killing was Chang's speciality. While some specialised in firearms and bomb-making, it was the traditional skills of the Asian arts of combat that Chang excelled at; hand-to-hand combat, the blade, the nunchaku, the garrotte.

Chang had taken care of the man in the office and had disabled him with no problem. Then, when he had reached the ground level of the Pink Lady, he had been aware of a female over by the bar as he ran to the door. He had been even more aware of her steadying herself and aiming a firearm at him in the darkness of the club.

Chang had hit the door at a run and was instantly out on the street, but not before the female had fired twice, hitting the door frame above his head as he exited. He moved fast, sidestepping pedestrians and street hawkers of every persuasion. He turned a corner without stopping and saw the Lincoln Continental parked where he had left it an hour earlier. Moments later, he was driving away.

Chang was confident that he had put enough space between himself and the Pink Lady Club. He would drive out of the area, change cars and then make his way to the airport. He would report to his Control and await his next assignment.

His training had taught him that when leaving the scene of an assassination, the assassin should always remain cool and collected; should walk and never run, in order to blend in and be one of the crowd. Running was for amateurs and...

His chain of thought was abruptly broken as he heard a noise in the distance – a growl, guttural, mechanical, like an angry lion gaining fast and letting its quarry know that it was near. And then he looked in his rear view mirror and saw the red-haired devil in her flame-coloured Mustang hurtling after him and gaining speed. He knew, in that moment, that escape wasn't going to be as easy as he had first thought.

It was a 1968 Mustang, flame-red and it reflected the personality of Nikita Brown perfectly. It was in-your-face and no-nonsense. Her knuckles were white as they gripped the steering wheel, the right hand occasionally moving down to the gear stick to either ramp up the speed or slow it down. She handled the turns expertly, slowing down and then speeding up to gain whatever advantage she could to catch the assassin.

She had no doubts that she could catch the Lincoln; compared to her Mustang it was big and cumbersome. The real problem wasn't the speed, it was the fact that two cars having a drag race in the centre of downtown New Orleans did tend to attract a lot of attention. So she had to close the distance quickly between the two cars, but not look like she was in hot pursuit.

In the passenger seat, Gorilla was being thrown from side to side. "Where the hell did you learn to drive? It's like bloody stock car racing!" he grumbled.

Eunice spun the wheel and skidded round a corner. Up ahead, she could see the Lincoln moving onto a main road leading out of the city centre. "I don't know what that is – stock car racing? I guess the nearest equivalent we have is NASCAR."

"Still doesn't explain why you drive like a bloody madwoman," complained Gorilla.

"Ha! I had a good teacher, an old boyfriend of mine who used to run moonshine in his truck. I used to yell at him to 'Kick it, Ira!' when I wanted him to speed up. He taught me how to drive fast and handle tight corners."

She looked over at him and winked. "He taught me a few other things in that truck, too, not all of them to do with driving."

Gorilla, feeling himself flush, grunted, "Yeah. Stop, I'm gonna be sick."

"Because of my driving? Or because you are jealous of an old boyfriend?" she teased.

"Just give me my bloody gun back!" he barked at her.

A smile played at her lips. "Sure. It's in my purse. You know how to use it?"

"Grrrr!" he growled, fumbling in the back seat and recovering the ASP.

The smile spread wider this time. Even in these moments of the hunt, when her mind should be on business, she always knew that she would love the game of teasing Jack Grant.

"Well, just so you know, Jack, I have a thing for blondes – even ones with a touch of grey. So it's your lucky day," she said, as she slammed the Mustang into top gear with one hand, while with the other, she flirtily ran her fingers along the nape of his neck.

Gorilla ignored her and chamber-checked the weapon. "Hands on the wheel and eyes on the road. Let's get him out of the city and into the country, then I'll take out his tyres."

"What were you doing back there, Jack? What's your interest in the Creole?" she asked.

Gorilla shrugged. "He's a link in a chain. I was hoping he'd move me further up that chain to the next link, all the way to the top."

"Is it a target?"

"I can't discuss that, Eunice, you know that."

"Jack, what are the odds that we were both after the same dead arms dealer on exactly the same day? I think we are after the same High-Value Target."

"Bullshit. Don't be crazy! I work for the French now, you know that and you work for…?"

"Let's just say for the land of the free and the home of the brave. I'm going to say a name to you, Jack. Caravaggio. Does that mean anything to you?"

He snapped a sly look over at her and she knew that the name had meaning to him. "I knew it! That sonofabitch Gibbs... *HANG ON!*"

She swung the car hard onto the freeway, as the guy in the Lincoln had upped his speed and had taken a sharp turn at the last minute in an attempt to lose her. But Eunice was better than that. She had him in her sights and she wasn't going to lose him now.

"Maybe we are and maybe we aren't," he said, "but that's something we can talk about later. Right now, let's just catch this killer and see what he knows!"

They came off the freeway and looped round onto the open country roads that ran along the levee. Once they hit the straight, both cars floored it. It was now a lethal drag race.

"Pull up alongside him," said Gorilla. "I'm gonna nail those tyres."

He wound the passenger window down and had the ASP ready, holding it in both hands. The Mustang surged and then shot forward, gaining on the Lincoln until, within a matter of seconds, both cars were nose to tail.

Gorilla craned his body so that his left wrist rested on the sill of the window. He flicked off the safety and centred the Guttersnipe sights on the black tyre and aimed for the thinnest part of the rubber near the hub-caps. He went with a double tap and was rewarded with an explosion of air from the tyre. The Lincoln swayed, almost spinning out of control, but the driver kept it in check.

Gorilla turned and yelled through the noise to Eunice, "All we have to do now is wait for that tyre to deflate!"

"No time, Jack," she called back, over the scream of the Mustang's engine. "We're almost out of road! Leave it to me. Just be ready!"

The Mustang was dodging and swerving either side of the Lincoln, jockeying for position and trying to cut in to get in front and slow it down. A truck heading from the opposite direction forced Eunice to pull in sharply behind the Lincoln until it was gone, and then she was right back out into the road again, harassing the Lincoln like an angry hornet, with revving engines, heavy braking and the smell of burning rubber on the road.

She swung the Mustang to the side so that it bumped the rear offside wheel of the Lincoln. The combination of the blown-out tyre and the impact of the bump caused the Lincoln to spin out and stop on a dusty roadside clearing.

The Mustang overshot the other car, and then Eunice completed a textbook hundred and eighty degree skid and the car came to a stop, fifty feet ahead of the Lincoln. The passenger door opened immediately and Gorilla rolled out onto the hard road.

Even in the roll, he had the ASP up, out and ready. He came to a stop in the kneeling position and fired immediately, throwing out rounds and peppering the door of the Lincoln. Inside, he could see the Chinese assassin flinching. Gorilla emptied the remaining rounds into the Lincoln.

He went to slide-lock and was in the middle of a tactical magazine reload when the driver of the Lincoln took advantage of the pause in fire to gun the engine and shoot past him, heading back the way they had just come. Gorilla knew that if the Chinese assassin could make it back into the city and dump the car, they would lose his trail fast.

He completed the re-load, decided against wasting any more bullets shooting at the fleeing car, and was about to turn back to the Mustang when he heard the squeal of rubber on the road as Nikita Brown and her Mustang sped off at in hot pursuit without him. Fuck!

Gorilla stood at the side of the road and watched as Nikita's car drove off into the distance, leaving a trail of dust behind her. She'd bloody tricked him again. This bloody woman and her bloody double-crosses!

What she didn't know, what she couldn't know, was what was on the one piece of paper that the Chinese assassin had dropped in the office at the Pink Lady club. It contained a list of numbers that looked strangely like bank accounts. Swiss ones.

It wasn't much, but it was a lead. If Sassi and the SDECE could narrow it down, he might have the advantage, even for just a little while, before Nikita Brown and the unknown Chinese assassin could get ahead of him.

Chapter Eight

It took him an age to make his way back to New Orleans. Most of it was on foot and supplemented by a bit of hitch-hiking. By the time he got back, he was dirty, exhausted and just plain old fed up with his job. He needed a drink and to quit... become a window cleaner, or anything. It had to be better than dragging his arse around America and dealing with this kind of hassle. But, in reality, he knew that was a lie. Who was he kidding? He loved it!

He was sitting in the Bourbon Bar across the street from his hotel when she found him. It was neither busy nor empty. The evening crowd hadn't quite filtered in and the afternoon crowd hadn't quite finished.

She sat on the barstool next to him and ordered a martini. He didn't even look sideways at her, simply took a sip of his bourbon and said, "You get him?"

"Not so as you'd notice. He got away. I lost him around the airport. He was fast. Dumped the car and disappeared," she said.

Gorilla grunted, satisfied that there was at least some justice in the world. "Pity," he said. "I picked up some useful information that I found at the Pink Lady Club."

"Would you care to share it?"

"Not really, love. Not after you left me out in the wilds of Louisiana."

"Oh, don't be sore, Jack. I was reacting to the situation, that's all. I'd have come back for you. Eventually."

"Yeah, sure," he grumbled.

She laughed. "Besides, I didn't want him to get away. Anyway, I've got a little bit of information, too. Hot off the presses. Maybe we could pool resources?"

"Fuck no!"

She frowned. "Jack! Tut-tut now… that's no way to talk in front of a sweet Southern gal like me! Fucks are for other people but not me. So please, baby, no fucks."

He looked at her, weighing up her words, being drawn in by those green eyes. "Okay, I'll risk it. What have you got?"

"Ah-ha, you first."

"No chance."

"Look, this is no way to start a partnership…"

"Who said anything about a partnership?" His voice had gone up an octave.

"Okay, let's call it a mutually beneficial business arrangement, if it soothes your sensibilities. How about I give you the outline of what I've got and then you do the same? Maybe, if we think it's worth it, we can hook up, help each other out. Deal?" she said reasonably.

He nodded. "Okay, let's see."

"I had a friend of mine in local law enforcement get the details of the Lincoln, who had hired it, and then I had another friend run the details of our killer to see if he had flown out from the airport."

"And had he?"

"Ah-ha! Not the details, remember? Now it's your turn."

He pulled a sheet of paper out of his pocket. "It's a list of bank accounts. I had my people run them, they are checking on them now. I should have some details of who they belong to within twenty-four hours."

"Impressive," she said.

His mind went back to the conversation in the car. "How did you get the name of the Creole in the first place?"

She shrugged. "It was part of the information that I got for this job."

"The source was good?" he asked.

She nodded. "Uh –huh. Seems that way. You?"

"The same."

The verbal stand-off continued. Gorilla thought it through. It probably came from the same signals intercept that the SDECE had got it from. Hell, Nikita was an American. Probably operating for the Americans, so it wouldn't have surprised him if the original source of information had come from the CIA or the NSA, anyway and the intercept had just been passed out to friendly agencies, including the French, as standard procedure.

"So what do we do now?" he said.

"Well, honey, I suspect that we will have another drink each and see where this crazy game of ours leads us."

He grunted.

"If you're lucky, I might flirt with you a bit."

"Don't bother."

"Why? Are you impervious to my charms?"

But Gorilla had already lifted himself off the bar stool and was on his way to the door.

"I'll meet you here tomorrow evening. Let me check out with my people to see if they know anything. Maybe you should do the same," he called over his shoulder, as he pushed open the door to the street.

Eunice smiled to herself as she watched him make his way across the street to his hotel. Watched again as he casually glanced back at the inside of the bar to see if he could spot her one last time. *Oh, you think you are so cool, Mr Grant. You don't need anybody, you're far too tough. Well, mister, we'll see about that!*

Eunice Brown slugged back the last of her martini and breathed a sigh of relief. This job had just gotten interesting.

Chang sat in the airport waiting for his connecting flight. His mission, for now, was done. The man from New Orleans was 'retired'. It had been a necessary step, vital, in closing down what was left of the Caravaggio network.

The only thing that bothered him had been the interruption by the man and the woman. Although they hadn't been able to identify or stop him, thus allowing him to make an escape, he still felt uneasy that he had been compromised. What was even more concerning to the overall mission was that Chang had recognised the man he had fought with – it was the gunman, Gorilla Grant.

Chang recognised him from the archives that his Control had insisted that he study as part of his training. The archives held the files of a list of individuals that operated in the same profession as he did. His controller stressed the importance of knowing all rivals from the intelligence world, but especially important competitors in the killing business.

So, Gorilla Grant himself was after the Creole? Now, that was interesting. As far as Chang had been aware, the man had been out of the profession for over a year. Nevertheless, he suspected that it was not a coincidence. Coincidence had no place in their trade.

The question was that, with this new intelligence, should Chang continue? His training and his instinct said that he should move onto the next target in the network quickly. But with new players appearing in this mission, Chang wondered if he would be forced to remove more than just his original targets?

He would go to his Control for the ultimate sanction.

Chapter Nine

They met the next evening as agreed. Gorilla was wearing his usual evening suit: black with a black shirt, open-necked. He sat at a corner table, nursing his glass of local bourbon and occasionally glancing at the couples dancing to the Cajun band. In truth, he wasn't sure that she would show up. To his cynical mind, he half expected her to blow out of town and get on with tracking the Chinese killer on her own.

So it wasn't an unpleasant surprise when, five minutes later, he looked up and saw her walking towards his table. But Eunice... oh my, she was dressed to kill, he thought. Her hair was tied back in a pony-tail and she was wearing a simple green cotton dress. A deep leather purse was slung casually over her shoulder. She stopped and rested a hand on her hip as she looked down on him.

"Drink?" he said.

She nodded and sat down. "It's a good place to start. A beer, please."

Gorilla got the attention of the barkeeper and motioned for two more beers.

"I do like a bad man in a good suit," she said, appraising him.

"Who says it's a good suit?"

She smiled. "You want we should eat, maybe talk a little business?"

They both decided on the jambalaya, which had a reputation for being excellent in the Bourbon Bar. They sat in the silence of their own company for a while, watching each other, weighing up the opposition. Was she playing him? Did he know more than he knew? For both of them, it was an internal battle, mainly because it was so rare that two such as they should come up against each other. Evidently, their mutual target was of enough importance to warrant the best contractors in the business having their gun-sights trained on him.

Gorilla couldn't stop himself gazing at her tanned arms, the smooth glide of her neck, taking in the glossy pony-tail and those stunning green eyes.

"I said, have you heard anything from your people?"

He came to, dragging himself back to reality and away from a teenage fantasy. Jeez, what was it with this woman? She had the ability to dazzle him, make him sway and, worst of all, lose focus. For an intelligence operator, that could be lethal.

"My people got a hit. A lead. You?" he said.

She reached out her hand and stroked one beautifully manicured green nail along his arm. "Of course, Jack, my people have the best information. But you go first," she said, winking.

He growled internally. Why was she always one step ahead of him, able to play him?

"The account belongs to a woman. Name of Thallia Dimitriou. The French have it on good authority that she's one of the best forgers in the business and that she operates out of Athens," he said.

"Oh, my! Good intel," she said, smiling.

"There's more, but now it's your turn."

She held him for a moment, kept him waiting with bated breath, then finally she said, "Okay. And our little black-suited Chinese friend, guess where his flight was heading to?"

Gorilla leaned forward, eager to hear. "No!"

"Yes..."

"Athens."

"Yes. Well, via Paris first, but eventually to Athens."

"Well, that's too much of a coincidence."

"I agree." A smile.

"Another drink?"

"I think we've earned it, so yes."

"So it seems we are definitely after the same target," said Gorilla.

"Another coincidence?"

He nodded. "Maybe… or maybe our bosses are just trying to be a touch too clever for their own good."

"What do you mean?"

"Well, two contractors such as us, in the same timeframe, after the exact same target. I think the people who employ us are leaving out some finer details."

Gorilla shrugged inwardly. It was almost always that way in the intelligence business. You never got the full story. He sipped at his beer, then said, "What do you know about the target? About Carravaggio?"

She picked a thread off the sleeve of his jacket. There was something seductive about the way that she did it. *Bloody hell, woman! Stop flirting with me,* he thought.

"Only what was in the file they handed me. But Caravaggio is a legend to anyone who knows their stuff in the spy business. We had rumours of him taking out people way back when I was with the Agency in Berlin. Rumour has it he did a hit from one side of Checkpoint Charlie to the other – long range sniper rifle. That was the rumour, anyway. What about you? What have you heard, Jack?"

"Mostly rumour. The odd piece of intel from the French files." Then he paused, caught himself, deciding how much to tell her and whether he should give a piece of his past to her. "I met him once, you know," he said, taking a bitter pull of the beer. The thought of the shootout in Nice still left a nasty taste in his mouth.

"You did? Where? Jeez, Jack, that's a story I really have to hear!"

Gorilla held up his right hand. "I used to be a right-handed shooter until he gave me this."

Eunice took his hand in hers. Her palm was cool against his skin. She looked closely at the round, puckered scar where the bullet had smashed tendons and obliterated his skills for almost half a year. "Mmm... looks like a 9mm," she said.

He nodded. "The thing is, when we went up against each other, one of us should have died. It's rare that people like us face off against each other and both survive. He had me dead in his sights and didn't kill me."

"He only wounded you? Interesting."

"Yes. My thoughts exactly."

"Then maybe you have a professional admirer, Jack. Maybe even two," she said, winking at him.

They were halfway through their second beers when Eunice said in a low voice, "There's a guy watching us just a tad too closely." She inclined her head subtly in the direction of the seated area on the other side of the dance floor

Gorilla glanced over and grunted. "Probably he's undressing you in his mind. Don't take any notice."

"You think he's working surveillance on us? For Caravaggio?"

"No. I think he's just a horny red-blooded male."

She laughed out loud and smiled, reaching in to kiss his neck. "Oh my lord, Jack Grant, you do make me smile. Tell you what, let's have a dance!"

"*What?* I don't dance!"

"*Pshhh...* of course you do. Everybody dances. Anyway, it's work. It will give us a chance to have a closer look at our would-be watcher. Come on."

She grabbed him firmly by the hand and pulled him onto the dance floor, moving through the crowd until they were on the periphery of the couples who were dancing. The atmosphere was alive and fun. People in the Big Easy sure did know how to enjoy themselves, he thought.

They danced to a slow Cajun number that the band leader said was called *Tramp Sur La Rue*. It was slow and sad and soulful and it allowed the couples on the floor to sway and hold each other close. Eunice was taller than him, even if she hadn't been wearing the heels. But despite that, Gorilla felt immediately comfortable dancing close to her.

"He's definitely interested in us," she said into his ear, her breath controlled and deep.

Gorilla nodded. "Plus he's packing. Handgun tucked into his waistband beneath his jacket."

"Lots of people carry guns in New Orleans. It's a rough town."

"Perhaps... It still doesn't explain why he's eyeballing us, though."

A man came up to them and tried to cut in. He was tall and smooth and impossibly good-looking. Gorilla would have termed him a *louche* lounge lizard. He knew the type. Gorilla immediately stepped back, his hands curling into fists ready to pop him if need be.

But it was Eunice who controlled the situation. She smiled sweetly and said to the dandy, "*Non merci, monsieur.* I only dance with my husband."

The man looked crushed, smoothed back his hair and went on his way, looking for an easier conquest than the redhead.

"Your husband?" said Gorilla. He was intrigued by her reply.

"It seemed like the right thing to say," she said knowingly.

They continued with their slow dance, half moving against each other and half concentrating on the man watching them. Eunice flicked a glance at Gorilla, caught his eye for just a moment, and then rested her body against him.

She felt him tense up for a moment, and then instantly relax. "You dance like my daddy would with Momma," she said.

"How do you mean?" he asked, holding her lightly, continuing to sway to the beat.

She smiled, remembering family parties and the dances on base. "He would take his time with her, he would always go slow and gentle, even though dancing wasn't really Daddy's thing, either. But he would always make the effort for Momma. And you know what? He always ended up enjoying it. He was actually quite good. I think you're the same?"

Was that a smile she saw at the corner of his lips? Had the angry mask of the Gorilla cracked and slipped, even just for a moment? She hoped so, because she didn't know what it was about Jack Grant – schoolgirl crush, infatuation, or maybe even possibly love – but he touched her in a way that caused her to open herself up to him.

And for Eunice, that was the first time she had felt like that with any man.

"We have company."

The music had switched to a different song, still slow but more up-beat. Several of the couples departed the floor, but Eunice and Gorilla continued with their slow dance.

The surveillance watcher had now been joined by a large, raw-boned man in a silk suit. The pair were standing and glaring at the dancing couple. Gorilla pretended not to notice. After all, why tip them off? But he did notice two other tough-looking hoods in suits watching them from the bar.

"You armed?" she asked.

"Only my razor. I only carry loaded when there is an active job on. You?"

"No firearms. I have something in my purse that might help, though. We'll see. How do you want to play it?"

"I think we need to slip away as quickly and quietly as we can. You have your car nearby?"

"Just around the block."

"Perfect. I think we need to grab our things and get out of town. We've definitely overstayed our welcome in New Orleans," he murmured.

"This doesn't feel like our target. This feels more localised, smaller in scale. The quality of the surveillance screams to me criminal, rather than professional," said Eunice.

"So not Caravaggio? You think it's to do with the Creole? Guillame?"

"I absolutely do. I think we were spotted, or there was a camera somewhere in the club that identified us. I think that these guys work – or worked – for him and they want a little revenge."

He looked around him and over her shoulder. "There's a service door down towards the toilets. We can slip out that way."

They waited until the band had kicked off with a rousing rockabilly number, causing more people to get up onto the dance floor, and then they slowly moved away and down toward the darkness at the rear of the bar. They bypassed the toilets and Gorilla quickly sprung the lock on the service door with his lock-pick. The door gave freely and they both stepped out into the sultry darkness of the night.

It was the click that they heard first, that of a revolver being cocked, and then the coolness of the barrel as it was placed against the back of Eunice's neck.

"Well hello, little lady," said a deep Louisiana accent, full of menace. "I think we need to have a talk."

They were surrounded within seconds. Shadows came out of the darkness and cut off their escape route out of the alleyway. There were four of them; two behind Eunice and two behind Gorilla. All dressed in suits. Not businessmen; they were more strategically clothed to make them look semi-respectable. Eunice knew the type straight away. Tough guys, hired muscle. Criminals. All had the meaty faces and swollen knuckles of street boxers.

Deep Voice seemed to be the leader. He had been the one watching them in the club and he was the one with the gun and doing the talking. "Give me the keys to your car, that red Mustang you got, lady," he said. She reluctantly handed them over and Deep Voice flung them over to one of his cohorts.

"A Mustang... nice. I'm gonna have fun with that," said an ugly bald man to his right. "I'm gonna take it down to the track and burn it out."

Eunice smiled. "Now, don't you be goin' doin' nothing too rough with my baby, fellas. That would make Mamma very angry."

"After what you did to our boss, you'll be lucky if you're gonna be able to walk anytime soon, let alone drive," said the lean man, who rested a restraining hand on Gorilla's shoulder.

"Yeah. You was seen running away from the club yesterday. Then the body of the boss turns up dead..."

"Shut your mouth, you guys. We don't need to tell them anything. They already know what they did. And now they got to pay the price," ordered Deep Voice.

So that was it, thought Gorilla. Eunice had been correct. The shootout at the club yesterday must have been witnessed by one of these goons. They had put two and two together and assumed that Eunice and he had killed Guillame. And now they wanted revenge for their dead boss.

"Let's get them out of here," said Deep Voice, motioning with the gun. "I got a date later tonight. I don't want this snuffing out to take all night! Chico, you get the Mustang. We'll pack these two into the trunk and take them out to the swamp. Do it there."

Slowly, they all started to move and then Eunice did something very deliberate. She dropped her purse and slowly bent down to pick it up. Two things happened in that moment. The curve of her dress rode up along to the top of her thigh and, because of the angle, her cleavage was exposed to reveal that beautiful 'V' shape between her breasts.

The men did an internal "Wow!" and paused for a few brief seconds. It was all that Eunice Brown needed.

Her hand moved in a blur. One moment the purse was clutched to her hip, the next, her hand was inside and out and holding a black tube with a leather lanyard wrapped around her wrist. What followed would later have to be slowed down by Gorilla in his mind.

The two-foot sprung steel lead weight extended out of the handle and crashed down onto the wrist of Deep Voice, causing him to drop the revolver. The man howled in pain. Eunice whipped the spring cosh back in a deadly arc, until it smashed into the side of the gunman's skull, sending him reeling to the ground.

Gorilla was also on the move. He smashed a reverse elbow into the face of the man to the side of him, sending the thug back against the wall. Gorilla turned into him and hit him with a hammer-fist strike to the nose, spreading it across his face, a mass of blood and flesh. Just for good measure Gorilla kicked and punched the man all the way to the ground.

The lean thug had taken a swipe at Eunice, but he was too far out of range with his fists to make contact. Unfortunately for him, though, Eunice's spring-loaded cosh wasn't. She swung it forward as if she were throwing a baseball and the spring extension shot forward under its own energy, the heavy ball connecting perfectly with the man's skull. He dropped like a sack.

She whipped the cosh back to a resting position against her right shoulder and it was then that she felt the final man grab her from behind in a bear hug.

"I got you now, bitch," he hissed into her ear.

Eunice tried to free herself but he had clamped his arms against her body, rendering the cosh useless. Even now, he was trying to drag her away from the fight scene.

"*ARGGHHH!*" cried her attacker as he suddenly let go. She spun out of the bear hug and saw what had caused him to release her. The man had fallen to the ground with his ankles opened up and blood pouring from the wounds.

Above him, glaring down, his face a mask of fury and holding one very bloodstained cut-throat razor, was Gorilla Grant. Gorilla had severed the tendons in the man's ankles. When he had tried to move, he had collapsed, his legs unable to support his bodyweight.

Eunice looked down at the man for a moment and then whipped the spring cosh in a short arc until it connected with the thug's head.

There was the inevitable *THOCK* as metal connected with bone and then their last attacker was knocked unconscious.

Gorilla looked up at her, his rage coming down… slightly. "Nice spring cosh," he said, wiping the razor on the suit of the nearest thug before folding it away.

"Thanks. It was my Pappa's. He was in the OSS during the war. It's a cosh that they gave to agents who were dropped into Europe. He always said that it would save my life one day," she said, slipping it back into her purse.

"Miss Brown, I think we need to get out of this town?"

"Mr Grant, I think you are right," she said sweetly. "I believe we have a plane to catch."

She glanced down briefly at the bodies that they had disposed of that night.

"No one messes with my Mustang," she said, as they walked calmly away with her arm linked through Gorilla Grant's. They were just a normal couple on a normal night out on the town.

Chapter Ten

Athens, Greece – September 1973

They had surveillance on her for nearly three days before she received the telephone call that set their alarm bells ringing.

Eunice had put in a request via Gibbs to the CIA Station in Athens. They needed a van, some directional microphones, cameras – the whole bag of tricks to conduct long term surveillance. CIA/Athens had kicked up a fuss. They weren't too keen about handing over their expensive kit to a 'freelancer', even if she had once been Agency.

Then the word had come back from Langley and the Station Chief and his officers had been told in no uncertain terms to pipe down. This was an operation that outweighed anything that CIA/Athens was doing at the moment and so Nikita Brown had received everything that she had asked for.

They had done an initial reconnaissance of the area and had found two possible spots that gave them direct line of sight of Thallia Dimitriou's apartment in the fashionable Kolonaki district of the city. Gorilla had dressed in old workman's clothes that had been filched from the CIA Station's wardrobe and he had driven the van. He parked it at the end of the street near the corner so that they had good access routes to escape in case they were discovered. The vantage point also gave them a good view of the target's apartment.

Eunice had taken the first twelve-hour shift while Gorilla got his head down to sleep. Not that it was easy, even with the air conditioning. The heat in the city was uncomfortable, to say the least. But they worked their shifts. Gorilla had the days, Eunice had the nights.

The first day, little had happened. Eunice had taken some shots on the camera as Thallia Dimitriou had left her apartment block and Gorilla had been the footman to see where she went. The second day was the usual dreary day hated by surveillance operators the world over. The 'honeymoon' period is over and the operator knows that he isn't going to get a quick result and is there for the long haul.

However, on the third day Eunice had been trying out the parabolic microphone, pointing it up at the apartment window as Thallia walked to and fro in the room. The microphone was a dish about a foot in diameter, with a directional microphone at its centre. The operator would listen in via a pair of headphones and record anything as needed.

The microphone picked up the ringing of the telephone and then muffled voices. Eunice pressed the headphones tighter to her ears and tried to move the directional mike into a better spot. She closed her eyes, concentrating. Voices... one female, one male. A brief outline of a conversation, most of it garbled, but a time and a place managed to make it through the static.

"We gotcha, lady," said Eunice to herself. It was the best information that they had and they would just have to make do. Her only hope was that the meeting time or location wasn't changed at the last minute. So they had a rendezvous time, a location and some brief details. Gorilla and Eunice reasoned that this could be their chance to 'acquire' the target.

They hoped so, and both operators knew from long and bitter experience that time was running out.

Gorilla and Eunice sat in their car in the underground car park of the Hotel Electra the next night and began the next phase of their covert surveillance. At least it was cool underground with all the stone and concrete. Anything was better than being stuck in that surveillance van again in the heat.

They had arrived at least forty-five minutes before their target was due to show, partly because they wanted to pick an advantageous spot so that they could see but not be seen, and partly to get the pulse of the environment. They wanted to watch the comings and goings and see if there was any other surveillance.

A variety of luxury cars came and went. Some contained guests and some were chauffeurs dropping off VIPs. Then there was a lull in the traffic for a while before a sporty-looking MG came gliding into one of the spaces near to the elevator.

"I think we have our target, Eunice," said Gorilla.

"Wait, Jack… Look! Who's that?" said Eunice, indicating a figure that had emerged from the shadows on the opposite row to where Thallia Dimitriou had parked. "The client, maybe?"

A large, bearded, bear-like figure in a dark business suit stood waiting behind one of the concrete pillars. He was shuffling from foot to foot. The big man could see the woman in the sports car, but he couldn't see the vehicle that Gorilla and Eunice were in. They were on his blindside.

"Shit!" said Gorilla.

"Who is he?" asked Eunice, searching her memory to see if she knew the face.

But Gorilla was already reaching beneath his suit jacket for the ASP and the silencer and fixing them together. "He's no client, he's the competition! We seem to have another freelancer taking part in this contract. It's getting awfully crowded."

Eunice glanced down at what he was doing. "Wait!" she said. "We don't have to kill him!"

Gorilla frowned. "Trust me on this, Eunice, there is no way that this guy will let us get close. I know him. We have to take him out. He's a killer. It's the Bulgarian, Brodsky."

The Bulgarian's name was Dimitar Brodsky. He was a heavyset, bearded man in his thirties with the look of a glowering bear. Brodsky was an operative of Service 7, a unit of the Bulgarian Secret Service responsible for the kidnapping, assassination and use of disinformation against Bulgarian dissidents and anti-communist activists in the west.

In his five years in S7, he had risen quickly to become one of its best assassins, so much so that the KGB had requested that he help them out with a little problem here or there in Europe from time to time. And when the Russians asked, the Bulgarian service jumped!

Not that Brodsky minded. The Russians usually gave him a little extra on top of his regular wages. Last time, it had been a suitcase full of Chinese narcotics that he was free to sell on the black market. And sell he had. He had made a nice chunk of money, which was just as well because Brodsky liked spending. Western suits, shoes, watches, expensive prostitutes.

His work brought him to the West frequently and he liked to treat himself to its riches. Of course, the secret account that the KGB had helped him set up in Switzerland made that possible. After all, what was the use of doing a little moonlighting for the Russians if you weren't actually allowed to spend what you had earned?

So it came as no surprise that he had been approached directly by the KGB to take on his most challenging operation for them yet; the hunting and termination of one of the so-called legends of the business. *Legends... pah!* In Brodsky's experience it was all hyperbole. He cared nothing for reputations, because the truth was that you were only as good as your last mission and, from what he understood, the so-called 'Master' would be an old man by now and had been off the radar for years.

Anyway, it was all irrelevant. The KGB had given him a good start point, a lead, someone that they knew who had been connected to Caravaggio. Brodsky may have come late to the game – in fact, he was sure that there were other contractors already working this operation – but he knew from experience that he had the skills to catch up quickly.

Which was why, today, he was in Greece and had made an appointment to meet with the best, and most exclusive, forger in the Mediterranean. The forger, according to the information given to him by his KGB handlers, was Caravaggio's personal paper artist, confidant and whore.

Brodsky considered this an excellent place to start.

The attempted kidnapping of Thallia Dimitriou, the forger, by the assassin Brodsky, took place at the Hotel Electra in the centre of Athens. She had been contacted by telephone the previous day at her apartment and was asked if she was in the market for a high-end contract to deliver forged papers within the next month. She had accepted in principle, but had assured the client that she would need more information before she could accept completely. The client had agreed and had booked a private suite at the exclusive Hotel Electra so that they might discuss business.

Her client for the evening was reputed to be a professional smuggler who needed to move some 'stones' across from Africa to the USA, and he needed the papers to be able to travel undetected and for some possible import. At least that was the story that she had been given in the telephone call to her private number yesterday afternoon. In truth, she cared nothing for the reason. The thing she cared about was if the client could pay.

Thallia Dimitriou was late forties, but with the youth and beauty of a woman fifteen years younger. She had the svelte figure and oval-eyed, dark beauty of the classical Greek woman, and the sensual grace of the professional courtesan. She had been a diplomat's daughter and as a young woman, she had travelled the world, studied art in Paris and Rome and had taught herself the skills of the tattoo artist throughout her twenties. In her thirties, she had been seduced by the mysterious Caravaggio who had played Pygmalion games with her mind and her body. For nearly a decade, she had been his willing slave.

She drove her car fast through the streets, comfortable in the knowledge that she would arrive on time, but also enjoying the freedom of driving her MG. The hotel was a luxurious palace in the centre of Athens, from the side rooms of which the lucky guests could see the Acropolis lit up of an evening. She drove to the side of the hotel, past the main reception area and down into the underground car park.

She had no sooner exited her car and headed towards the lift when she felt a strong hand grab roughly at her arm. Brodsky jammed a pistol into her ribs. "Miss Dimitriou, please don't struggle if you want to live. I have a room in the hotel, we can have a little talk there. Don't make any untoward movements or try to alert any –"

In her peripheral vision, she was aware of a black metal tube pushing its way forward to her rear. It moved past her at head height, aimed at the kidnapper's skull. It spat twice and the noise was that of a steel brush against steel, a sweeping *swoosh*, nothing more. Thallia caught a gust of wind from the shot and then felt the weight of the man who had grabbed her suddenly disappear. She heard the body hit the concrete floor and then felt her other arm being taken in a confident but gentle grip. She hadn't even missed a step, it had happened that quickly.

The arm that guided her now belonged to a tall, red-haired woman in her thirties. The redhead steered her around and back to her sports car. "Just keep walking, sweetie," she said. "You don't need to see any of that. Now, please let's me and you go for a little drive. And no trouble, please. I don't want to have to get rough unless it's absolutely necessary."

Thallia had been in enough danger in her life not to argue with her new abductor, woman or no woman. She opened up the sports car and they both got in.

"Just drive, sweetie," said the redhead. "I'll give you directions once we hit the road."

They turned left and moved up the ramp towards the exit. A final look in the rear view mirror showed her the red-headed woman's accomplice, the man with the silenced gun, dragging the dead body of the kidnapper away.

The safe house was a rented apartment, discreet and off the beaten track on the edge of the city limits. Eunice took control and moved the other woman out of the car, in through the door and down into a seat in the main lounge.

"Please make yourself comfortable," said Eunice, handing Thallia a glass of brandy. "Here, drink this. It might help calm your nerves."

"I'm fine. I am not nervous," said Thallia.

"Good for you, sweetie, good for you," said Eunice.

They had sat in the apartment waiting for Gorilla to arrive, making small talk. Eunice thought that the Greek woman had an ethereal quality to her. She had that confidence that beautiful women the world over have; a combination of poise and serenity.

The door opened and Gorilla walked in. He nodded to both women, locked the door behind him and sat down across from them both. Thallia noticed a spot of blood on her shirt collar.

"Are we ready?" he asked Eunice.

Eunice nodded. "I think so, yes." She turned to Thallia and smiled. "Miss Dimitriou, first of all can I assure you that you are in no danger. I'm sorry you had to witness the unpleasantness in the car park. Events did rather overtake us and my friend here was forced to take extreme action. But *we* are friends. We mean you no harm. We are here to help if we can."

"So I am free to leave?" said Thallia defiantly, testing them.

Eunice smiled. "Alas, for the minute, we hope that you will stay seated and listen to our proposal. So let's just say that you are our guest and we would like to buy your company for the next few hours."

Thallia shrugged. Eunice took that as acceptance that she was willing to listen. "We understand that you receive a monthly income. The source of the money originates from an account in Switzerland. Is that correct?"

Thallia stared at them both, her face betraying nothing. "I cannot talk about that."

Eunice led the pitch. In this respect, it was more her area of expertise – Eunice the talker, Gorilla there to do the manual labour. "Thallia, look, we know the source of it. We have a few questions that we want to ask you. Nothing that would compromise you in any way, you have my word."

Thallia smiled. "Then if you know the source of the money, what do you need me for?"

Eunice shrugged. "We need some background information. We have been instructed to offer you a cash amount for information – twenty thousand US dollars. Here, now, tonight."

"Background information? About the money?"

"About the source of the money, about Caravaggio," said Eunice.

Thallia caught herself, took a breath and calmed down.

"I think you at least owe us for saving your life? If whatever that kidnapper had planned for you had happened... well, my guess is that *you* would be dead by now, rather than him," said Gorilla. "Plus, we are offering you some serious money just for a few hours of your time."

The Greek woman turned and glared at them. "You wish to know about Caravaggio, yes? I would urge you to turn back now. Forget this. Forget that you ever heard his name. There is only death in that name for you."

Gorilla and Eunice glanced at each other. Even though her words sent a chill down their respective spines, they knew that turning back was never an option.

Thallia sighed. "Very well, if you will not, that is up to you. I will tell you what I can."

"That is all we ask, sweetie. Tell me about him."

She nodded, steeling herself, unsure where to begin. In the end, she just spoke plainly, with no embellishments, only the truth. "Caravaggio was an enigma to me, a mystery to most people. He was a man of many faces. He was also the best lover that I ever had. I was his lady and I was treated as such. Monte Carlo, St Moritz, Bermuda. We travelled everywhere together. We lived the lifestyle of gods. Nothing was beyond our reach, no experience, no taste, no pleasure was unattainable. "

"Did you know who he was, what he was? What he did for money?"

She shook her head. "Not at first, no. To me, he was just my Caravaggio. That is the only name that I knew him by. He was wealthy, influential, and confident. He said that he was a businessman, that he had inherited his wealth from his family."

"What does he look like?" asked Gorilla, keen to put a face to the name.

Thallia smiled. "He is a man, as a woman expects a man to be. He was like a Greek god, tall and blonde and beautiful. He found me alone and sad on the Island of Kos. I was escaping from a failed romance and I was lonely and scared. He romanced me and made me believe that I was the centre of his universe… and, for a while, I was. He even bought some of my paintings. He said they were beautiful and that he admired them."

Gorilla nodded to himself. It was the perfect recruitment pitch. Take a target when they are at their most vulnerable, say the right things and then whisk them away in a whirlwind of action so that they don't have time to think, or consider that things might not be as straight up as they seemed. It worked notoriously well with agents and beautiful women, it seemed. Always had, always would. It's what made them so bloody easy to recruit.

"It sounds perfect, too perfect," said Eunice, flicking a glance at Gorilla.

"We would fly around the world together. He would work on what he said were business deals and I would be given free time to spend money. I wanted for nothing. We lived in grand style in his houses and apartments around the world. I never asked where the money was coming from or where it was going. But over time, I missed my family. I wanted to see them, talk to my mother and father. But Caravaggio said that we would make time to visit them soon, after his work was done. But 'soon' never came. I became distracted. I chose to lose myself in money and my art."

"Friends?"

"Only those he chose for me, people he did business with and their wives. Most weeks, the only people I spoke to were the servants, and then only briefly. I was watched constantly by his bodyguard, a man called Chang. It was as if he didn't wish to share me with another human soul. He chose what clothes I would wear, what I would eat, who I could talk to. I was weak and I let him, because I thought that was how love was meant to be in our world.

"Soon, several years had gone by and, aside from my artwork, I had nothing to do but sit around and feel bored and unfulfilled. Then one day I snuck out from our villa in Malaga and drove into town. I found a payphone and called an old friend of my father's. I explained who I was and asked if he could pass a message to my *patéras*, my father.

"The man told me that my parents had died in a car crash in Cyprus a year earlier. My parents were dead and I didn't even know about it! I had become blinded and isolated. I was a fool."

Gorilla knew that was another aspect of successful agent recruitment; isolation. Starve them of a support network so that the agent relies on the handler completely. It was a sordid and dirty world that they operated in, taking advantage of and manipulating weaker human beings.

"When Caravaggio found out that I had contacted people from my old life, he became angry. He raged and spat at me. I had never seen him like this before. He was like a violent maniac. He smashed up the bedroom in the villa and stormed out. I did not see him for two days.

"I cried all the time. I felt even more alone. I had no parents and now my lover had abandoned me. When he returned, he was apologetic and we sat and talked. He said that he had something important to tell me. It was a great secret. The reason that he hadn't told me this secret before was because he wanted to protect me."

"From what?"

"His enemies. Dangerous people. He said that his business activities, all the wealth, the cars, the houses, the travel... it was all just a cover, a front for his real work."

"What was that?"

"He said that he had been recruited to work for several intelligence agencies... that he was trained to carry out special operations for them. He was committed to fighting tyranny and injustice. When he looked into my eyes, I could see he was sincere and honest.

"My mind was dizzy with what he had just told me. My lover, the man that I had spent all these years with was a spy, a secret agent? It could not be, surely? How fortunate was I, as a woman, that he had chosen to share this secret with me. To give me that level of trust!"

That was a facet of successful source recruitment, thought Gorilla. Embody in them that level of trust, that they have been admitted to a great secret, that they are working for a higher calling. Gorilla knew that it was all crap. This beautiful and intelligent woman had been deceived by a fraud and a liar. Caravaggio, if his files were to be believed, wasn't a moral crusader. When you boiled it down to basics, he was just a grubby little killer.

Thallia continued. "He took me to a secret room in the villa that held the tools of espionage. Weapons, knives, guns, secret cameras, code books. He let me see everything, he shared it all with me, and he said that he would never withhold anything again. We made love there on the floor of that room... we lost ourselves in our passion.

"Eventually, he included me more and more in his conspiracies. I met some of his people, his network. I became his personal forger, making documents, travel passes, passports. I was trusted with his work, so much so that eventually I would know when he had killed."

"How would you know that?" asked Gorilla.

She looked at each of them in turn. Eunice noted that there were tears in her eyes

"Here, let me show you," said Thallia.

She stood and slipped off the shoulders of her black dress, allowing it to fall to her feet. She was naked underneath. She was an incredibly beautiful woman and Gorilla, even Eunice, could not fail to notice her sensuality. But her nakedness and beauty were secondary to what was on display.

The tattoos that stretched across her body began just above her pubic area, across the flat of her stomach, over her breasts and over onto her back. Most were symbols, but some had writing next to them, Asian, Sanskrit, Arabic. Most had dates attached. She turned, twisting her body so that her audience could see the artwork from every angle.

"Each one signifies a target, a life that he has taken. I would wear his kills on my body. He was an artist, he said. He was like the old masters who would paint their great imaginings on canvas – though he preferred to tattoo his kills on my body. Caravaggio was a natural artist. I taught him my skills and he would tattoo them himself, using my needles and inks. Eventually, he became my equal."

"Oh, my God!" said Eunice in disgust, her eyes absorbing what she was seeing. "And you let him do this to you, willingly?"

She nodded. "I was conditioned to accept whatever he wanted. I was brainwashed. It is my shame."

"So what changed?"

Thallia pointed to a tattoo on her left breast. The artwork was of a small bear and a date. She covered herself once more with her dress, suddenly aware of her nakedness.

"This one here was my own work. I was able to do it myself, despite the angle. This is the one that I am both ashamed and proud of. Ashamed because of what I had to do to earn it, and proud because it marked the end of my subjugation."

"I was told that I was to fly to Buenos Ares to meet Caravaggio. A suite was booked at the best hotel in the city. Everything was provided

– a private jet, a limousine to meet me in Argentina, even the dress and shoes that I wore had been had hand-picked by him.

"When I arrived at the suite, Caravaggio was not there. I was confused. The only thing waiting for me was a handwritten letter. I opened it. It was from Caravaggio. He said that he was on an important mission and that he would be delayed. He needed my help. He needed me to do something very dangerous to help him with a mission."

"What was it, Thallia? We can stop and have a break if it's too much," said Eunice, stretching out a hand to her.

"No, no... I have to tell this. I have never spoken of any of this. It helps me." She composed herself and continued.

"The letter said that a man was coming to the suite. The man was an enemy, a target. He was dangerous and in order for Caravaggio to complete his mission, the man needed to be distracted. I was to seduce him, get him to lower his guard, but that I was not to worry because Caravaggio would enter the suite and rescue me before things went too far.

"I was shocked, but what else could I do? I felt sick, but Caravaggio needed my help. I trusted him. I truly believed that he would arrive in time to rescue me. He had promised me."

"While I was considering this, there was a knock at the door. I opened it and saw the target for the first time. He was the epitome of the Arab playboy – middle-aged, obese, corpulent, open-necked shirt and too much gold dripping off him. He revolted me instantly. His hands were all over my body. I assume he had been told that I had been paid for, that I was his gift for the night.

"I let him carry on for a while, hoping desperately that it would provide enough time for Caravaggio to arrive and complete the mission. But the Arab quickly lost patience and began to get rough. He ripped off my dress and pushed me onto the bed. He forced himself upon me. He was too strong. I tried to fight, but I couldn't hold him off. He raped me.

"I closed my eyes and just prayed that it would be over quickly. But it wasn't, the fat pig took his time. His sweat was on my body, his grunting was in my ear and his hand was across my mouth to stifle my screams.

"When I finally did open my eyes, I was aware of another person in the room at the foot of the bed. It was Caravaggio! At last, my Caravaggio had come to rescue me! But... but he just stood there watching – watching this animal fucking me... fucking *his* woman! My eyes bored into him. Why didn't he just kill this pig and save me, and complete the mission? *Why?*"

This time when Eunice reached out a hand to her, Thallia took it. It comforted both of them.

"Caravaggio stood there and watched for another five minutes... watched his enemy raping his woman. He had a strange look on his face, part amusement and partly as if he was aroused. Finally, he pulled out a silenced pistol and shot the Arab in the back of the head. My face was covered with the dead man's blood and brains.

"I began to cry but Caravaggio never said a word. He just turned and walked out. That was the last time I ever saw him."

"Oh my! Where did you go?" asked Eunice, shocked.

"I just grabbed what was left of my dress and ran from the hotel. I had nowhere to go and very little money. I was lost. I realised that I had outlived my usefulness to Caravaggio. I was now expendable and I needed to be disgraced, so what better way than to see me abused and treated no better than a common whore off the street?

"Why he didn't kill me, I don't truly know. Perhaps there is a part of him that is still human, but I don't think so. I think he likes to be cruel to people weaker than he. Maybe one day you could ask him."

"Oh, I'll do more than ask him, sweetie," said Eunice, through gritted teeth.

"I walked the streets of Buenos Ares that night in the rain. I found an alleyway and went to sleep there underneath some cardboard boxes. The next day, I found a café with a telephone, thrust whatever money I had at the owner and put in a call to someone who I hoped could help. I was lucky, he answered the phone. This man arranged to get me to a safe house and then get me out of the country. It was a gamble, but it paid off. Within a week, I was back here in Greece," she said.

"And Caravaggio?"

She shrugged. "I told you, I never saw him again. Six months after the incident in Argentina, I received a phone call from a man. He sounded American, from New Orleans. The man said that his employer was willing to offer a generous stipend in exchange for my complete silence and co-operation.

"I told him to go to hell. It didn't make any difference. The money has been paid into my bank account every month for the past five years. I have not spent any of it. I give it away every month to charities, the poor, the Church, anywhere, but I will not spend it, no matter how hungry or impoverished I get."

"So, where do you think Caravaggio is now?" asked Gorilla.

Thallia shrugged, as if it was a ridiculous question. "I do not know. If he's not already dead, then he is to me. Men like Caravaggio take their toll, they have no end point. All they do is suck the life from you and leave you like a hollow shell. I just count myself lucky that I was able to be released from that nightmare life.

"If you wish to discover something about someone, there is no point in asking those close to them, old lovers and friends like me. No, if you want to know the real truth about a man like Caravaggio, then you must go to the ultimate source, find the one person in the world that knows, or has discovered, all of his deepest, darkest secrets."

"Is there such a person?"

"But of course there is! You must go to his oldest enemy. He is the man who rescued me from my ordeal in Argentina. You must find the South African, the man they called the *Chirug*."

They asked her a few more sundry questions, but Gorilla and Eunice were both experienced enough to know that the source of information had now run dry. Gorilla put the twenty thousand dollars cash in a leather shoulder bag that he had bought in the market and said that he would walk her safely to her car.

She had laughed at him. "Ha, my kidnapper wants to protect me. How ironic."

Gorilla had insisted regardless. Thallia had collected the bag and left the safe house with Gorilla close behind, just to make sure that she was safe. At the last minute, she turned and looked at him.

"Will you be the man to stop him?"

"It's a possibility," he said simply.

"And does my new-found protector believe in evil?" she asked.

The question took him aback. "I've seen enough to know what evil is," he said cautiously.

"You have not known true evil, my friend. I have looked into the eyes of true evil, I have made love to true evil, have tasted its breath upon my lips. It is both sweet and toxic."

He shrugged, not knowing what to say.

She smiled at him. "Can I give you one final piece of advice, stranger?"

"Of course."

"If you do get the opportunity to look evil in the eye, when you shoot, shoot to kill. Do not miss."

Chang knew the value of patience. It was a necessary skill for the professional assassin. But, even more than patience, he knew the advantage of not acting hastily and of holding back in your actions. That, too, was a lesson he had learned at an early age.

He had been on surveillance for the best part of the day, watching his Master's former mistress. He had most of it. He had bugged her phone line and had listened to the call with the supposed client, then he'd been in place in the car park of the hotel, waiting for her to arrive. He had seen the incident with the man who attempted to kidnap her, and witnessed his execution at the hands of Gorilla Grant and then the abduction of Thallia Dimitriou by the redhead known as Nikita.

So he had held back and waited for another opportunity. Patience.

He had followed the man known as Gorilla to see where he would lead and the surveillance took him to an apartment way out of the city. Chang guessed it was a safe house. He assumed that she had been questioned and had revealed what she knew.

Over the past year, the operatives that made up the Caravaggio network had been quietly snuffed out, silenced. The Hungarian in Nice; the Creole in New Orleans; several other minor members and couriers. He had hoped to be able to eliminate Thallia Dimitriou from what was left of the network before she had the opportunity to be interrogated by his Master's hunters. But it was not to be.

After a few hours, he decided that if Grant and Nikita didn't kill her themselves, then they would release her and, at some point, she would make her way back to her own home. All he had to do was to wait for her there. His plan had been simple. Enter covertly and then kill her to make it look like one of her clients had murdered her. It would take just seconds to snuff out her life.

So he had sprung the locks on her apartment, reset them, and then waited in the darkness for his next kill. Patience.

Four hours later, just as darkness was fading and daylight was beginning to emerge, the woman, his Master's former mistress, had entered the apartment. She had looked exhausted.

Chang had simply stepped out from the next room and hit her once on the side of her neck, just at the right angle. She had dropped like a stone, her head twisted at an unnatural angle and her eyes already beginning to glaze over. Her life would ebb away within the minute, but by that time Chang would be away and ready for his next mission. He doubted that her body would be found for weeks.

Chapter Eleven

Tenerife, Canary Islands – September 1973

The little hire car was struggling to cope with the hills and at one point Eunice thought it would blow a gasket and die on them. The little Fiat was no Mustang, that was for damn sure!

Gorilla was wilting in the fierce heat and had removed his jacket, donned his sunglasses and leaned his head back to get some rest. It was the intelligence operative's version of the Spanish *siesta*. Not that Eunice would let him have it all his own way. She would, on purpose, steer the car over a particularly rough patch of road to keep him awake. It amused her to annoy him from time to time.

It had taken them several weeks to trace the whereabouts of *Chirug*. Following the interview with Thallia Dimitriou, Gorilla and Eunice had set up a temporary office in Madrid. A bed each, a couple of telephone lines, a desk and they had started the slow process of tracking down leads. Both had put in a number of search requests to their respective agencies for a trace report.

For over a week, they had nothing and in the end it was Eunice who had struck gold. An informant she had used in the past had some information – a rumour, certainly, but a good one and two thousand dollars. The whisper had turned out to be true and they had been passed along a series of cut-outs until they had a location and an address.

Then it was a whirlwind of activity as they packed up camp and took the first available flight out to the island of Tenerife, the Spanish-owned Canary Island, off the coast of North-West Africa.

The little farmhouse was perched up on a hillside in the village of Masca, a tiny hamlet with notoriously steep inclines and winding roads that was located on the north-western side of the island. They had called ahead, introduced themselves and said that they were in the market to purchase some information.

The woman who had answered had a soft Spanish accent, but was resolute in her words. "He does not wish to speak to you. He is sick, very sick. Please leave us alone."

Eunice had played the wild card, just to see if it got a reaction. "I understand. We don't wish to disturb him, but this is very important. Can you please just pass on a message to him?"

There was silence while the woman considered the risks. In the end she said, "What is your message? I promise nothing."

"Thank you. Can you please tell him that we are looking for an artist that he may have known in the past? A Master, in fact? We wish to acquire the rights to this Master, perhaps put his works into storage once and for all so that he can no longer paint. We were told that the surgeon could help us achieve this?"

There was a pause, as if she didn't know what to do and then: "Wait one moment, please."

Eunice heard the phone being placed down and footsteps walking on a tiled floor. There was a long silence and then, in the distance, the sound of raised voices and pleading. Eventually, the footsteps on the tiles returned.

"He says that he would like to meet you. He says that you have intrigued him, that you have caused him to remember his past," said the woman.

They made an appointment to travel to the small farmhouse in the mountain hamlet the next day. Eunice pulled up into the private dirt road and stopped the car. She nudged Gorilla in the arm to wake him up.

"We are here, sleepyhead," she said.

In the field by the side of the house, several large black dogs roamed free. Eunice recognised the breed immediately. They were *Presa Canario*; large, Molosser-type dogs that were used to herd livestock. But because of their power and the ease with which they could be trained, they had been used more and more as guard dogs.

Gorilla and Eunice moved up to the front of the farmhouse, vaguely aware of the kitchen curtain twitching as they approached. They had chosen, as a sign of trust and openness, to come unarmed. Gorilla had even left his razor back at the small hotel they were staying at.

The door was opened to them by a small Spanish woman dressed in the uniform of a nurse. She looked at them with mistrust. Gorilla fancied he saw the outline of a gun in the pocket of her nurse's uniform. "I am Rosa. Come with me. He is waiting for you."

She led them through a small hallway; the coolness of the farmhouse was in stark contrast to the inferno-like heat on their journey to Masca. Without ceremony, she led them into the main bedroom. It was plainly furnished, just a bed, plus some chairs for visitors. The walls held a monumental collection of photographs from days gone by. It was Coetzee's life as a young man, his parents, his youth in South Africa, his days as a soldier, various places... Egypt, Asia, Europe. The man in the picture looked the epitome of a tough and seasoned soldier.

The figure in the bed, however, groaned and lifted himself upright with an effort. Hs face was gaunt and ashen; his once blond hair was now thin and wispy. The man looked as if someone had broken him and put him back together again in the wrong order. The pain and weariness of illness and life was clearly etched upon his face.

"Nikita and Gorilla, I assume. Those are the cryptonyms that Rosa told me you would like to be known by?" He produced a small, slim Walther PPK from underneath his bed sheets and hovered its front sights temporarily over their bodies for a moment, before placing it on the bedside table. "I apologise. I had to be certain that it wasn't our mutual friend... or, should I say, mutual enemy?"

In his day, Leon Coetzee had worked under the codename *Chirug*. The word was Afrikaans for surgeon, and it was with the same clinical mindset of a medical surgeon that Coetzee had operated as one of the foremost political assassins. He could get in and out undetected, eliminate his chosen target and leave no collateral damage by way of innocent civilians. A former French Foreign Legionnaire, he had quickly turned mercenary after the war and had never looked back in the post-war political melting pot of intrigue and assassination.

"By the way, you can keep your money. I have no damned need of it," coughed Coetzee, when Eunice said that they were willing to buy the information that he had for a sizeable amount.

Gorilla hadn't thought that the South African would accept the cash amount that Sassi and the SDECE had offered, but he at least had to offer it. Besides, Gorilla knew why Coetzee was agreeing to help them; revenge, pure and simple.

"How did you connect me to Caravaggio?" asked Coetzee.

It was Eunice who answered. "It was Thallia Dimitriou. She helped us."

"Aah, such a beautiful woman, she was poorly used by him. I'm glad I helped her to escape."

Eunice nodded. "We know, she told us how you rescued her from Argentina. She suggested that if we wanted to track down Caravaggio, we should find his greatest enemy and ask him his secrets."

Coetzee nodded as if he were remembering a long-forgotten movie. "Thallia is right. I can think of nothing more satisfying than helping to put a nail in his coffin. But please, can you tell me why you want to find him?"

Gorilla and Eunice had discussed this at length back at their hotel. Should they lie or tell the truth? In the end, they had both agreed that if they were going to get the best out of their next source, then a watered-down version of the truth was the better option.

Gorilla leaned forward and whispered. "He's played too long at the big game. He's pissed off the people that used to run him... on both sides of the Atlantic, even on both sides of the Cold War. There may be others like us hunting him, ready to take his head, we don't know for certain. But what we do know is that we're the best at what we do."

"I see," said Coetzee. "I suppose it was inevitable that he would overextend himself too far and make one too many enemies. I'll be honest – it is a day that I've been waiting for. I hope that you succeed where others in the past have failed."

"Will you tell us what you know?"

"Of course! Caravaggio and I met in Algeria, just after the war. The place was crawling with all kinds of soldiers, mercenaries and would-be killers. It was a bleddy melting pot of distrust and chaos. We were both there – so we later discovered – to top the same target."

"How did that work out, Mr Coetzee?" asked Eunice.

"I got him. He didn't." He winked. "After that, we met again sporadically, usually when we passed each other in transit at an airport. In time, we started to work together as partners. We shared contracts. It was a very profitable relationship for both of us."

"Were you friends?"

Coetzee thought for a moment, then answered, "Yes, I would say that we were, or as much as anybody in our profession can be. We shared a profession and a level of professionalism."

"What was the reason for the split? Why the animosity. It sounded like you worked beautifully together," said Gorilla.

Coetzee barked a harsh laugh. "My friend, things are never as they seem. Let me tell you my story. It's a story that I have been waiting to tell for many years."

"We were in Africa. It was a job for the Americans, your Office of Policy Co-ordination, which was later part of the CIA. Caravaggio and I had worked with them several times and we liked the way they operated.

The job was the usual type – to remove a politician who was stopping US influence within the country. Two long-range sniper rifles on a high-rise building. Caravaggio was to take out the driver of the motorcade and I was to deliver the kill shot to the politician. I had a reputation as a marksman, I was clinical, precise, hence my work name – the Surgeon.

"Initially, most of our CIA work came through Caravaggio, he was the contact man. But over time, the CIA talked to him less and less and began to approach me more and more. I suppose they figured out that he was a difficult man to control and accommodate, which he was. He had a love of his own image and grandiosity. In normal people, this can be seen as an annoyance, but to a professional assassin it can be a liability.

"However, this particular job went according to plan. We got out and we got paid. What more can a contractor ask for? But then in the following months… well, things began to turn sour between us. Caravaggio accused me of double-dealing behind his back, of speaking to the intelligence agencies without his knowledge, to cut myself a bigger slice of the pay-off. All of this was untrue. We argued – it never became physical – but we decided to go our separate ways. Then things began to turn sinister."

"In what way?" asked Eunice.

"A woman I was seeing at the time went missing. Her body was found several months later. Several of my covert weapons stashes were raided by the police in several countries. A number of my false identities happened to get 'blown' to Interpol."

"Caravaggio?"

"I had no proof, but it was a remarkable coincidence and the timing was… suspicious, to say the least."

"Why do you think he turned on you?" asked Eunice.

"My dear… Caravaggio is an incredibly narcissistic man. He basks in his own image and self-worth. He thinks he is a God to the great game of espionage. For many years, he saw himself as being the epitome of the perfect intelligence operative. He was successful, good at his work, reliable. His reputation had grown during the war and had continued post-war. Add to that the way the intelligence business works… a case officer will flatter and bolster ego in order to make their agent do what they want. Caravaggio was no less susceptible to this than anyone.

"You have to remember that really, up until the start of the Second World War, the intelligence business was run by amateurs. Both spy agencies and agents alike. So a man like Caravaggio, with his resources, iron will and charisma, would have thrived. However, during and after the war there were an awful lot of newly-trained people from all sides of the espionage divide coming through. Many had been through just as much as Caravaggio, some even more so.

"By 1945, he was no longer the first among equals. I would say that there were an even dozen of us worldwide who could claim to be on a similar footing as Caravaggio. And for a man with an ego like that, a man who is used to getting his own way, that would have been a devastating blow both personally and professionally."

Gorilla frowned, not quite understanding. "So what are you saying? That he decided to eliminate the competition?"

The old man nodded. "I'm saying that's exactly what he did – or at least tried to do. He is both a sociopath and a psychopath. That's a dangerous combination. Over the past few decades, slowly, quietly, several high-ranking assassins have disappeared. Most people just assume that it is an occupational hazard, that some enemy has taken them out. But I hear whispers… rumours… that someone else took up their outstanding contracts. I suppose that is good business practice."

The old man started on another coughing fit that lasted for several more minutes. Rosa appeared at the door and looked in, her face a mask of concern, but Coetzee waved her away with a weak hand.

"She worries about me. Anyway, where were we?" he said, sipping at his beaker of water. "Ah, yes…

"Over the following year, we fought. First, he tried to take me out when I was visiting Sarajevo, but he fucked it up. The next time, he attempted a car bomb in Spain. After that attempt, I'd had enough and I started planning how to fight back.

"This game of cat and mouse continued for another year. I understand that Caravaggio became obsessed with eliminating his rival, the Surgeon. But every time he failed, it only made him more insane. During this time, I set about using all my contacts and resources in order to find out everything I could about this man – every morsel of information, anything that could give me an edge.

"Eventually, everything fell into place and I had a plan to lure him out. I concocted a false operation – fake client, fake contract, and fake target. I had it set up perfectly. When Caravaggio was due to attack the supposed target, I would be concealed on a rooftop with a rifle to kill him.

"I had paid an actor to take on the role of the target. He got a limo, driver and bodyguard for a few days and was told that he had to report to an office block in Cairo on the third day. There, he would receive a bonus. Caravaggio was to attack him on the pavement between the vehicle and the building. It was a simplistic scenario and one that he could have done in his sleep.

"On the day, everything went according to plan. I had been in position in my sniper's perch on the roof since dawn of that day. The target was due to arrive at ten that morning. It was perfect. The car arrived, the bodyguard got out, the target got out. And then I saw him… saw the figure… a tall man wearing a dark coat and hat… the same build, the same gait when he walked. I knew that I had him!

"The dark figure had his back to me as I looked at him through the sniper scope. I saw him walk to the target, pull a gun and shoot the bodyguard first and then the target. Both head shots. The third shot was mine. It was a clean head shot, a definite kill! I saw the dark figure of Caravaggio drop onto the pavement and I knew that I had won."

"What happened then?" said Gorilla, knowing what was coming next, but eager to hear the details.

"I did what I always do. I paused and took a breath. In the moments after a sniper fires and a target is dropped, there is always panic and confusion on the street and this is the perfect time for the assassin to make good his escape. Then, when I was satisfied the time was right, I stood up and made ready to break down the rifle.

"I never heard the shots that took me out, perhaps because he was using a silencer, or because it was just out of my hearing range. All I know is that they came in rapid succession. One moment I was standing, the next, there was traumatic pain and I dropped and toppled over the side of the high-rise.

"I came to on the roof of the building next to it – I had probably dropped about thirty feet. I believe it was that fall that saved my life because the next shot would have taken my head apart."

"But you survived. He didn't complete the hit," said Eunice.

"Yes," said Coetzee bitterly. "I survived. I was found several hours later by some workmen, half dead and dehydrated from the Cairo heat. Most of it was a blur... a hospital... eventually flown to Europe, and then the last eight years here in my private villa. I know that I will never leave this place."

"And the 'fake' Caravaggio? Who was he?" asked Gorilla.

"Oh, he was just some small-timer who had been paid a pittance to get dressed up and gun the target down. Caravaggio often employs such decoys, apparently. They are disposable and have a very short shelf-life."

Gorilla and Eunice went quiet for a moment, weighing up this new information. Finally, it was Eunice who spoke. "So why doesn't he come back and finish you off? Why do you deserve his generosity and be allowed to live? Why doesn't he just come back and put a bullet in you?"

"And complete the job!" said Gorilla, finishing the sentence.

The old man turned one rheumy eye to his inquisitor and snarled. "Just look at me, lady, *look at me*! I'm alive because of tubes and drugs.

I haven't taken a piss on my own for years. That bastard Caravaggio...
it amuses him to know that this is how I live. Frail, bed-ridden, eking
out an existence for years until death finally takes me. Now, you tell
me which would give a man like Caravaggio more pleasure – a bullet
for a quick kill, or watching his enemy suffer for decades in misery
and pain?"

He broke into another coughing fit. Gorilla was about to say something, but Eunice glanced over at him and shot him a warning glance
– *don't push it too far, Jack!*

Gorilla thought about it for a moment, but decided to pose one last
question to the broken man before him. He leaned forward, his hands
clasped together in front of him. "If you had the chance to get to Caravaggio again, to kill him, how would you do it? How would you find
him?

"That's easy. Isn't it obvious? I always said that Caravaggio's downfall would be his own ego, his over-inflated sense of himself. If you can
find a way to prick that ego, well, it might just buy you enough time
to kill him, to get inside his guard. Maybe..." said the old assassin.

"And how to find him?" pushed Gorilla, once again ignoring Eunice's stern looks out of the corner of his eye.

"Oh, my friend, that's the bleddy easy part! You won't need to find
him. If he catches even a rumour of someone like you on his tail, *he'll*
find you! But I have something for you, a file, or at least what's left of
it. Who knows, there may be something of use to you in there?"

He pointed over to an old briefcase leaning against the wall and
beckoned for Eunice to take it.

"If you want to catch the devil, you should always follow the money.
That's how they caught Capone, so I'm told. It wasn't guns or dawn
raids or shootouts... always follow the money and it will lead you
right back to the source.

"Caravaggio is no different to anyone else in that respect, he still has
to have money to operate, although in his case it is vast sums of cash.
And he needs to have someone manage it for him – hide transfers,
disguise accounts, assets, the whole mix. He always said to me that he

would like to retire to the mountains in the North... to a cabin, snow and ice, isolation.

"But I always had a sneaking suspicion that he was being evasive. Europe was too risky for him, he would be too exposed there. He had made too many enemies in the Middle East. Asia is a possibility, but it doesn't feel sophisticated enough for a man like him, Africa, the same! And as for America... *tsh...* never. He hated the Americans, despite the vast amounts of money he took from them."

"South America?" asked Eunice hopefully.

"It's a possibility, which may be something your people can help with. Perhaps they can lean on their contacts in those countries. At least it would narrow the field down. But for me... no, it doesn't feel right."

"So where?" asked Gorilla.

"I would guess that he would stay near his money. He can't declare it openly, so he needs to hide it, probably somewhere with loose laws that international criminals can take advantage of. There was a man I discovered years ago who was suspected of taking a cut of Caravaggio's money, but it was never confirmed what for. I always suspected that he was his money-launderer."

"Who is he?"

"It was only a rumour, but look for a man named Alvarez. Louis Alvarez. He's a fixer, a middleman. He runs and gambles big on illegal knife-fighting tournaments. If it was me, I'd look to head south."

"South where?" asked Eunice.

"To Mexico," replied *Chirug.*

Chapter Twelve

Virginia, USA – October 1973

Gorilla had control of the Mustang, hands on the wheel, foot on the accelerator. Beside him, Eunice slept. The flight home from the Canary Islands had taken it out of her and she had been about ready to crash when they landed at Washington Dulles International, so he had offered to take the wheel and drive them to Virginia.

He was having one of his 3 a.m. moments, when all his doubts about whether he was doing the right thing or which direction his life should go in, came and haunted him.

Eunice Brown fascinated him. It wasn't just that she was a strong, independent woman in a very male-dominated trade… it wasn't even that she ticked all the boxes for him physically, with her height, her red hair, slim figure and green eyes. It was more than that. He felt as if he were seeing a different aspect of her every day and, to a man like Gorilla with his straight-down-the-line attitude, he found it hard to get a handle on her different facades. She intrigued him.

He had seen Nikita; the hard-bitten professional bounty hunter. Then he had seen the cool interrogator of the South African hit man.

He had seen the sophisticated and glamorous woman wearing designer dresses in Paraguay and Argentina. And here and now, he was seeing the relaxed girl from Virginia; asleep, skirt pulled up to her thighs and dusty old cowboy boots resting on the dashboard. To him, she was an enigma.

He had known women in the intelligence world – he had known women as friends, family and lovers – but he had never known one who transcended both of his worlds so easily. He loved the way she slurred and drawled her speech in the southern way; even though he wanted to correct her pronunciations every time, he held back because it was what made her who she was.

She was strong and feisty and independent. She could be both hard and gentle, and she was one of the best damned operators that he had ever had the pleasure to work with – or against!

But still, she was that enigma. That unqualified puzzle. The question was, could he trust her? Or was she just using him to get the target and fulfil her own contract?

Sometimes he hated this bloody business.

The ranch was called *Lafayette*, according to the gatepost.

Gorilla spotted it from half a mile away. It sat on an incline, isolated from the rest of the area and he guessed the nearest house was a good two miles away. It was a pretty, green, two-storey hacienda-style building complete with a front porch and rocking chairs. Gorilla thought it looked like something out of a William Faulkner novel.

They pulled off the main road and onto the long drive that led up to the residence, to the side and rear of which there were at least six acres of land, with stables and several horses milling about.

From a tactical point of view, it was perfect. There was clear line of sight in every direction, so anyone attacking would have trouble staying hidden. The only downside that he could see was that it was isolated, but he guessed that was what Eunice Brown was after. And let's face it, he thought, she could handle herself, so back-up would be a moot point in the grand scheme of things.

As they approached the ranch, Eunice clicked a button on the dashboard and the garage doors began to open. He drove the Mustang straight in and parked up. Two very large German Shepherds came running out of their kennels to greet them.

For a moment, Gorilla did what he always did with strange canines, especially very big strange canines – he paused and braced himself, ready to fight. He had never been a dog lover by any stretch of the imagination; a battle to the death with some Japanese fighting dogs several years earlier hadn't changed his opinion any, either.

But he needn't have worried; Eunice calmed them with a command from her voice. "Axel! Ada! Heel!" The dogs immediately came to heel.

"They bite?" asked Gorilla cautiously as the dogs sniffed at him.

"They'll only nibble you, Jack." She laughed. "See, they like you."

The dogs were good for security, either as an alarm or to take down intruders. He had no doubt that there would also be an array of weaponry concealed in various stashes around the property in case of an attack. He also had no doubt that Nikita Brown knew how to use all of them to lethal effect.

The dogs kept watch outside as they both entered the coolness of the interior. It was open-plan and simply furnished. Eunice made her way to her ground floor office while he perused the bookshelves. It was something he always did in people's houses or at parties, rummaging through books.

"Holy shit!" she cried from the office.

"What is it?" he called from over his shoulder.

She came back holding a sheet of computer paper from a teleprinter. "It's from my controller at EXIS. It seems that your people and my people have been in touch. I wonder how that came about?"

He shrugged. "And?"

"It seems that they want us to work together, pool resources."

"You mean, exactly like we have been doing for the past few weeks?"

She laughed. "Yes! But now it's official. I mean… you know how it works, Jack. Nothing real exists until some seat-shiner gives the order. How the hell would we cope without these people? It's a wonder we can go to the bathroom by ourselves without them providing us with instruction!"

"Maybe the agencies have been in touch all along. Maybe they've had us all competing over the same contract? Whatever it is, they all certainly seem to want Caravaggio's head."

She nodded. "I agree. I think this is something a whole lot more than just terrorism."

"Is that what they told you?"

"Yes. Only the bare details. Something to do with a terrorist plot to bring down an airliner."

Gorilla raised an eyebrow at that. "The SDECE told me that he was going to kill the President of France!"

She shrugged. "Well, let's forget about it for now, at least until to-morrow. Drink?"

"Please. Bourbon," he said. He needed a good drink more than ever tonight.

"You've lost weight since we first met in Paraguay," she observed, pouring him a Wild Turkey with a splash of water, just how he liked it.

"Some," he admitted. "I had some time away in a private medical fa-cility recently. The hand injury. The medical professionals insisted on a healthy lifestyle while I was there. I've carried it on. You approve?"

She nodded. "Absolutely! You've lost that bulk. You look leaner, harder, fitter… you wear it well. It suits a man of your age." She handed him the glass and for a brief moment both their fingers and their eyes locked in an intimate embrace. The silence was palpable.

"Maybe tomorrow I can show you around before we get back to work. Take you into town and introduce you to some good, old-fashioned southern food? Meet the locals, that kind of thing."

Gorilla nodded. "Perhaps, although I think we should concentrate on getting back on the road. I don't want to lose Caravaggio's trail."

She flushed and a hint of defensiveness and embarrassment crossed her face. "Oh, I agree, Jack. We will, but I think we need a breather first. Even just a day or two," she said, moving closer to him, touching his arm in that intimate manner that Americans seemed so comfortable with.

Gorilla felt his body instinctively respond to her touch and her proximity. He could sense all of her; her natural heat, her scent, her eyes on him. He could hear her breathing deeply. He knew that even something as simple as a touch from this woman could stir things in him that he hadn't felt for a long time.

"Eunice, I don't –"

But she cut him off before he could say any more and turned away. "I've made up the guest bedroom downstairs. You should be comfortable. I don't know about you, Jack, but I could probably sleep for a week. That flight was a killer!"

She stood in the doorway, hands on hips and he thought she was going to take the conversation further. But instead, she simply said, "Goodnight, Jack."

"Goodnight, Eunice," he said quietly. And then she was gone.

She came to him that night. He had gone to bed early. The day's travelling had worn him out. He had lain down in the downstairs guest bedroom and listened to the sounds of the night, but his thoughts were busy. Busy with the route that he had taken to get here and the information that they had gathered to find Caravaggio. Busy with how he could find this man, his target. Busy with how he would get close to him – get close enough to be able to kill him.

But most of all, his thoughts were with Eunice Brown who was asleep upstairs.

She fascinated him, she intrigued him, but most of all she stirred emotions in him that he thought had long since been buried. Oh, there had been women, certainly, but no one who had connected with him so clearly and on so many different levels.

Finally, around 2 a.m., he drifted off, sleep eventually taking hold of him. He slept hard, his dreams of the woman with the red hair and the sassy manner prominent. He imagined her scent, her touch, how it would be to kiss her and hold her.

Then there she was, standing over him in the darkness of his room. Not a dream, but reality, wearing a leather aviator jacket to keep out the cold and very little else. "Can I join you?" was all she said.

He nodded and she slipped off the jacket to reveal herself to him. Her body was just as he had imagined it; slim, lean, the curve of her hips, the swell of her breasts that were partly covered by the cascade of her red hair. But it was the eyes that held him. Even in the dark, her eyes searched for his and never let him go. Her hand reached out for his and they interlocked their fingers; it was both an innocent and deeply personal act.

Then they were together between the sheets, skin to skin, holding each other.

"You think we should?" he asked, knowing that he wanted to more than anything.

"Jack, we've waited for so long, let's not put it off any longer."

They started a kissed that lasted for minutes, neither one of them wanting to break the connection and, when they finally did, it was only to explore each other's bodies with their hands and tongues and eyes. They both found that they had a similar style of lovemaking; physical and passionate. It was as if two long-parted souls had finally found each other and had been reconnected once more.

Eunice took control and straddled him, gasping as he entered her. She took it slow, grinding on top of him, his hands rested on her hips, moving with her to bring her on. The warm night had brought with it an electric storm and intermittently, their lovemaking was illuminated by a flash of blue lighting.

Eunice began riding him more passionately now, with power behind the thrusts, and she moaned when Grant moved his hands up to caress her breasts to the rhythm of their combined beat. When she came, she came hard and the inevitable scream of their mutual orgasm was drowned by the crash of thunder from the storm. "Oh Jack, oh Jack... Oh my God!"

They lay in each other's arms for a while, talking, whispering to each other, joking at times, comfortable with each other's skin, their bodies entwined. The talking only stopped so that they could kiss some more.

"Well, aren't we a pair, Mr Grant?"

"We certainly are, Miss Brown."

She got up and slipped on the jacket. "I'll be back. Don't go away." Moments later, she came back with a beer for each of them. It was cold and refreshing and it suited both their moods. She sat on the bed, her knees drawn up to her chest inside the jacket.

"That's a nice jacket."

She smiled. "It belonged to my dad. It was his old motorcycle jacket. He'd wear it all the time."

"It's an aviator jacket. Was he Air Force?"

"No, Dad was Army. Special Forces, then later, assigned to intelligence duties. He just liked the jacket. He got it off an old buddy of his. Dad went missing in action when I was young. Every time I wear that jacket, I think of him. It reminds me of the last time I ever saw him. He was walking out of the kitchen, he turned and waved and... and that was it. He was gone."

"You miss him, Eunice?" That was a stupid question. Why had he said that? Of course she would miss him!

He saw a single tear roll down her cheek and fall onto the pillow. "Jack, honey, I miss him every day. He was the strongest, sweetest, kindest man I ever knew. You remind me of him in many ways."

Grant lay back, not speaking, not knowing whether to say 'thank you' or let her talk herself out. It didn't feel right to intrude on her thoughts.

Finally, she broke the silence. "Have you ever lost anyone like that, Jack? Parents, lovers, a friend?"

He lay back onto the pillow and thought. He didn't have to search hard in his memory for the pain of loss. He remembered a night, many years ago. Cold, dark, standing in front of a barbed wire fence, holding a baby in his arms, wrapped inside his thick winter coat; the Smith &Wesson 39 that he had been given, gripped tightly in his other hand, ready to be used to protect himself and the child.

He had stared across the no-man's land to a man who mirrored his own actions. The man was in uniform. Tall, arrogant, he too was holding a child in a similar fashion. At his feet lay a dead body, the body of a woman. The man was staring at him, hate in his eyes. Only the barbed wire fence separated them. In the distance were the sounds of klaxons, shouting, automatic gunfire, and the random strobing of flashlights as guards searched the gloom, drawing closer all the time.

Jack Grant had taken one final look, tears in his eyes, and then he had run... run as hard as he could into the forest, his legs pounding, still cradling the baby, putting distance between him and the fence. Some way behind him, he had heard the man calling after him, "You can never run from me, Grant, I *will* find you... you can't hide!"

He came back out of his thoughts and turned towards her, his hand resting on her thigh. "We all lose people, Eunice, it's a part of life. It's how we learn to deal with it, live with it... that's what counts. There are certain things, certain pains that will never fade away no matter how much time I give them. I think they will only stop when I take my last breath."

"I notice you didn't answer my question," she said.

He thought for a moment, unsure what to say, then he said, "This isn't the time. One day it might be. That's the time when I will tell you all about it. But for the moment, I don't want to feel pain as I lie here with you, I just want love."

She looked into his eyes and said, "I agree." Then she rolled over and snuggled her body against his.

The next morning after breakfast, Eunice took him out to show him the land. She grabbed his hand and held it as they walked. "Oh, don't you go all shy on me now, Jack Grant. Not after last night."

Grant smiled. It was funny how she could put him at ease. They walked around the ranch, finally coming to a stop at the horse paddock. The horses came over, eager for a treat and they petted them, rubbing their heads.

"I have a question for you," she said.

Gorilla nodded. "Ask away. I'll do my best to answer."

"How do you reconcile what you do, Jack? The redactions, the killings?"

"Who says I have to reconcile anything? It's just a job," he replied.

Eunice frowned at that. "State-sponsored assassination. I know your background. First for the British, even though they would deny it forever and a day, and now for the French."

He shrugged. "Eunice, you're not the first person to ask me that. I suppose I don't think about it the way you do. It's a job I'm good at and qualified to do. On the whole, I remove people who are similar to, or worse than, me. By taking them out, I hope I will have saved innocent lives. How many? Who knows? It's not the job of the field agent to question that, just to complete the operation. If it wasn't me, someone else would do it."

"And that's okay with you?"

"The only person who I answer to in real terms is my daughter. When and if, and it's a big 'if', I get to heaven, the only person who has the right to judge me, and the only person whose opinion of me matters, is my little girl."

She looked at him for a long minute, as if weighing up his answer. But Jack Grant wasn't finished with the conversation. "Anyway, what about you 'Nikita'? We aren't that different in what we do."

She came back at him instantly. "Well, pardon me, sir," she said, the Virginia drawl coming out as she began the process of correcting him.

She had her hands placed squarely on her hips, which Grant was fast learning was the code for 'I mean business'!

"I don't kill on contract. I bring my targets back alive, that's what I do," she said haughtily.

"Have you ever killed anyone? Directly?"

She shook her head. "Not in cold blood, no. Only in self-defence. There's an art to tracking a man and bringing him back to face justice. Killing someone isn't a badge of honour, Jack."

"No, you're right, it's not. But it's part of what I do," he said. Gorilla stroked the horse's head, felt the warmth of it against his hand and smiled. "My daughter would love this," he said. "She always wanted a horse."

"Maybe she could come and visit us here. What's her name?"

"Katy. She'd like that."

"Do you have any other children, Jack?" she asked innocently.

He caught himself for a moment, then said, "What breed of horses are these?"

She looked at him for a brief second. Gorilla wondered if she was unsure whether to press the point, but she obviously decided against it. "They're Palominos," she told him.

"They're beautiful," he said. "What about you? Children, marriage? Any of that ever play a part in your life before all... this?" He waved a hand.

She smiled sweetly. "Oh, I'm not that type of girl. I've always had one eye on the next challenge, the next adventure. For most of my life, all of that would have just been in the way. Maybe I'm just a selfish bitch."

He nodded to himself. He understood that guilt that he had held within himself for a long time. The pull of family and the pull of who he was and what he was good at. It was a bind that had tortured him for many years. Thankfully, his life was now in balance.

"Or maybe I just never found the right partner to make me want those things," she added.

"Maybe," said Gorilla Grant. All at once, he felt vulnerable, because he was sure – no, he *knew* – that this woman was making him think about possibilities and choices that he hadn't considered in a long, long, time.

After their walk, Eunice had retired to her office and Grant had lain down on the bed. His mind was a hurricane of what to do next regarding the operation. Finally, admitting defeat at getting any rest, he went in search of her. In truth, he was eager for some news of the operation.

As he entered the office, the teleprinter kicked into life. Eunice was behind her desk, her feet propped on top of it. She swung them down, went over and ripped off the computer paper.

Her eyes scanned the paper. "It's from EXIS. They feed me updated information as and when they get it from the CIA. Oh my God, Jack, look!"

She held up the printout from the teleprinter and handed it to him. It read: *BODY OF THALLIA DIMITRIOU FOUND. ATHENS – GREECE.*

"Maybe we shouldn't pass any more operational information back to our controls for a while? As a precaution," she said.

"You think there is a leak?"

She nodded. "Could be. Either that, or we still have someone tailing us."

Gorilla thought it through. "The Chinese? Is he Chinese Intelligence, or is he Caravaggio's bodyguard? The one that Thallia told us about?"

"Whoever he is, he seems to be snuffing out anyone connected to Caravaggio. So far, we've been lucky and have been ahead of the game, so at least we have good information. Let's keep it that way."

Chapter Thirteen

Chang sat upright in the darkness. He was naked in a meditation position and had been that way for the past two hours, the sweat glis-
tening on his body, as he waited in this cheap motel on the interstate,
watching the clock tick down. He had been here for the past few days,
waiting by the telephone for the call from his controller.

12.35 In the morning. The call would happen soon.

He breathed in, slowly and steadily, his mind clear and focused.
Even the ringing of the telephone did not disturb him when it hap-
pened. He slowly stretched one arm over and picked up the handset.
He spoke the recognition code clearly: "*Mortis.*"

"Is the team ready?" said the voice of his controller. Strong, clear,
in control.

"Yes. They are on standby. I have a surveillance operator watching
the house. The assault team can be at the target location within the
hour," said Chang, his eyes still closed.

"Good. Then send them in," came the order.

"To kill or to capture?"

The voice of his controller laughed softly. "Oh, to kill! Let's see if
Grant and Brown are worthy of our time and effort. If they survive,

then we will move them onto the next rung of the ladder. If they fail, then they were not worthy of our time in the first place."

"I understand. It will be done," said Chang.

He replaced the handset and made the call to the assault team stationed at a rented warehouse on the outskirts of town, giving them the green light. He heard a mumbled "Okay" and then the call was cut. Chang would have preferred to have been given the opportunity to eliminate Gorilla Grant and Nikita Brown himself, but he understood that they had to be tested first.

The Master was nothing if not thorough. He would view it as an almost Darwinian test, a service to the profession that they had chosen. The weak were killed, but the good would survive and even go on to excel.

It was the dogs that alerted them both. They had been wrapped in each other's arms after a night of lovemaking when the two German shepherds lying at the base of the bed had started to bark uncontrollably. Eunice was instantly awake and alert. She knew her house, she knew her dogs and they never barked like that unless there was something in the vicinity that wasn't supposed to be there.

"Jack. Wake up, we have a problem," she whispered.

She jumped out of bed and started to grab clothes. Jeans, boots, a sweater. She rubbed the ears of the two large dogs to calm them. "Easy, Axel, easy, Ada, hush now."

Gorilla roused himself from sleep and checked the clock. 2 a.m. He reached for his ASP, half dragging on some clothes and shoes. "What is it?"

"The dogs don't like it. They don't spook easily. They sense something," she said, rubbing the fur of the large dogs. The dogs definitely didn't like it. Their faces were curling into a snarl and a low rumble of aggression was bubbling beneath the surface.

"Weapons?" said Gorilla. "We should check it out."

"Under the bed. Just reach a hand down and pull. Pass it to me."

Gorilla finished dressing quickly and knelt down, snaking a hand under the frame of the bed that they had slept and made love in only hours before. He felt the cold, hard steel of a weapon and pulled it free from its harness. It was a Mossberg Pump-Action shotgun with a fully loaded ammunition bandolier/sling. He threw it across the room to her and she caught it one-handed.

In the distance, they heard the faint smashing of a window being broken. The dogs' aggressive tone ramped up to a full-on growl. Eunice hushed them and slung the shotgun over her head by its sling. She did a quick chamber-check, racked the slide and flicked on the safety. She looked over to Gorilla and saw that he was going through the same procedure with the ASP.

"Whoever it is, they'll be in the house in seconds," he whispered, moving closer to her and the dogs.

She nodded. "How you want to handle it, Jack?"

"We keep the high ground as long as we can. Let's see what we are dealing with before we turn things noisy," he said.

They moved into position, Eunice by the bedroom door and Gorilla primed and ready behind her. Even in the darkness of the house, she had a perfect view from the crack in the door of the dark-clad figures, weapons up, starting to spread out across the hall and move cautiously towards the stairs.

She could make out four of them, all armed with semi-automatic pistols and all fitted with silencers. That at least confirmed that this wasn't a planned robbery. Burglars don't use suppressed weapons. This was a hit.

Gorilla padded across the bedroom to the en suite bathroom. The bathroom had two separate doors. One led to the bedroom and the other one led directly out onto the hall. He waited behind the half-open door, the ASP at the ready. He could hear the slow tread of footsteps moving along the landing hallway. He just hoped Eunice could keep those dogs quiet.

The masked figure passed the hallway door to the bathroom and gently nudged it open with his boot. His weapon was up and leading into the room. Gorilla appeared through the door and hit the intruder full in the face with the business end of the ASP. Instinctively, the gunman fired off two silenced shots, both rounds hitting the floor, before Gorilla hit him again, this time shattering teeth and busting the man's jaw. He hit the floor with a *clump* and Gorilla finished off the assault with a full-force stamp to the head, knocking the gunman unconscious.

At the same time, Eunice emerged from the bedroom at full pace, the pump action shotgun up and aiming at the dark figures that were starting to head towards the wide staircase. The shotgun boomed twice, illuminating the darkness, and took down the gunman farthest away, killing him. The man looked as if he had been pushed backwards and into the wall by an invisible giant hand.

At the same time, the dogs were let loose and the combined weight and fury of Axel and Ada launched themselves at the gunman who had begun to make his way up the staircase. The dogs impacted into him, Ada, the female, in the lead, leaping at the man's throat. The gunman screamed and managed to get a silenced shot off that took her in the leg. Ada yelped in pain but continued with the assault on the attacker.

The second dog, Axel, joined in the fight and his huge mass knocked the gunman off his feet and caused him to topple backwards. The man and the two animals crashed down the stairs in a tangle of limbs, fur and teeth.

Right behind them, and crouched low, came Eunice and Gorilla seeking out targets and shooting on the move. The chaos of the dogs had caused the other two gunmen to split into defensive positions behind the walls to the kitchen and Eunice's study area. As Gorilla passed the dogs that were ripping at the downed gunman, he nonchalantly shot him in the head and moved onto the next target.

The gunman nearest the study went for the hero option and tried a full-on assault, but Eunice was in a perfect tactical position on the staircase and a solid round blast from the shotgun took the man in the chest, dropping him permanently. The final gunman, still concealed near the kitchen, had decided that enough was enough and tried to make a run for it. But he had not counted on the speed and ferocity of the large male dog, Axel.

"Axel – attack!" shouted Eunice. The man had barely made it five feet before the dog had taken him down, his huge jaws clamped tight around the gunman's wrist, dragging him back to his mistress. Gorilla stood over the terrified man and finished him off with a bullet to the head. Then there was silence. Gorilla looked around him at the scene of carnage.

The whole thing had taken no more than a few minutes. He looked at Eunice, the shotgun's butt resting easily on her hip, the barrel pointing skyward.

"Are you okay? No injuries?" he said.

She shook her head. "I'm fine. Not exactly how I want to spend my nights, but... I'm fine. Although maybe we should have kept one alive to see if we could learn anything?"

He nodded. "Don't worry, we soon will. The one upstairs is just unconscious. I'm going to talk to him right now."

"I'm going to check the grounds with Axel... see if we can track down anyone else."

"Be careful."

"Don't worry, I will. Just keep an eye on Ada for me. She's a brave doggie, I'll deal with her when we get back," said Eunice.

Gorilla watched her go out through the kitchen door and into the night, the large German Shepherd trotting protectively at her heels. He settled Ada on the floor, placed a rug over her and rubbed her ears. She whimpered, obviously feeling sorry for herself. The bullet had hit her in the thigh. It wasn't a life-threatening injury, but she'd feel the pain for a while.

He had made it to the top step of the stairs when, from outside, he heard a single blast from Eunice's shotgun. She had evidently found the last member of the hit-team.

Poor guy, thought Gorilla with a smile.

Chapter Fourteen

Gorilla rolled up his shirt sleeves to just above his elbows and went to collect his prisoner from the hall where he lay semi-conscious. The floor was a mass of blood and teeth. Gorilla ripped off the balaclava to reveal the damaged face of a heavyset man with a drooping moustache, covered in blood. The man's eyes were bulging wide in terror and his face was a mask of sweat.

Gorilla knelt down in front of him, the ASP hanging loosely in his hand. When he spoke, his tone was matter-of-fact.

"Now, you listen to me, sunshine. I don't have time to fuck about here. So here's what's going to happen. I want to know who you are, who hired you and what you've been told. I'm not going to count to three, or any of that bullshit – you understand me? This isn't the movies and I'm not George Lazenby.

"You get one chance to talk. If you say nothing, I'm going to put two 9mm rounds in your kneecaps and drag you down to the basement. Yes, we have a nice big basement here with lots of room. Then I'm going to throw you in there, bleeding and smelling the place out.

"Then I am going to give you a cellmate to keep you company – one very big and pissed-off German shepherd who has already acquired a taste for human blood. Add to that the fact that he's just seen his mate been shot by one of your team and… well, I wouldn't fancy your chances against him for very long."

The man continued to look at him without speaking.

"So," said Gorilla. "Who are you? Who hired you? What else do you know?"

The man continued to glare silently. Gorilla let out a frustrated sigh and quickly placed the barrel of the ASP against the man's kneecap and fired. There was the sudden smell of burning flesh and bone. The man screamed. So Gorilla shot out the other one, too. A second howl of pain came from the bruised and battered hit-man.

But Gorilla was in no mood to be forgiving and immediately began to drag him from the bathroom by the collar of his jacket, along the hall, down the staircase and towards the door to the cellar. A trail of blood marked the wounded man's route. Gorilla ripped open the door and threw the screaming man down the small flight of stairs and onto the musty stone floor.

"Eunice! Where's that bloody dog? Axel, come here, boy!" shouted Gorilla, as Eunice and Axel entered through the kitchen. The big dog's mouth was already drooling with blood from his recent victim.

Scenting an intruder down in the basement, Axel started to bark, deep, woofing roars of anger. He looked at the door, looked at Eunice. She nodded. "Go, boy," she said, and the dog bounded down the stairs. At once, the barking increased.

Gorilla kicked the door closed behind him. Then the screams started.

Despite the late hour, the phone rang at the appointed time. "This is Control."

"Yes, Master?"

"Did they survive?"

"Yes. They survived."

"And the freelance team?" asked the controller.

"It appears they were all eliminated. Only the surveillance operator escaped and that was only because he was hidden too far away in the woods," said Chang.

"Excellent! Then it seems that they are worthy opponents!"

"What would you have me do next?"

There was silence from the controller as he ruminated on his next move. Chang thought that he was like a Chess Grandmaster or military strategist, always ready to instigate the next part of his plan.

"For the moment, nothing. Close down the operation there. Return home to the island. I have already taken steps to ensure that Grant and Nikita Brown will find their way to Mexico," said the voice on the phone.

"And then?"

"Then, let's test these star-crossed lovers further. Let's spilt them up and see how they react. For what is love if not pain?" asked Caravaggio.

Chapter Fifteen

Standard operating procedure, when there has been any kind of compromising intelligence operation in the field, is to call in the clean-up crew.

A good clean-up crew is worth its weight in gold to an intelligence operation. They can dispose of evidence, even bodies, and make it look as though nothing untoward had ever happened. Eunice called the duty officer at EXIS, who immediately put her through to Gibb's private number. Eunice knew that Gibbs would call in his own dedicated team to help. It was part of the terms of her contract, and CIA money went a long way with logistical support.

"Yes," said Gibbs irritably, when he answered the call.

"It's Nikita. There has been an incident. I would like your people to clean it up for me," she said simply.

"Uh-huh. Tell me the details."

She could imagine him reaching across his bedside table for a pen and pad. So she told him the details and what she would need; body bags, cleaners, and an emergency vet for the dog. Plus, for someone to have a quiet word with the local Sheriff's Department to tell them that the ranch was a no-go zone for them.

When she had finished, there was a moment or two's silence as Gibbs jotted down his final notes.

"I'll have a team there within the hour," said Gibbs. "I'm glad that you handled the situation. However, perhaps we should retire you from this operation?"

"Negative. No way!"

"You seem to be compromised, Miss Brown."

"Don't you dare, Mr Gibbs. This is my bounty. I'll find the target and take him down. It will take a lot more than a few thugs in ski masks to scare me off," she said, her temper rising.

"Of course, Miss Brown, however –"

"However nothing. If you take me off this operation, I will simply offer my services to another vendor to bring Caravaggio in. This is more than just a job now. This is personal," she barked back at him.

"But personal is not always professional, Miss Brown."

"Oh, I'll be professional. You don't have to worry about that."

Gibbs paused. He could tell that she was serious. And headstrong. Better to have her onside than not, he reasoned. "Very well, Miss Brown. You can continue to have primary on this mission, but I want to be kept informed of any unusual occurrences."

"Mr Gibbs, it will be my pleasure," she said, before slamming down the phone.

She came out of the office and noted that the door to the basement was open and Axel was at the top, guarding it. From inside, she could hear the panting of a desperate man and the slow monotone of a patient interrogator. It was Jack... no, Jack was gone. It was Gorilla questioning his prisoner.

A few minutes later, Gorilla emerged from the cellar and went to the kitchen to wash the blood off his hands. She came up behind him and hugged him. Gorilla turned into her and kissed her. Then, when the affection of the survivor was behind them, he was all business.

"He's part of a low-level mercenary crew. Ex-military. Sounds like they do contracts for a few organised crime families up the East Coast.

The only thing he knows is that it was a Chinese man who briefed them and paid them," said Gorilla.

"And they were paid to kill us? Not capture?"

"Seems that way."

"How is he now?"

"He's passed out. A smash in the face, a knee-capping and being extensively mauled by a tame wolf have taken it out of him. I figured we'd leave what's left of him to the CIA clean-up crew," he said.

The CIA crew were as good as their word and were at the ranch within the hour. A compact, no-nonsense team of five men plus one tame vet came in and began to move about the house, assessing what needed to be done.

The vet looked at the injured dog and declared that the bullet had gone "in/out" through her rear left leg. A shot to dull the pain and some bandages had fixed Ada up within the half hour. She would sleep for the rest of the night.

Gorilla and Eunice needed to get out of the area and travel incognito, so the Mustang was left at the ranch. Instead, they loaded up Eunice's old Ford truck with the dogs, weapons and clothes that they would need for their eventual trip to Mexico. They needed to disappear completely for the night, just to regroup. Eunice said she knew the perfect place. They were heading into the Appalachian Mountains. She said she knew a man.

"He's my uncle. Well, not my real uncle. He was one of Dad's closest friends. They grew up together. He'll look after the dogs, feed Axel and take care of Ada and check on the ranch while we are away."

While *we* are away. Already, she was referring to them both as one entity, noted Gorilla.

"Can he be trusted?"

"Of course. Those mountain folks have a code of silence that would put the Sicilian Mafia to shame," she said. "And besides, he's family."

The drive took them a little over two hours. Twice, they stopped and pulled over just in case they had picked up a 'tail'. Once they were satisfied, they would set off once again. Gorilla was fascinated by the road trip. It was the America, the 'lost' America that he had never seen. Up until that point in his life, America had been a blur of airports, chain hotel rooms and busy cities. So this was something new, something refreshing. A hidden secret that was whispered in corners.

They arrived in the small town of Galax, Virginia, just around sunrise. Galax was the gateway to the Blue Ridge Mountains and the air got cleaner and crisper the nearer they were to the mountains. The town itself was small and unremarkable, nothing but a single row of stores and businesses. You could have done a day's worth of shopping in less than an hour.

"Does he live here in town?" asked Gorilla

"No way! Jeb lives out in the boonies… another few miles into the country up a dirt road. He only goes into town for supplies or to pick up his mail."

An hour later, they were deep into the wilderness of the mountains. The roads had all but disappeared, dwindling to nothing more than dirt and dust tracks. Gorilla thought that the decision to use the truck was the right one. The Mustang would have struggled.

Jebidiah Smith was a tall bear of a man in his sixties. He was dressed in denim coveralls and heavy work boots. His beard was wild, long and grey. He looked like the archetypal mountain man. In his day, he had been one of the most renowned bootleggers in the State and even today, he still indulged in making a little moonshine for his close acquaintances. To almost everyone who knew him, he was simply referred to as 'Uncle Jeb'.

He had been chopping firewood on a block out front of his cabin when he heard the engine of the truck approaching up the dirt road to his isolated property. He calmly put the axe down and stood his ground, picking up his sawn-off shotgun in case of trouble. Uncle Jeb had a few notches on his belt from the past and he could still sling some lead about if he had to. Violence and murder had always been a part of the illegal moonshine business. Probably always would be.

Moments later, an old and mud-spattered truck pulled up and parked. Two people got out, the man first, dressed in a suit and then the woman, tall and red-haired, in flannel shirt, jeans and boots. The big man squinted and then smiled. "Euney? That you? Well, laws alive, if it aint Euney Brown come to see her ol' uncle!"

"Hi, Uncle Jeb. How are you?" She went over and embraced the big man.

What followed, at least to Gorilla Grant's Anglo-Saxon ears, was a rapid-fire cacophony of gibberish and patois. Gorilla guessed that these hill people had their own unique language and way of speaking that was totally foreign to outsiders. Occasionally, he would pick up the odd word that he recognised, or a smattering of a phrase. It was English, just not as he knew it. He thought that he would have to get Eunice to interpret for him otherwise he'd be left in the dark.

"And who's this young fella?" asked Jeb suspiciously.

"Uncle Jeb, meet my friend Jack."

Jeb looked at the smaller man as if deciding whether he liked him or not.

"Pleased to meet you," said Gorilla, holding out his hand in greeting.

The big man shook it and then raised an eyebrow. "Well, he sure *dooo* have a real pretty mouth, don't he? Where'd ya get that crazy accent from, boy?"

"I'm from Texas," said Gorilla, with no hint of irony. British sarcasm was his forte.

Uncle Jeb squinted to see if this tough-looking 'furner' was poking fun at him. When he decided he wasn't, he let out a big, bellowing laugh and slapped at his thighs.

"Well, I darn well heard everything now! Texas? Texas, you say? I know that kinda accent... I seen dem picture shows up in the big town. You sound like that guy that played the explosives fella in *The Guns of Navarone*."

Gorilla thought he had never sounded like David Niven in his whole life. And never would.

"Well, come on in. Y'all must be hungry. I got some food cooking. I don't eat as well as I used to since Kitty passed on," he said, "but y'all more than welcome to enjoy some good, ol'-fashioned Southern hospitality."

The kitchen was small and basic, but comfortable. It smelt of old wood, coffee and diesel. Eunice and Gorilla sat at a big kitchen table, the dogs at their feet, while Uncle Jeb dished out a meal of collard greens, fried chicken and large biscuits.

"That right there," Jeb pointed to the biscuit and laughed, "is called a cathead, 'cause it's as big as a cat's head!"

"Now Jack, I'm gonna tell you, Uncle Jeb was quite a character back in the day," said Eunice playfully.

"Back in the day? I'm still alive and kickin'. This little lady only remembers the old, friendly uncle. Your daddy and me... whoo boy, when we were young'uns, we were too big for our britches," said Jeb, chewing on some food.

"You still making the shine, Jeb?" asked Eunice.

Jeb held his hands up as if to say 'okay, you caught me'. "As long as the stream be flowing, I be making the moonshine. So tell me. I won't ask too many questions, but... something's happened, hasn't it? Let me help if I can," said the big man, concern in his voice.

"Now, Jeb... You know better than to ask li'l ol' me about my work. But yes, something's happened. But it's been taken care of. We just needed a place to regroup for a day. We'll be out of your hair before tomorrow evening."

"There's no danger to you, if that's what you are concerned about," said Gorilla.

Jeb waved a dismissive hand. "Hell, I ain't worried about a fight. I was rough-housing it when you were still sucking on your momma's titty, young fella."

Gorilla laughed. "I have no doubts," he said.

Uncle Jeb nodded. "So, what do you need?"

Eunice laid a hand on the old man's forearm. It was a touch of genuine affection. "Let us rest up here for the day. We'll leave first thing tomorrow. I also need you to look after the dogs for me, especially Ada. She took a bullet for us. The ranch is fine. I got people who can take care of that and the horses."

"How long will you be gone?" asked Jeb.

"I don't know. Could be a few weeks, or it could be a few months. But once I'm finished, I'll come back and collect the dogs. They're good animals. They won't cause you no trouble. Take Ada to the vet in town, just to make sure she's healing well. I'll leave you some money to cover everything."

Uncle Jeb said nothing for a moment, and then turned to Gorilla, one eyebrow cocked quizzically. "Boy, she got a way of handling men, don't she? She was the same when she was a slip of a girl. Those boys would flock round you, Eunice, and you could twist them around your little finger."

"Oh, hush now, Jeb or you'll be giving Jack here the wrong impression of me!" said Eunice, a twinkle in her eye. "Besides, us ladies need to have big, strong men to help them every now and again, don't we?"

That was Eunice Brown completely, decided Grant. Soft and gentle when she needed something, but with a core of steel inside when the going got tough.

Later that evening, both men were sitting on the porch, staring off into the distance of the woods and swigging occasionally at their beer bottles. Eunice had gone in to town to pick up some supplies as a thank-you to Jeb. The men sat easy in each other's company. Plus, they had a love and affection for the same woman, so their alliance was grounded.

"It's a little airish out here. You alright, Mr Jack?" Jeb stated.

"Airish?"

"Yeah, airish. Um… I guess you'd say it's chilly."

"I'm fine. Thanks."

"So… you a bounty hunter like Eunice?"

"In a way."

"What way?"

"Best you don't know kind of way."

"Guvment?"

"Not anymore."

Jeb accepted this and changed tact. "Is it you that's dragging her into this? Or, knowing Euney, it's more 'en likely the other way around?"

Gorilla nodded. "To be fair, we're both equal passengers on this train."

"Well, I don't know you too well, mister, but –"

"Hang on, is this the bit where you warn me off of her? If I get her hurt or break her heart, I'll have you to deal with? Is that the way this conversation is going? I hope not, Jeb," said Gorilla.

Uncle Jeb paused and frowned. "Well, no, I don't suppose I am. I guess we're both a little too old for all that." He seemed to be about to say something else and then thought better of it. There was a long spell of silence, until finally Uncle Jeb sat forward and smiled, as if remembering a half-forgotten memory.

"I had a dog when I was a young'un. Old Lab, great huntin' dog. Kip, he was called. Whoo, boy, could he track! But he had a crazy streak in him. He would go and go and go until he'd found the kill. I used to struggle to keep up with him. No matter how much I would yell and holler at him, he'd just keep on going and going until he tracked down whatever we were huntin'."

"Relentless, was he?" asked Gorilla.

"Well now, yessir, he was. Like I said, crazy. He became fixated. That Fall, there was a big ol' buck that I had taken a shot at, but I'd only winged it. Hit it in the haunches. And boy, did it run… left a trail of blood after it. Well, of course old Kip, he sets off at full pace… he's got the scent and ain't nuttin' stopping him. And there's me, o' course, screaming at him to 'come back, you damn fool hound!'

"I thought I'd lost 'em both. They took me miles into the woods. Finally, I saw them both heading upwards towards the top of a ravine. The buck was nearly done, but he still kept going. So did Kip. I hollered and hollered. I could see what was going to happen as clear as day, if that fool dog didn't quit. And it did. Both of them bolted and ran right off the edge of that cliff. The buck in blind panic, the dog out of that crazy fixation he had.

"I got to the cliff's edge, tuckered out of breath, and looked down. Buck and dog were dashed to pieces all over the rocks below. Shame. He was a good dog, aside from his obsession."

"That's a sad story," said Gorilla.

"Oh, I got much sadder than that one, Mr Jack," he said, with a grin. "You see, I know Eunice. And in my time I've known men like you. Sometimes, mister, you just gotta know when to stop tracking and running to ya doom. Stay a while, I'll show you them mountains... show you how to shoot a gun. You furners don't know much about firearms, do ya?"

Gorilla, the professional gunman and assassin, laughed in spite of himself. "No, I guess we don't. Too busy playing cricket, I suppose."

"Well then. Let *me* teach you the ways of the Appalachians! Come on – what's the harm?"

And, for that brief moment, there was a sadness and longing in Gorilla Grant. He would have liked nothing more than to spend time in this man's company and get to live among the mountain people. Perhaps even go native with Eunice? But he knew it was a dream, a fantasy and he shook himself out of his indulgence.

"I'm sorry, Jeb, I wish I could. But I can't... *we* can't. Maybe one day I can come back. I hope so. But we have to leave soon. We have a job to do."

Uncle Jeb looked at the smaller man and nodded. He knew that he wouldn't be back. Because this Englishman had the same intense look in his eye that his old hunting dog had, right before he had plunged over the side of a ravine to his death.

Obsession, Uncle Jeb decided, could be a killer.

Chapter Sixteen

Private suite, Hotel Obrigado, Lisbon, Portugal – October 1973

Theodore Gibbs, former CIA officer, and now Comptroller of EXIS, a private and corporate intelligence business, guessed the only reason that he was in this predicament was that he was the victim of his own success. Oh, everyone knew that EXIS was nothing more than a front company, bought and owned by the CIA and that Gibbs, at the end of the day, took his orders directly from the senior men at Langley.

Gibbs had been a promising intelligence officer after his military service in the Second World War. He had fitted into the newly-formed CIA well and had risen steadily, so much so that he had been given a niche position within the Clandestine Services; handling the freelance burglars, kidnappers and contract specialists for wet-work. Within the CIA, they were referred to as the SSM – the second story men. In other words, they were deniable operators that didn't officially exist.

Based out of a secured warehouse in Alexandria, Virginia, the SSM were pros through and through.

If you needed an operation to break into an embassy in Warsaw, the second story would do it for you. If you needed to sandbag a courier in Brazil, the SSM would provide the team to knock him out and fleece him of information. Gibbs had never worked with such a good bunch of operators.

But even within a closed unit such as the SSM, there were even more deeply run assets that Gibbs had to deal with; namely the freelance assassins that the CIA was occasionally called upon to use.

By the early 1960s, many of these agents – former war criminals and mercenaries – had been pretty much retired or eliminated by the Agency. The military Special Forces had begun the transfer of power for specialist covert paramilitary operations by that time, thanks in part to President Kennedy's influence. Gibbs and his people still had access to a few operators, though; after all, one never knew when a deniable asset would be needed.

Then, one day in May 1965, Gibbs had been called to a private meeting, out in the Virginia countryside and away from Langley. His contact was the then Deputy Director of Central Intelligence, Roy Webster. Out of the office usually meant that it was ultra-sensitive.

"You have an asset on your books, I understand. The contractor has a proven track record, is discreet, reliable, and professional. He goes by the cryptonym of Caravaggio," said the DDCI.

Gibbs stood looking out over the Virginia countryside while he thought through his assets list. Caravaggio. Of course he knew of him. Caravaggio was a legend within their little milieu; a ruthless contract killer who had a penchant for pulling off the most impossible assassinations. He was also the most expensive contractor, with his fees regularly running into six figures.

"I'm aware of him," said Gibbs cautiously.

"We have a target. A CIA traitor. His identity is known to only a few at the minute and we'd like to keep it that way. This is all highly classified, Theo. You understand the sensitivity of this?"

"Of course. Who is it? Who is the traitor?"

"Higgins, the Deputy Director of Plans. He decided to go rogue and get the CIA involved in a shit-storm," growled the DDCI.

"What?"

"You don't need to know the full details. In fact, it's better if you don't. But we have a rather delicate job that needs doing, a problem of catastrophic proportions which, if it isn't resolved, will have damaging consequences for the Agency. He has betrayed the Agency and has left us vulnerable.

"That alone would be bad enough. However, we believe that Higgins is planning to blackmail the CIA at some point in the future. Whether it is to fleece us of cash or to buy his freedom, we don't know and we don't want to take the risk. The Agency already has oversight committees baying for our blood. Higgins's testimony would finish us all off for good," said Webster bitterly.

Gibbs had known Higgins on and off for years. He knew him to be a good operator and a solid man. He couldn't believe what he was hearing, but if the DDCI said it was so…

"We have an information pack for you to pass on to Caravaggio. We've disguised Higgins's identity; let the contractor think that it is just an operational target. Under no circumstances should he be made aware that it is a former CIA officer of Higgins's standing," said Webster.

Webster stood glowering down at Gibbs. "There can be no foul-ups in this, Theo. Get it done. You can write yourself a blank cheque at the Agency when you succeed, but screw it up and it won't be a good career move for you."

The threat was subtle but clear. Arrange this and keep your mouth shut, or face the consequences. Gibbs was smart enough to know that unemployment, financial ruin and possibly being murdered didn't suit him at all. He was an Agency man through and through and so, when the DDCI – and, by default he supposed, the Director of Central Intelligence – gave the order to recruit a contractor to 'remove' a CIA traitor, he would do it to the best of his ability and no questions asked.

After that, things had moved fast. He had been given a special directive, along with special resources, in order to organise the contract on Higgins. It had been rudimentary by normal standards; a flight to Europe, a meeting with a representative of Caravaggio's, an agreed-upon price and the details of what was required. That was it. After that, Gibbs's part in the recruitment was over.

The next he heard about anything was four months later, when Higgins had been reported dead. A heart attack while scuba diving in the Caribbean, the news reports said. That was, Gibbs noted, one of Caravaggio's great skills; making murder look like an accident.

As a reward for his part in the operation, the DCI had given Gibbs a promotion, a raise and a covert program to run. A deniable 'off the books' commercial enterprise that could handle the dirty jobs that the CIA couldn't officially take on. It was basically the second story boys working in private business, and so Executive Information Services, or EXIS, was born.

Fast-forward eight years and things had changed radically. Webster was now the DCI of the CIA, the old DCI was now a leading member of the President's inner circle and now, the viperous head of Caravaggio had risen once more.

This time *he* was the one trying to coerce not only the Agency, but potentially one of the President's most trusted advisors, using the threat of blackmail. Some very powerful people had a lot to lose by allowing such a killer to carry on living. And so DCI Webster, not a man who was known for letting his subordinates off the hook, even if it was eight years later, had recalled Gibbs to be part of a multi-intelligence agency task force, with the aim of tracking down the rogue agent who went under the name of Caravaggio.

The two other men – the Frenchman and the Russian – arrived at the allotted time for their meeting. Security was discreet and, for this particular occasion, was under the control of the Russian's people. All were of a similar age, early sixties, and all were retired intelligence officers, or at least they had been until this crisis had arisen almost a year ago. Now, they had been forced out of retirement to be the deniable face of negotiating a solution to a problem.

The suite was on the top floor of the hotel and had a private balcony. Later, when the business of the day was at an end, the three spies would adjourn to the dining table that was already laid outside, where they would enjoy a hearty meal of sardines, cod and Portuguese beef steak complemented with a light Portuguese white wine. Their view would be that of the harbour and the deep blue Mediterranean Sea.

But now, for at least the next hour, it was purely business as they sat around the small conference table and looked over their individual notes. It could be any board meeting anywhere in the world, except that this board meeting had potentially fatal consequences for any number of individuals across the globe.

It had been a year of negotiating, tracking, failed attempts at gathering intelligence, not to mention having the reality of blackmail hanging over their heads – or at least the heads of the intelligence networks that they represented. The three men knew that there were probably dozens of intelligence networks that were being threatened with being blown, but that it was really the big three – CIA, KGB, SDECE – that would have the most to lose. Hence, the smaller spy agencies would fall into line and do as they were told. For now!

It was the Russian who began the meeting in his usual blustering style. "We have to dispose of this threat once and for all."

The Frenchman nodded. "I agree. If we don't, it exposes not just us personally, but potentially every operation for the last thirty years."

"Not to mention several of our political masters. The result would be catastrophic for everyone. I can't believe we have been so stupid for so long," replied Gibbs.

"And yet here we are, comrades and the question is, do we have a reasonable chance of eliminating the threat and protecting our people?"

"We should have controlled this threat long ago. We got greedy. We thought we had a tool that we could use to our own ends. In reality, what we had was a rogue wolf, something that we couldn't control," said Gibbs.

They had all, as representatives of their chosen agencies, met several times over the last year and all, up to a point, had co-operated with each other to resolve this problem. Now, it seemed that things were unravelling.

"So... the contractors?" asked the KGB man.

"It seems, Yuri, that your man got a little... exuberant," said Gibbs.

The Russian snorted. "The Bulgarian was not my man. I would have chosen a good Russian operative if I'd had my way. As far as I am concerned, the Bulgarian was expendable and got what he deserved. He was what was pushed upon me for this mission by the KGB. What about the other freelancers? Are they any nearer to finding the threat and the information?" asked the Russian.

It was the French intelligence officer who answered. "Following the incident in Athens, we gave orders that our man and the American contractor should pool resources and work together. It seems that our man and the American contractor have formed a workable alliance. As I understand it, they have gone underground."

"Perhaps to recover?"

Gibbs nodded. "That is more than likely," he said noncommittally.

He didn't feel like sharing the information that the two contractors, Grant and Brown, had recently come under a lethal attack in the heart of the Virginia countryside. Besides, his EXIS operatives were dealing with the fallout and 'cleaning', to make sure that no evidence existed.

"Whatever they learned in Athens, it is assumed they will act on it once they have analysed the information."

"Are they any good?" asked the Russian.

"The American is, for a female, one of the best trackers in the business. She is quite remarkable," said Gibbs.

"And the French operative?"

The former SDECE man replied. "Actually, he is British. His reputation as a covert intelligence operator and 'wet work' specialist is second to none. It's why we recruited him."

"So, up until the time that they decide to resurface, we continue to wait?"

"Yes."

"And after? After they have neutralised the threat and recovered the information that we need? What then?" enquired the Russian.

The three men looked at each other. They all knew the stakes of this operation failing or being compromised any further – not only for the agents and networks across the globe, not only for the careers of high ranking career intelligence officials that had authorised their secret operation, but for their political masters that had the most to lose.

"There can be no leaks, no more witnesses to any of this. Our agencies can't afford to go through this again. It sets a bad example," said Gibbs.

"I agree. Once the information is retrieved, it is imperative that we tie up any loose ends. Do we agree?" said the Russian.

They all knew what that meant and how it would work. One of the final two contractors would take out the other, and then the final one would also be terminated by an independent third party. It was the normality of the business that they were in. Contractors and freelancers were expendable, they owed allegiance to nobody.

And the thought of one contractor not taking out another, especially if the money was right, was just ridiculous in the extreme.

Chapter Seventeen

Mexico City – October 1973

Gorilla and Eunice's journey to Mexico City had been a long one. Once they had left Uncle Jeb and the dogs in Virginia they had contacted Gibbs, who had arranged for a CIA-owned private jet to get them across the border into Mexico. The private jet was a bonus. It speeded up their journey considerably and it also made it easier for them to take their personal weapons with them into Mexico.

On the flight manifest, they were awarded the title of 'Government Contractors' and were issued with temporary American Diplomatic status, hence their valises were protected, sealed and couldn't be inspected by the Mexican authorities. Gorilla guessed that this operation had cranked up a notch, at least as far as the CIA was concerned. Whatever it was that the Americans wanted Caravaggio for, it was evidently important enough to allow two freelance contractors the use of a luxury private jet usually retained for high-ranking CIA executives.

They had set off early and a four-hour drive got them to a covert military base in Williamsburg, Virginia. Camp Peary, officially referred to as the Armed Forces Experimental Training Facility, was a 9,000 acre site that hosted the CIA's infamous training school for its operations and paramilitary officers – The Farm.

It was here that Eunice had completed her original CIA training way back when, so for her, it was like returning home. Camp Peary also had a private airfield and it was there that the CIA Lear jet had picked them up. For Gorilla, it was a taste of the high life. He was used to travelling at best first class on commercial airliners and at worst, coach.

But this was something else. The interior of the jet was roomy and expensively decorated with four tan leather bucket seats for maximum comfort. There was the usual high-end pull-out table and a drinks bar located at their disposal. There was even a shower room. It was an executive hotel suite but at thirty thousand feet.

"You don't seem impressed?" said Gorilla

"Huh?" said Eunice, throwing her grab bag into the overhead locker. "I've been on private jets before – some for the Agency, some for some Middle Eastern clients. They're very nice and all, but they are just a means to an end. A way of getting us over yonder, that's all."

Gorilla grunted. Well, *Miss* Eunice might not be impressed, but he was bloody impressed and he was going to make every moment count! He settled himself, admiring Eunice's long legs as she sat opposite him, and helped himself to an eighteen-year-old Macallan whisky from the bar, which he thought was superb. But really, by the end of the flight, he had to admit to himself that it was just the same as any other flight, which dampened his spirits a little. Next time, back to the commercial jets. Still, it had been a nice dream while it had lasted.

They had flown into Tenochtitlan Airport and had hit the ground running in Mexico City. It was to be their jumping-off point and their base until they came up with some leads that could narrow down the search. As they were now on a combined CIA/SDECE ticket, they decided to pool their operational expenses and book into one of the best hotels in the city – The Marquis Plaza on the Paseo de la Reforma.

They settled in well and on the first day, Gorilla had covertly contacted the SDECE Station and requested additional cash funds for possible informant payments, as well as the usual contact procedures for receiving up-to-date intelligence that might help them to track down Alvarez, Caravaggio's suspected money-launderer.

The French Station Officer told him to sit tight and they would be in touch once they had anything. Gorilla wasn't going to argue. The hotel was luxurious, to say the least, and the thought of having a naked Eunice in his king-sized bed would help them both to kill the time.

They were three days in when they had a breakthrough. They had spent the previous days making love, double-checking and going over the information that they had so far, but really it was about sitting it out and waiting. So, when the contact call came from the French Service, both of them were more than ready to act. The CIA had nothing, so it seemed, but the French had contacts in all kinds of interesting places that the Agency didn't.

"You okay to make the contact alone?" asked Eunice, as she watched Grant get dressed. She had virtually been a full-time resident of their bed for days now, and, while the sex was good and physical, even she recognised that you can have too much of a good thing. She needed to 'shake her ass' out of bed and hit the streets.

Gorilla was fixing his tie and attaching the holster to his belt. "I'll be fine," he said. "It's only a handover with one of the SDECE blokes. I'll be done in a few hours."

He bent down and kissed her, their tongues meeting. Eunice kept the kiss going longer than she meant to. She couldn't help it; they were just so good together. When she finally broke away, she smiled up at him.

"You sure I can't tempt you back in?" she said, pulling back the covers to reveal her slim, tanned and very naked body underneath.

"You know you can," said Gorilla. "But you've worn me out over the past seventy-two hours! If I don't take my mind off your body and do some *real* work, I may just end up having a heart attack or dying from exhaustion!"

"Okay, Mr Grant, be on your way. I may go and check out the surrounding area, go for a walk and stretch my legs. Don't worry, I'll be careful. Just come back to me in one piece. Deal?"

"Deal," he said, heading to the door.

Once he had gone, Eunice stretched herself out in bed one last time. "C'mon girl, time to get up" she told herself. Maybe that's what she needed; to explore the city. She flung herself out of bed and grabbed her clothes.

The sniper had been in position since early that morning. He had a good spot on the roof of a building that gave him a clear line of sight up and down the Paseo del la Reforma and to the target's hotel. He was in the shade, he had water, he had been provided with a good weapon, and he was being well paid. He was happy.

He had learned his trade from the Americans during his time in Bolivia and Honduras. He could think of nothing better than lying up in a hide at long range and firing on a target. It was what he was born to do.

But the requirements of this job were unusual, to say the least. Not least the strange rifle that he had been provided with. It would certainly not have been his usual choice. But he didn't care. He was being paid by the mysterious Chinese man and his controller. Whoever that was...

He had been given photographs of his targets, the primary and the secondary. The secondary was a tough-looking individual; his face and body lean and hard inside a compact frame. But the primary target, the one he was ordered to shoot on sight... *Madre de dios*! She was quite a looker – tall, red-haired and with a slim, athletic body. Beautiful. Not that he cared what the target looked like. To the sniper, a shot was a shot. It was that simple.

Twenty minutes later, he saw the tough-looking man, the secondary target, leave the hotel and get into a taxi. He took his finger off the rifle's trigger. He should only fire at the secondary as a means to draw out the primary target. He eased his eye away from the scope and relaxed slightly.

Patience was the best skill of a marksman. Not the ability to shoot. Patience. And it was this patience that rewarded him thirty minutes later. He saw her exit the hotel and begin walking up the street, heading towards him. She was wearing a white trouser suit, sunglasses and scarf. She looked and carried herself like a catwalk model, confident and aware of her own sexuality. The sniper thought she looked stunning.

The target paused to look into a boutique window. It was all the opportunity that the sniper needed. He fired. Heard the silenced *phut* of the condensed air as the pellet left the barrel of the high-powered air rifle, and saw, through the telescopic sight, the impact as it hit the target on the side of the neck. He saw the target's hand instantly reach up to feel what had hit her.

For the sniper, the job was done. Now it would be in the hands of the kidnap team. Oh yes, he was very happy.

Eunice felt a sting on the side of her neck. Nothing really, something similar to a mosquito bite. She winced and looked around. She knew what it was; knew straight away. She'd been shot – but this wasn't a bullet in the classic sense of the term. This was something smaller. More discreet and low impact. An air pellet. A small pea of lead. The streets were busy, it could have been anyone, anywhere.

But within a few seconds, she knew… knew she had been hit with a fast-acting chemical agent, a poison. Already, she could feel her hands going numb and she had no doubts that in a few minutes, her legs would start to go as well.

The hotel. She knew she had to get back to the hotel… to Jack… to her Gorilla…

Her vision started to swim, her focus going in and out. Whatever it was that was coursing through her bloodstream was fast-acting and potent. The crowds around her on the street were swaying. In the distance, she managed to make out the upper part of her hotel. It became a beacon that she aimed her body towards. Left foot… right foot… left… right… foot… foot…

She felt her knees buckle and then strong hands lifted her under her armpits, which was just as well, because her legs had given out completely. By that time, she didn't care, she was just so sleepy… so sleepy.…

She felt herself being lifted, then there was the familiar noise of a van door being opened, the smooth burr of rollers as the door moved. Then she was thrown onto a dusty blanket in the interior, which became pitch dark as the doors closed. Then came the gunning of an engine and the jerking movement as the van drove away.

She knew all this because it was something that she had done herself – something she had organised many, many times. It seemed strange that one of the best bounty hunters in the business had been taken using tactics that she herself had perfected. But of course by this time, she didn't care. She was just so sleepy, so tired.

A woman collapses and is thrown into the back of a van. It didn't even raise an eyebrow. It was a normal day in Mexico City.

The local SDECE man was called 'Marcel', or at least that was the name that he had given Gorilla. This Frenchman was no refined, dandy intelligence officer. Gorilla looked at his hands and the scars. This man had been a soldier and had a no-bullshit attitude about him. Gorilla suspected that Marcel had been a part of the Action Service at some point, maybe even one of the feared *Barbouzes* from the 1960s. He had the look of a tough Marseilles drug dealer, complete with moustache and long hair.

They were in a restaurant not far from the city centre. But it was in enough of a side street to enable them to spot any hostile surveillance easily. Both men were nursing a cold Mexican beer and ignoring some burritos that they had ordered. Marcel was talking and Gorilla was listening.

"Our agents in the Mexican police say that he operates out of a place called Puerto Vallarta. It's a sleepy town on the coast. They say that in a few years' time it will boom, due to the tourists discovering it. But for now, it's quiet and discreet enough for Alvarez to run his little illegal operations, like the snuff movies he makes and the fights to the death. Plus, if he's laundering and moving money for someone on the scale of Caravaggio, then he's connected in all kinds of ways."

"So where do we find him? How do we narrow him down?" asked Gorilla, taking a sip of the beer.

"Alvarez and his people are understandably cagey, they don't want to be caught doing what they are doing. But even they recognise that, at some point, they have to tell someone about where the fights are happening, otherwise they would have no customers! The police soon get wind of it, but don't seem too eager to act on the information."

"They being bought off?"

Marcel laughed. "Of course, this is Mexico. Everything and everyone can be bought. What we know is that the next fight will be held in the fighting pit in a few days' time. If we hurry, we can make it. I have the address."

"If I can get close to him, I can make him talk," said Gorilla.

"Or maybe your current partner, Nikita, can. Perhaps she could infiltrate his inner circle? I'm told that she is an expert at getting close to a target," said the SDECE man.

Gorilla was about to tell the Frenchman to mind his manners, but then thought better of it. The longer he kept his private relationship with Eunice a secret, the better. Instead, he grunted something non-committal.

"I can get you all the details by tomorrow. Do you need me to come with you? La Piscine said that whatever it is you are doing, it is to be given the highest station priority," said Marcel grumpily.

Gorilla thought about the offer. For the moment, he wanted the operation to be carried out by just himself and Eunice. They had started it. He wanted the two of them to finish it together.

Finally, Gorilla shook his head. "For the moment, no. But just stay by the phone in case the situation alters."

Marcel nodded in understanding. Less than three hours later, the SDECE man would think back to how prophetic the words of this English gunman had been.

The moment he touched the door to the hotel suite, Gorilla knew – he just knew – that something had gone badly wrong. When he pushed the door open wide and saw the scattered clothes and overturned furniture of their suite, it had been confirmed. "No, no, *NO!*" he cursed.

He didn't think, he didn't pause, he just blasted into the room. He didn't care if there was physical danger there, he just had to find Eunice. The room had been expertly ransacked. Gorilla suspected it had been done more for show than for actually searching for anything. He drew the curtains in case of a sniper or surveillance, pulled out his ASP and did a quick security check of the suite, to make sure that no unwanted visitors were still present. Nothing.

He scanned the room, trying to organise the visual chaos in his mind, all the time looking for a clue or some tiny piece of evidence as to what had happened here to Eunice. He didn't have to look far. The evidence that he needed had been left in the perfect spot for him to find it. There was a beautifully folded note waiting for him on the centre of the bed's rumpled sheets.

The note was printed in a clear, strong hand. It read: *Find Alvarez and he will lead you to Nikita Brown. Good luck. Caravaggio.*

Chapter Eighteen

Twenty-four hours later, Gorilla was still in a rage.

He was furious with whoever had kidnapped Eunice, furious with this job, and most definitely furious with himself. He had taken his eye off the ball and allowed himself and Eunice to become distracted with each other. It had cost them dearly. His woman had been kidnapped and he was now in a position of weakness. His enemy, the unseen phantom, had outsmarted him. And that was a position that Gorilla Grant didn't like being in.

To calm himself following the ransacking of the hotel room and the discovery of the kidnap note, he had tidied the room and put in an emergency call to the SDECE agent who was handling him.

"I need to find Alvarez *now*!" he had barked into the phone. "Get me a car, on a plane, or on a fucking boat! I don't care what you have to do, but get it done quickly! What? I don't care that you're busy! Any problems, contact Sassi at the Action Service. This mission takes precedence over anything that you have on at the moment. Understand? And no, I don't care what your boss says... Oh and by the way, you're coming with me. So start packing!"

Then he had slammed the phone down and waited, cleaning and oiling the ASP to help focus his mind. The action of disassembling and cleaning the gun helped to bring his heart rate down and calm him enough to start thinking clearly. For now, anyway.

That evening, Marcel, the SDECE agent from the Mexico City Station, arrived in an anonymous Embassy car. "Get in! We have a flight to catch," said the French intelligence officer.

Gorilla flung a small holdall in the backseat and off they had set; one in sullen silence because he would far rather be dealing with his own agents that night on the diplomatic cocktail circuit, and the other simmering with barely contained rage at having his woman kidnapped and his mission blown out of the water. Well, almost.

The SDECE man was to be his guide, get him into the fighting pit and help him find Alvarez. He threw a stapled-together paper file into Gorilla's lap.

"Read this," he said. "That's all we have on Alvarez. But we do know where he'll be tonight. One of our sources in the police keeps a track on illegal fights. Alvarez is the main organiser. He takes a cut himself and likes to gamble heavily on the bouts."

The SDECE man didn't want Gorilla travelling with French documentation – the less of an official French trail, the better, in his opinion. "Do you still have the diplomatic papers that the Americans gave you?" he asked.

"Yes."

"Good. Use them. If it all goes to shit, we can always claim that you were working for the Yankees," grumbled Marcel.

The journey south to Puerto Vallarta only took a few hours but, to Gorilla Grant, it was an eternity. His mind was a whirlwind of 'what ifs'. How had she been taken? Was she even still alive? How had she died? Had she been assaulted? His mind ran through all the nightmare scenarios.

He knew that if he was to have any hope of getting her back, of finding her, he would have to remove the emotion from his thinking. They had left a note saying that they had her, so it was unlikely that they would kill her. He tried his best to think logically. Eunice being used as bait. She was the next step in a chain that was drawing him closer to Caravaggio.

The rest of the flight passed in a blur with Gorilla being lost in his own thoughts. He barely remembered getting off the flight; hardly remembered the car that picked them up at the airport or the journey to the SDECE safe-house.

"Get a few hours' rest," said Marcel, checking the apartment. "We leave later tonight. You'll need to be ready."

Gorilla lay down on the bed. He closed his eyes, but he did not sleep. All he could see was the green eyes of Eunice Brown and, in the background, in the darkness, was the shadowy figure of Caravaggio towering over her.

That night, there was a storm in the Puerto Vallarta area, causing flooding in several streets. For the criminal element of the town, that was good; it kept the good and righteous people off the streets, leaving it open to the street rats and gangsters.

The fighting pit was an underground car park in a disused office building in the centre of town. It was one of several disposable venues that were used to run the knife duels. Within hours, bodies would be removed and they would be cleaned and returned to their usual state of dilapidation.

Gorilla arrived a little after midnight and the place was heaving. Gamblers, fighters, voyeurs, hookers, even a few off-duty policemen. The atmosphere was one of tension, sweat and money, a lot of money, and the gamblers and bookies were doing a roaring trade.

The fighting pit was full of Mexicans, the odd adventure tourists and a group of over-the-top Texan businessmen who were flashing the cash and being loud. Gorilla and the SDECE agent made their way along to the circle of bodies that were fighting in the latest bout. They edged near to the front and spent five minutes watching the combat.

Two whip-thin Mexicans, stripped to the waist and drenched in sweat, were at a standstill and held traditional *Navaja* blades, ready to make the next cut on their respective opponent. He watched as the two fighters went through a series of thrusts, parries and slashes. There were the inevitable cheers from the ramped-up crowd as one fighter began to take cuts again and again. Gorilla started to walk away. He knew how these things played out; the fighters would close the distance, grappling would take place and, sooner or later, one would dominate and start pumping the blade into the other. Death would follow.

Both men moved along, glancing at the various bouts. It didn't take long to ID Louis Alvarez. The SDECE man spotted him first and pointed him out to Gorilla. "That's him," said the Frenchman. "It fits the mugshot that we got from Mexican Police Intelligence."

Gorilla glanced over to a thin, lanky figure at the centre of the crowd. The man looked like the epitome of a dandy gambler, pimp and lounge lizard. Once they had ID'd the Mexican, Gorilla told the French agent that he could go.

"You've been a great help," he said. "Wait outside for me in the car. As soon as I know how this is going to play out, I'll let you know. You don't want to be here when things start going south."

The agent nodded and left Gorilla to his own devices. He had better things to do up in Mexico City, and transporting a crazy Englishman around wasn't high on his list of intelligence priorities, so sitting outside seemed like a fair compromise.

Gorilla watched Alvarez for the next thirty minutes. He appeared to be gambling big and large amounts of cash were exchanging hands with the bookies. The Mexican clearly knew his fighters, judging by the amount of dollar bills he had pocketed.

An hour later, Alvarez decided enough was enough for one evening and pushed his way through the crowd to the car park exit which was guarded by two armed crushers. He nodded to them on the way out and exited onto the street.

Gorilla followed the same route and quickly caught up with the three men.

The crushers were the first to go, thanks to the silenced ASP. A single shot to the head of each dropped them without any worries. Then Gorilla headed straight for the dandy Mexican, hoping to intercept him before he made it to his Cadillac that was parked on the outskirts of the disused car park.

Gorilla moved fast – he knew he had to, if he was going to keep the initiative.

"Alvarez?" Gorilla went straight in, no build-up, no talking, just violence. He grabbed the tall Mexican by the fancy shirt front and started throwing punches into his face, not even giving him time to answer.

"Where is Nikita Brown?"

The punches turned to elbow strikes and when the Mexican's body began to drop to the floor, they turned to kicks.

"Where is Nikita Brown?"

The Mexican was huddled in a ball on the floor with Gorilla standing above him, his face red with rage and his hands clenched, ready to deliver more beatings. He looked around the empty street and noticed a collection of empty beer bottles. He picked one up, tapped it firmly against the wall and watched as the body shattered, leaving a handle with a jagged edge in his hand.

Gorilla pushed it dangerously close to the Mexican's eye.

Alvarez held up a hand to protect himself and screamed, "I have a message for you! The woman! Caravaggio has the woman!"

"*Where*? Tell me now or I'll fucking blind you!" roared Gorilla.

"No, no… don't do that! I can get you there. There is no need for that."

"Bullshit. You've got one chance. So talk!"

"Caravaggio is expecting you. That is the message. He has your woman. He wants to meet you."

"Where?"

"You have to go to him, to his island," said Alvarez.

"What island?"

"La Isla del Diablo. The Devil's Island!"

"Where is that?"

"It is off the coast, here at Puerto Vallarta. It is Caravaggio's private island. I am the man that can get you there. Please put the bottle down. There is no need for this!"

"How do I get across?" said Gorilla, pushing the bottle into the other man's face, drawing blood.

"*Ahhhhh…* please stop! I have arranged it all. I was expecting you. Talk to the ferryman, he will take you there!"

Gorilla looked at him and growled, "If you try to fuck me over, Alvarez, I will find you. You read me?"

Gorilla told Alvarez to wait in the Cadillac and he went off in search of the SDECE man. The agent's car was parked two blocks away and he was sitting inside, smoking a cigarette. Gorilla climbed into the rear seat and took a breath.

"How did it go?" asked the French agent cautiously, glancing at him in the rear-view mirror.

"Good. Okay. I got what I needed."

"Excellent! Then we can go?"

Gorilla shook his head. "Not exactly. You can head back to Mexico City, but I have to go a different route."

The SDECE man frowned. "Monsieur, I'm not sure that is a good idea…"

"It doesn't matter. It has to happen. Can you do me a favour?"

"But of course."

"Get in touch with Sassi at the Action Service. Tell him that Gorilla is still in play. Tell him to let the CIA know that Nikita has been kidnapped, but that I'm tracking her down. I can't tell you where I'll be going as there are risks involved for other people, but if it plays out like I think it will, then tell him I'll be able to get close to the target. If I can get close to him, I can finish the mission. Do you understand?"

The SDECE man nodded.

"Oh, and make sure he gets this," said Gorilla, unhooking the ASP and holsters from his belt and passing it across to the agent in the front seat. "Tell him to return it to the USA cache."

"But monsieur... you are going... wherever... unarmed?"

"I've got a feeling that where I'm going, it won't be needed," said Gorilla and with that, he got out of the car and walked away into the darkness of whatever fate had decided for him.

Chapter Nineteen

Alvarez was as good as his word and drove Gorilla to a small harbour three miles down the coast. During the drive, neither man had spoken. Gorilla had sat and fumed, barely containing his anger. Alvarez had sweated and kept his eyes on the road. Gorilla wondered who the Mexican gambler was more frightened of; him or Caravaggio.

Eventually, Alvarez pulled up and Gorilla quickly got out, eager to move onto the next stage of his journey. "End of the jetty. You can't miss him. He is the ferryman. He's been told that you are coming. Good luck, Senor Grant," Alvarez called from the car, before speeding off.

Gorilla made his way along the jetty, a series of small lights illuminating his way in the darkness until he reached the end. He stopped and stared down at the figure that sat in an old and abused panga, a small Mexican fishing boat that was traditionally used to move contraband. The boat looked as if it would hold about three people, but no more.

"You are the Englishman? The one that wishes passage to La Isla del Diablo?" said the ferryman.

"Yes."

"Then hurry please, senor. The moon is against us tonight, but the tide is with us. We will leave soon."

The ferryman was old, hunched and crooked. He was bent over like a man who had spent a lifetime of hard manual toil on the sea. His face was thin, bearded and covered with a cowl to keep out the cold of the night. Only a pair of bright eyes occasionally glinted from the darkness of the hood, and a thick, guttural voice came from within.

"Have you been the ferryman here for very long?" asked Gorilla.

"I have always been the ferryman here, senor. I take the mail to the island. Occasionally supplies, nothing more."

"And do you take things from the island to the mainland?"

"No, senor. I would not trust anything from that place in my boat. It would be cursed."

"What do you know of the island?"

The ferryman swore under his breath, hawked and spat into the water. "I do not like to speak of such things, senor. It is bad luck."

"Please. I would like to know."

The ferryman grunted. "The old ones say that it was a place of the insane, where they would send the mad and the crazed. It was a place of evil. Many people died there, many people."

"And now?"

The ferryman shrugged. "The locals speak of bad things. Strangers go missing. People who visit never come back. They say that there is fornication… witchcraft… unnatural things."

"And of the man who lives there? What of him?"

"El Diablo? I have never seen him. They say he is a genius, but that he has sold his soul to the devil. To own an island like that, he must be very rich, very powerful."

"I suppose he must," said Gorilla.

"Do you have business there, senor? Do you have business with El Diablo?" asked the ferryman.

"Yes."

"And you will not turn back? You will not let me take you back to the mainland? There is still time."

"No. I can't. I have to go there," replied Gorilla, watching the flow of the water as the panga cut through the tide.

"Are you a man like El Diablo? Have you sold your soul, too?"

Gorilla shrugged. "I don't know anymore. I hope not."

"Then I will pray for you. It is all that I can offer you."

Gorilla sat in silence, listening to the paddles gently moving the water. He was happy for the conversation with the old ferryman to end. It had disturbed him and he needed his own thoughts. It had been what...? A few months, maybe more, that this hunt had been ongoing. What had started as a mission, a job, nothing more, had morphed into becoming a reason for revenge against the man who had disabled him all those months ago.

Then, somewhere in this dark quest, it had changed. He had found witnesses, talked to sources, travelled the globe hunting this mythical figure. The motivation had changed again when he heard the stories about this man. They intrigued him. To Gorilla, he was an enigma. Now, it was less about revenge and more about solving a mystery.

How had he reached this point? When had duty become obsession for him? When had revenge turned into that single-minded focus so beloved of the addict?

Maybe he was more like Caravaggio than he cared to admit. And if he was being honest with himself, that thought scared him more than whatever he might find on this island.

La Isla del Diablo was located two miles off the coast of Puerto Vallarta and was a heart-shaped ten acres of jungle and swamp. The one main access road split the island like a crack in the heart shape and led from the main quayside on the south of the island, to the private residence and grounds that had been purposely built on a hill in the north. The quayside was where the owner of the island kept his personal yacht and where special visitors to the island would dock their motor launches.

Gorilla and the ferryman, however, would be taking the shorter and more covert route, which involved moving along the west coast of the island to a small jetty the ferryman knew about, in an open part of the swamp. It was Gorilla's strangest and slowest journey into enemy territory in his entire espionage career to date.

The journey across from the harbour at Puerto Vallarta to the outskirts of the island had been uneventful. Once they had left the sea behind and had turned off into the rivers surrounding the island, the ferryman had cut the engine and taken out his paddles. Gorilla offered to help him row, but the old man had declined his offer.

The ferryman had found an inlet along the coastline that led to a small lake and then into a dark and oppressive swamp. Gorilla sat with his hands resting in his lap, trying to ignore the heat, humidity and the brooding jungle that lay beyond the water. This journey up the river had become similar to his hunt for Caravaggio himself; it had been a long and winding path that was now forcing him into a chokepoint, drawing him nearer to the mystery.

"We are almost there, Senor. Please, no sudden movements," warned the ferryman, crouching low in the boat. He had lifted the paddles out of the water and was letting the boat coast into the shoreline under its own momentum. Gorilla turned and nodded in understanding.

"When we dock, it will be a quick drop-off and then I will be away. I do not like to stay here any longer than I have to," said the ferryman.

He pulled the small boat into an improvised makeshift jetty that ran along the edge of the swamp. In the distance, Gorilla could hear the eerie sounds of wildlife and the nocturnal predators of the island. He reached into his jacket pocket, pulled out a roll of cash and pushed it into the ferryman's hands.

The old, hunched figure nodded his appreciation and jumped out of the boat and onto the jetty, quickly securing the rope to stabilise the boat. He shook Gorilla's hand. "Good luck, senor," he said quietly, his head bowed.

Gorilla climbed out, straightened his suit and patted the razor in his trouser pocket. It gave him comfort and reassurance. Through the darkness of the trees, he could see lights shining in the distance from some kind of structure. Caravaggio's villa on the hill, he guessed.

Carefully, he began to move forward, readying himself mentally for dealing with whatever was waiting for him. Then, as an afterthought, he called over his shoulder to the ferryman, "Be careful on the way back, my friend."

There was a bust of loud, brash laughter. "Oh, I am not going any-where!"

The voice had changed beyond all recognition. It was no longer the guttural voice of a Mexican peasant. Now, it belonged to a cultured European. The effect was jarring. Gorilla Grant slowly turned round to see if there had been someone else on the small boat with them all this time – a ridiculous idea, he knew, and yet...

The ferryman was going through a transformation. He was hunched over and gnarled no longer. Now he stood stretched to his full height, and he was tall, very tall. He stared at Gorilla, his arms outstretched in a messianic way, welcoming the visitor forward.

"It was so good of you to join us, Gorilla Grant. You are our welcome guest," said the ferryman in his new-found accent. Gorilla realised that he had heard that voice before – on the beach in Nice.

He started to reach for the razor in his pocket, but he was way too late. A strike to the side of the neck stunned him and then dark, slender arms enveloped him from behind, snaking around his neck and throat, tightening up and cutting off his blood supply. Dimly, he recognized that unconsciousness would happen within seconds.

The last thing he saw before he sank into the blackness of his mind was the determined face of the Chinese assassin, whose arms cradled his head and opposite him, the smiling face of the 'ferryman' who was Caravaggio.

Chapter Twenty

Gorilla awoke shivering in the darkness. He was naked except for the hood that had been placed over his head and sat handcuffed to a hard, metal-framed chair. He could feel the coolness of the room and could faintly hear the drip, drip of water onto a stone floor.

His wrists were locked behind him and he flexed them to see how strong the handcuffs were. Nothing. No give in them at all. He wasn't going anywhere. He tried to rock the chair using his own momentum. Again, nothing; it was fixed to the ground. He *definitely* wasn't going anywhere. So he did what he had been trained to do in these situations. He sat, calmed himself, slowed his breathing and waited.

Drip... drip... drip.

He heard the word, "Chang" before the hood was whipped off his head. So far, he hadn't seen this man's face. In Nice at the casino, it had been hidden behind a mask and on the beach it had been in silhouette. On the ferry across to the island, it had been heavily disguised and now, here in this dungeon, the man was seated far back in the shadows.

The only visible parts of him were his large, strong hands, which were crossed casually in front of him on a plain wooden table that was illuminated by a small desk lamp. The man wore a black shirt and the only concession to colour was a huge steel wristwatch on his thick wrist. His body and head were laid back in the blackness of the room.

"Caravaggio?" mumbled Gorilla. He wasn't scared yet. That was to come, he was certain. But for now, it was an open game.

"Indeed," said the voice from the blackness. "Please allow me to introduce Chang, whom you have met intimately but not formally."

Gorilla glanced over his right shoulder to the dark corner behind him and was aware of a stern-faced Chinese man dressed in a black suit. The man had the mannerisms and composure of an android. He was unnerving, to say the least.

"Chang is my manservant, bodyguard and apprentice. I have trained him since he was a young man and I have high hopes for his education. I truly think he could be one of the greats of our profession, Mr Grant. Chang has been your shadow in your quest to find me. He has protected you on many occasions, in order that you could follow my little clues," said Caravaggio proudly.

Yeah, and taken out quite a few witnesses, thought Gorilla.

"Did the hand heal well?" Caravaggio enquired. "I am truly sorry that I had to do that, but I needed to slow you down."

For the moment, Gorilla couldn't connect the dots, then he remembered. Nice... the shootout on the beach. "It took a while, but now I'm better than ever with a gun in my left hand. You'll find out soon enough," Gorilla snarled.

"I have no doubt."

"Why didn't you just kill me there and then?"

"Mr Grant, surely it is obvious, no?"

"Not to me. No."

"Let's just say that I hate to waste promising talent. But that is for later. Here and now, we have more pressing matters."

"Such as?"

"Such as you telling me all you know about why you were sent after me."

"And if I refuse?"

"Oh, Mr Grant, I had no doubts that you would refuse at first. After all, you are the great Gorilla Grant, a hard man, a tough guy with an international reputation as an expert with small arms. A crack shot. But I doubt that you have met anyone like Chang. He has his own reputation, too," said Caravaggio.

Chang stepped out of the darkness behind Gorilla's shoulder. His face was still just as impassive and betrayed no emotion.

"So, it's questions, is it?" asked Gorilla.

"All in good time," said Caravaggio from the shadows. "First come the pain and the brutality, then come the questions. It is necessary to show you that I am a man of detail. It is vital that we concentrate your mind on what can happen if you don't co-operate."

Chang had worked him over diligently for twenty minutes. It had been hard and brutal and, for a small-framed man, his strength and power were remarkable, thought Gorilla.

He had fluctuated between strikes to the body and pressure points to the nerves. There was very little bruising on Gorilla's body, it had been mostly internal pain, but that didn't alleviate the amount of agony that had been inflicted upon him.

The questions, when they came, were not delivered with the bark and rapidity of a torturer, but with the flow and smoothness of the practised interrogator. Caravaggio was an expert in taking his time. The voice that spoke from the darkness came with the usual operational questions beloved of spies and their need to know the bigger picture: *What was your mission? Who gave the orders? How did you meet the woman?*

Caravaggio didn't have the bad habits of a less experienced interrogator. No questions were incessantly repeated. Instead, he gently probed his subject, coming in wide and narrowing the focus. He was a professional, looking at his subject through the critical eye of one who has been both the torturer and the tortured in his time.

But interspersed throughout these standard points were questions that dug deeper into Gorilla's mind. These weren't questions to do with what he had been hired to do, these were questions that he believed Caravaggio wanted to know, in order to better understand the man that he had trapped here: *Tell me about your first kill? How did you feel? Have you ever turned down an assignment? Have you ever failed to complete a contract?*

If it hadn't been for the regular pain received from the little Chinese torturer behind him, Gorilla would have thought he was being interviewed for a job. It was if the dark man in the shadows needed to get to the heart of what made Gorilla Grant tick.

And all the while, as this persistent questioning continued, Gorilla was steeling his naked, shivering body for the next round of pain delivered by Chang – pain inflicted by hands, metal, wood and electricity. Gorilla would gulp in a huge breath, grit his teeth and wait for the agony to begin. Often, he would pass out. Every time, he would scream. His life had been condensed down to moments of violence smattered with a journey deep into his psyche.

"Tell me about the woman?"

It was another session. Gorilla guessed it had been hours since the last one. In all of his interrogations, he had tried his best to limit his answers to Caravaggio. Information was the currency at the moment and Gorilla needed as much collateral as he could if he was to survive this thing.

On the whole, despite the torture to his body, he had fielded the questions well. But occasionally, Caravaggio would throw in a wild card question, trying to get under Gorilla's skin to find that gap in his armour. *Nikita.*

"She's a contractor. She's the competition," mumbled Gorilla, his eyes cast down at the wet stone floor where his bare feet lay on top of one another.

"So she is an ally?"

"No, she's a contractor like me. We decided to share information so that we could get closer to the targ… so we could get closer to you. But, at the end of the day, we are on opposite sides. Like I say… she's competition."

"Do you always sleep with the competition, Mr Grant?"

"A gentleman never tells."

The shadow barked out a harsh laugh. "Oh, come now, Mr Grant, let us not pretend that you are a gentleman. You are a rough diamond."

Gorilla was about to hurl back a rebuke, but before he could finish his sentence, the dark man in the shadows threw down a series of black and white photographs at Gorilla's feet. They lay splayed across the damp floor.

He managed to catch a glimpse of the top photo that showed Gorilla and Eunice making love. She was riding him, her head flung back in ecstasy, her breasts flung outwards at the moment of orgasm, while Gorilla had his hands on her hips to aid in the rocking motion of their lovemaking. Across their naked bodies were the horizontal shadows from the window blinds as the electric storm had raged that night.

Gorilla remembered the moment immediately. It was at the Ranch in Virginia. Caravaggio and his people had had them under surveillance even there.

"Do you love her?"

Gorilla remained silent. Let Caravaggio take what he wanted from his silence. He couldn't even admit it to himself, let alone a man who was his captor. "Where is she?" he asked instead.

"She is safe here on the island. She has been treated with respect. She is a beautiful woman. I congratulate you. I, too, understand the allure of a beautiful woman on a mission. They can be either an asset or a hindrance, depending on the task at hand. I was on a job for the Germans during the War and I, too, fell in love with a woman not unlike your Nikita.

"I would risk my life to go and see her. On every corner, there were informants ready to kill me if I showed my face in public. It didn't matter. I would prepare elaborate ruses to remain undetected just so that I could hold her. She was one of the bravest and most passionate women I have ever met."

Caravaggio stared at the seemingly broken man before him. "When they come for you, they will not come at you directly. Learn from one who has travelled this road before. They will come at those that you love and those that you hold dear. It will be a friend, a saviour, a blood brother that will try to wield the knife, the gun, the strangling hands against you. Very rarely will it be an enemy."

"Then you do have a weakness. Love," said Gorilla weakly.

There was a deep, throaty laugh from the darkness, but one without humour. "Of course not, Mr Grant, I am a professional. I had a job to do. I killed her."

It was another day… or night, Gorilla wasn't certain. Being stuck down in the dungeon altered your state of mind.

Once more, he was the prey of the man in the shadows, the dark man, with only his huge hands visible, that large metal watch glinting in the ambient light as he rested them on the table in front of him. At some point over the last few days, the questioning had stopped. Whether Caravaggio had run out of questions, or whether he had simply become bored with the answers, Gorilla wasn't sure.

But something had changed. Now, the dark man talked and his captive listened. Now, instead of it being an interrogation, it felt like a confessional. It was as if Caravaggio was absolving himself of his sins and had decided that Gorilla Grant would be the man to hear them; to hear them and to understand.

The voice of the dark man was hypnotic. It was the same voice that had brought him here and had taunted him for days; that deep, rumbling bass voice that at once both seduced and educated.

"I once spent a year getting close to a target. To a man I had been paid to kill. That was my commitment, my level of professionalism.

I took on no other contracts, no other work. I became obsessed with this man, with how I would assassinate him. I could not make love… could not relax until I had him in my sights and had pulled the trigger.

"To be an assassin, I think, requires a great deal of love and empathy for our fellow man, do you not think? People assume that we are all cold-hearted killers. Perhaps the amateur ones are, or the people who boast of it, but to a professional, a dedicated craftsman of the art, it requires a level of understanding of what it is to be a human being."

The voice stopped for a few moments, as if it were considering where this train of thought was going. "Have you ever felt emotions for your targets, Mr Grant? Have you ever been disgusted with yourself at your actions?" said the voice.

Gorilla thought back to a dark night in Cornwall many years ago, an operation of the past, when he had a man tied to a chair, a chair not unlike the one he was shackled to now. He had interrogated the man, pumped him full of drugs and then cut open his veins in order for him to bleed out. He had caught the blood in a bucket. Then he had rushed to the door and puked all over the porch steps. He had been ashamed of the way he had murdered that particular target.

Gorilla raised his head and looked in the direction of the dark man's hands.

"No, never," he lied weakly, through split lips.

The dark shape stared back at him from the shadows for many moments. "I don't believe you, Mr Grant. But we will talk of this again when you are feeling more… receptive. Chang?" he added softly

The figure behind him, the iron fist in the Master's velvet glove, moved in. Gorilla felt the expert touch of the Chinese man's fingers as they dug into his nerve points, the points that only an expert in torture and pain would know existed, and he felt his head explode.

He screamed.

That night, Caravaggio once again visited his new 'pet Gorilla', as he liked to say. He sat in the shadows again, a bottle of red wine and a single glass on the table before him. The wine had been poured and left to breathe. Gorilla could make out the aroma of the strong, fruity grapes. Its colour reminded him of blood.

The Master took a delicate sip before returning the glass back to the table. Chang had been dismissed and the guard from outside the dungeon's door had been ordered out of earshot. For now, it was a private audience of two, the Master and the Gorilla. No other players were allowed.

"So, Mr Grant, let us begin properly. The time for questions is over and our time together will soon be at an end. So, I would like you to hear my story – my confession, if you like. I would like you, Gorilla Grant, to bear witness to my tale."

Chapter Twenty-One

"I was born Nicolai Vlcek. My father was a Czech industrial engineer, very successful, and my mother was an Italian music protégée who played the violin and had performed all over the world. They met in Rome and their love was one of the greatest love affairs of the age.

"I was raised on the island of Sardinia. My family had wealth, status, opportunities and respect. My father arranged to have the best tutors in Europe teach me. I was a scion of Italian aristocracy. I had privilege.

"As a young man, my life was as luxurious as my childhood. But now, I had the opportunity to travel and have adventures, and travel I did – Europe, the Middle East, Asia, the Americas. I was ravenous for experiences, to see the world and explore. I climbed the Matterhorn in my twenties. I have run illegal narcotics in Asia, hunted wild animals in Africa and have been a regular at every luxury hotel across Europe several times over.

"I was known within high society. In my life, I have bedded lovers of both sexes and have fathered many children, none of which know my name or who I am. But all this, all these adventures, never truly satisfied me, Mr Grant. Quite soon, they all lost their edge. I was constantly searching for the next fix, the next thing that made me come alive. I was already rich from my family inheritance, so even money could not excite me or motivate me."

"I was first recruited by an intelligence organisation in the 1930s. I was naïve and was embarrassingly green about the whole spy games milieu. But I was a quick learner, Mr Grant. I had to be. Well, you know this. After all, our trade has no time for poor players.

"The Russians taught me the tradecraft of espionage, the Germans taught me the skills of sabotage and assassination and from the Japanese masters I learned the ways of silent killing, the way of the blade and the use of poisons. I excelled in all of them. I have been an agent, a double agent, even a triple agent at times, throughout many wars and conflicts. I have been a whore in who I have worked for. It mattered not to me. Ideology was a luxury that only affected lesser people.

"I have killed on contract more times than I can remember, but I will always remember the face of the first man that I killed... always. I have lied, cheated, deceived and manipulated and I regret none of it."

Gorilla thought back to the rumours that he had heard about this man from fellow spies, enemies, and lovers. Could he be all of these complex characters rolled into one living body? This was no ordinary hit man, in Gorilla's opinion. This man had been an integral part of the espionage trade for nearly half a century and had survived. He doubted that the rumours did the real man justice.

"Do you know who Janus, was Mr Grant?" said Caravaggio. "He was the Roman God of gateways, duality and passages. He is often depicted as having two faces. These faces look to the past and the future at the same time. That was who I was. I was known on the international stage as a wealthy Italian aristocrat and playboy. That was my outward persona and it was a good cover. But my true life, my real personality, the one I relished more than any other, was that of my cryptonym, Caravaggio. Mr Grant, I was born to the life of espionage. It is my calling."

The dark man stopped and took another long pull at the red wine, then refilled the glass. He waited, as if unsure of where he wanted to go next. Then, once again, those smooth, deep, hypnotic tones flowed into the gloom of the dungeon.

"When you are perceived as a legend, you take on a level of commitment to your chosen profession. For me, it was never about the money or the ideology. It was never about revenge. At one point in my life, I used to think that my secret lives, my missions, my adventures, were all about the experiences. To live to a different beat than my fellow man, to be something beyond the norm. That may still be true, but it is not what has motivated me for a very long time.

"It was always about being the best in the world – to be the best intelligence agent, the perfect assassin, to test myself. It was always truly about being an artist at my craft. The original Caravaggio was one of the greatest artists, a great master. He could create beauty upon his canvas. My version of Caravaggio was to be an artist in death and deception and the Cold War was my canvas. The rifle, knife and garrotte were my brushes. The targets were my muse. It was my job to bring all these elements together to make one perfect kill."

He paused, took a sip of wine and continued.

"Mr Grant, I have a secret I wish to share with you. For a man like me, 'secret' is a dangerous word, but you are the only person I wish to share this with. I think that you are probably the only one that will understand.

"For many years, I have wanted to retire, leave this life and be free of the constant bickering of the Cold War and the spies who run it. Like my earlier life, their adventures were becoming passé, boring... predictable. Another double agent assassinated, a coup organised, a kidnapping... there were too many amateurs playing in games that they had no business being involved in as they lacked experience.

"I had become disillusioned with the intelligence game. I wished to be free of it. But unfortunately, a legend does not get to leave, it seems. The spymasters were constantly trying to pull me back in – with money at first, then later, with threats. I grew tired of their feeble attempts very quickly. So, I decided to play them at their own game. I cut my links with all of my former contacts – eliminated them in some cases. Anyone that could lead back to me had to be removed."

"Like in New Orleans and Athens?" said Gorilla

"Exactly. Why would I take the risk that someone would betray me?"

Caravaggio then turned his thoughts to something that they had in common; the assassination of the Hungarian in the Casino in Nice.

"The Hungarian spy, Szabo, had also been a part of my private network for many years. He was someone who I had worked for and who had worked for me. It was a mutually beneficial relationship. However, he decided to betray me and pass on what he knew of my operations to the French when he defected. He should have known better. He had worked with me long enough to know that I would not tolerate betrayal. Hence he had to die.

"Although I will admit that it was a surprise to find you there protecting him!" he added. "That, I had not expected."

"I hope I didn't disappoint," said Gorilla. "A bullet in the hand tends to do that."

"On the contrary, Mr Grant, I was emboldened. I had wanted to meet the great Gorilla Grant for so long. I had heard many good things about you. Now, I had a chance to witness them for myself," said Caravaggio.

Gorilla snorted. Even in his weakened state, he was not going to fall for flattery.

Caravaggio returned to his story. "I have in my safe here on the island, a dossier compiled against the Americans, the French, the Germans and the Russians of every intelligence mission and dirty operation that I have conducted for them. The information in those files would be explosive to the right people. It has the potential to rip apart spy networks across the globe. The details stretch from the lowest spy on the ground, all the way up to the intelligence officials that run them... even up to their political masters that own them. I am not exaggerating when I say that it could bring down governments.

"So you see, the SDECE and the CIA have lied to both yourself and Miss Brown. Your mission to track me down and Redact or capture me wasn't because I had planned to assassinate the Presidents of both countries. It was because I had enough blackmail material to frustrate their efforts to control me. After all, an agent out of control, one who has gone rogue, is a dangerous weapon to have roaming free. Spymasters fear what they cannot control."

Too right, thought Gorilla.

"Despite my wishes to retire, and my various former employers' attempts to try and stop that, I still crave the need to pit myself against the best. Retiring from the secret world is one thing, but the desire to constantly test myself is something else.

"I have watched you, Gorilla Grant. I have watched you for many years now. Several times now, our paths have almost crossed. I have seen the way you have risen in our business. I like the way you carry yourself. Oh, you can be a little crude at times, a little rough around the edges, but I can recognise someone of a similar ilk to myself. I can feel a kinship.

"You were born to do this type of work, Mr Grant. You are a natural like me. It is who I am and I do not think that will ever go away. So it was fortuitous when the French Secret Service decided to send the one operative that I would wish to test myself against, to track me down and kill me – assassin against assassin. It is why I orchestrated your visit to my island."

Gorilla cocked an inquisitive eyebrow at that. Could it be true that every aspect of this operation, all the tracking and killing, had been for nothing, just so that he and Eunice could be brought here at Caravaggio's bidding? In the darkness, he could sense Caravaggio smiling to himself, secure in the knowledge that all along, his pet Gorilla had had no idea that he was being lured here.

When Caravaggio continued, it was as if he were reading Gorilla's mind. "It was easy really, a rumour that we planted here or there, a paid informant to give you information, even finding the clues that Chang had dropped on purpose. It was all a part of the road that led you to this island. But, please… do not concern yourself with the details now, Mr Grant. It is done.

"Can I ask you, do you know the tale of *The Scorpion and the Frog*? No? It is a relatively recent fable that is based on much older ones. The tale is an apocryphal one that I would like to share with you. A scorpion and a frog meet on the bank of a stream. The scorpion asks the frog to carry him across on its back. 'How do I know that you won't sting me?' asks the frog. The scorpion says, 'Because if I do, I will die also.'

"The frog is satisfied and agrees. They set out across the stream. Halfway across, the scorpion stings the frog. The frog feels the onset of paralysis and starts to sink, knowing that they will both sink and drown. He has just enough time to plead, 'Why?' The scorpion replies coldly, 'I had to. It's in my nature... it's what I do.'

"It is what we are, Mr Grant, it is stamped on our soul. We cannot change what we are, any more than we can change the colour of our eyes or the genetics that run through our body. We are like the scorpion – we act because it is what we know we must do."

Somewhere in these confessions, Gorilla began to see beyond the myth that had surrounded this man. At the beginning of this operation, the man known as Caravaggio had been nothing but a target, a ghost at best. He was unidentifiable, unknown, a man without thought or emotions. He was just a figure that Gorilla Grant had been sent to kill. When Gorilla had started in this business more than a decade ago, the international assassin known as Caravaggio was one of the few operatives that could be called truly legendary. His exploits had been taught and analysed on the training programs of fledgling spies the world over.

And yet here he was now; the man, the real man, stripped bare and exposing his soul. The fact that he was telling his deepest, darkest secrets to a man like Jack Grant was not a coincidence. Perhaps the only person who would understand was someone like him, another killer.

Caravaggio sat in silence for a while, as if contemplating all that he had shared. Eventually, he leaned forward and clicked off the desk lamp, leaving the room in a gloomy darkness.

Gorilla, in his weakened state, was aware of the other man getting up and moving slowly toward where he sat. Caravaggio stood over him and rested a gentle hand on Gorilla's head.

"That is enough for one night. Rest now. There is still much work to do, but for now... sleep," cooed Caravaggio. And with that, he pressed a thumb into the nerve behind Gorilla's right ear.

There was a flash of white light in Gorilla's head, a stab of pain, and then he passed out into the darkness of unconsciousness.

Chapter Twenty-Two

THE DAY OF THE DEAD – 2nd November 1973

Gorilla awoke to find his hands resting gently in his lap. He was no longer handcuffed to the chair, as he had been for the past few days. Instead, he was lying in the foetal position on a mattress in the corner of the dungeon.

He slowly sat upright and took stock of his surroundings. Things were different. For one, his whole body had been washed and cleaned. The dried blood and detritus had been replaced with clean, oiled skin. Secondly, his wounds had been treated with some kind of ointment, he assumed to help them heal. He looked around him.

On Caravaggio's interrogator's table, there was a brightly lit desk lamp that gave the surroundings a warm, comforting glow. Next to it was a small plate that contained a little rice, some vegetables, and bread. A glass of fresh orange juice sat beside the plate.

He stood, stretched, heard his bones click as he elongated his spine, and then he ate quickly. He didn't know if this was a trick, perhaps one of Caravaggio's mind games, and to be fair, he didn't care. He was starving and he knew that if he was to have any chance of escape, of finding Eunice, he would need the energy that the food and juice could provide.

Once he was finished, he picked up the lamp and shone it around the rest of the room. In the opposite corner were the two chairs. On one was a steel wash bowl with face cloth and towel and on the other was a zipped-up holdall.

Gorilla splashed some cool, clean water over his face and neck and then wiped his whole body down with the towel. Once finished, he unzipped the holdall and took out its contents. Inside were his light-coloured linen suit, shirt, shoes, socks and new underwear. All had been freshly laundered. He dressed quickly and was surprised to find his watch and cut-throat razor in the jacket's inside pocket. He put the watch on his wrist – it showed 8.30 p.m. – and the razor in his left-hand trouser pocket.

He walked towards the dungeon's door. When he pushed against the heavy wooden door, it yielded easily. Surprised to find it unlocked, he opened it wide and stepped through. No guards, no alarms, nothing, only thick stone steps that led upwards.

Gorilla started to ascend and the further up the winding steps he got, the more he could hear… snatches of music in the distance, subdued voices. At the top of the steps there was a second door. Once again, he pushed against it and again it opened wide. He walked out into a glass-fronted lounge area.

The furniture was expensive and chosen by someone who had good taste – Italian designer chairs, French tables, Greek statues. Beyond the glass-fronted walls was an expansive lawn with a large, kidney-shaped swimming pool at its centre.

It was night and there was a party or celebration going on. A Mariachi band was playing a soft, slow tune. But it was the guests… Gorilla took a step nearer to the glass to get a better look. He opened the patio doors and stepped out into the warm air of the night. He breathed it in and then focused on the scene that lay before him.

There must have been at least fifty people down on the lawn, all wearing the same mask – a white skull with dark, hollowed eyes.

At one time, the men must have been dressed in black suits and the women in black gowns. But not anymore; now, it was an orgy.

There were men and women in various states of undress and in various stages of carnal sex. Gorilla imagined that this was what it must have been like for the Ancient Romans. A woman was making love to two men at the same time, her mask pushed up so that she could perform fellatio on one of them while the other man entered her from behind. Couples were everywhere, some as a duo, and some as a threesome. A fat woman was eating out a tall black woman, the woman shrieking as she finished her orgasm.

There was one group of people, Gorilla wasn't sure how many, that reminded him of a pit of snakes, limbs intertwined and slithering against each other in a soup of sweat and semen. In one corner, a tall, skinny white man was sodomising a naked Mexican man while a group of women watched them and masturbated.

The sounds and smells of sex permeated the night, clothes were scattered everywhere and watching it, detached, from a distance, Gorilla thought that the orgy resembled a living thing, undulating, sweating and moving in rhythm to the slow tempo of the band. It was like watching a car crash; you wanted to look away, but the spectacle kept drawing your eyes back to it.

"Isn't it a beautiful sight?"

Gorilla froze at the sound of the voice from behind him. Then he slowly turned his whole body to see who had spoken. He would know that voice anywhere. It was the voice that had tortured him. He turned and he looked. He took in the dark suit in the tall frame, he took in the skull mask and he shuddered. The figure lifted one elegant hand up and removed the mask.

Gorilla saw the devil.

Chapter Twenty-Three

The face was not that of a killer, at least not initially. If anything, he had the look of an aristocratic nobleman. It was long, patrician in nature, the bone structure strong, the skin tanned.

The jet black hair, with streaks of grey at the sides, was swept back dramatically, giving his face a sleek quality. The mouth was a cruel slash that held both contempt and sensuality in equal portions. But it was the eyes that held Gorilla; dark and brooding, hidden beneath the hollows of the sockets and flanked with the lines of age.

Physically, the man was tall and slender with the poise and build of the natural athlete. The hands were large and strong, the fingers long and elegant. They were hands that could play a piano concerto or strangle you with equal measure, thought Gorilla. He knew that the man was in his early sixties, but he had a life-force and vitality radiating from him that made him look at least twenty years younger.

It was only when the man moved across the room towards him, that Gorilla truly saw the cat-like presence and contained power of Caravaggio as he walked. The tall man stopped a few feet away.

"Would you like to indulge, Mr Grant?" said Caravaggio, indicating the orgy outside. "I'm sure it can be arranged."

"No. Not my thing."

"Each to their own," said Caravaggio. "It is something that I do annually. Today is the *Dia de los Muertos*, the Day of the Dead here in Mexico, when the spirits of the deceased are honoured by their loved ones. I tend not to believe in such things, so instead, every year I throw a celebration and I invite a specially selected list of guests. There are gangsters, corrupt politicians, drug lords, killers, business people and members of several large organised terrorist groups. All are rich and powerful. None of them have ever met before.

"They have all employed me as an assassin in the past, although none of them knows me by the name of Caravaggio. They think I am a wealthy playboy who likes to host elite sex parties. None of them have any clue as to my real profession.

"When they arrive, they are welcomed by my staff and are offered drinks laced with a special chemical cocktail that I appropriated from the KGB's Special Warfare Division many years ago. It dramatically lowers their inhibitions. The more they drink, the more the drug takes effect. Nature takes its course and inevitably, the allure of sex arises. Within the hour, the orgy is usually in full swing."

"Is there a point to it all, or is this just how you get off these days?" said Gorilla dismissively.

"Oh, there *is* absolutely a point to it, Mr Grant. We film everything here, we have visual, and we have audio. I have carried out many parties like this one. I assure you it is not for my own personal gratification."

"So what? You use the material for blackmail purposes?"

"Exactly! It buys my protection and funds my operations. You would be amazed how many wealthy people can be coerced. In the past, we have had the wife of a certain President become pregnant by his closest political rival! Can you imagine how much they would pay to keep that quiet? Even now, looking down by the pool, I can make out a leading member of one of the American La Cosa Nostra families, a good Catholic and family man, being pleasured by the wife of a German terrorist leader. Imagine how much that Italian would pay to have those images *not* released!" said Caravaggio.

"As long as they keep drinking the champagne, they will continue with... this?"

Caravaggio shrugged. "It's the type of operation that I would run in the past for many, many intelligence networks. It's what we do, isn't it? Blackmail, threaten, murder. I simply decided that I would use it for my own enterprise."

He seems to revel in being the master manipulator, thought Gorilla. *He likes to view himself as holding all the threads and controlling the puppets. It gives him a sense of identity.* In truth, Gorilla thought he was a fucking idiot.

"But enough of distractions," said Caravaggio, changing the subject. "I thought we might play a game, Mr Grant."

"What kind of a game?"

"Oh, the game that we play every day in our profession. A game for assassins!"

"A duel?"

Caravaggio nodded. "In a way, but with a most interesting prize. Something that we both want. To be the best!"

"Eunice? Where is she?"

"Ah, yes. Miss Brown, of course. She is not far. Chang is keeping her quite safe. We will visit her soon, I promise."

"You were saying something about a prize?"

"Indeed," said Caravaggio. "If you win, you get the luxury of killing me and completing your mission – in short, you get to safeguard the secrets that I know about. I will hand over the files to you. I win, I take your head and the head of the beautiful Miss Brown, return them in a box to the SDECE and the CIA and release some of the agents' names and the operations that I have been privy to. I'm sure the western press would be enthralled by my information."

So Caravaggio was going for the big prize: murder and the release of intelligence information. Even the limited amount of information that he had at his disposal would put hundreds of agents and operatives in danger.

Gorilla took a breath and looked down at the continuing orgy. Whatever Caravaggio had drugged them with showed no signs of abating – if anything, it seemed to make the men more rampant and violent. A small, petite blonde woman was being held down and gang-raped. Gorilla felt like he wanted to puke.

Gorilla glared at Caravaggio and said, "I want to see Eunice first."

"Then we must go to the Arena," said Caravaggio.

They had to walk through the throng of the orgy and past the pool. Gorilla ignored the spectacle around him and tried to focus his thoughts on what Caravaggio might have in store for him. A duel, he had said, or at least hinted at. Not that Gorilla was unarmed now. He still had the razor in his pocket and his fists, too, of course. But a perverse part of him wanted to see this through to the end.

They walked for another five hundred feet, the noise from the party fading with each step, until they had reached a clearing on the extreme of Caravaggio's estate that was surrounded by swamp and jungle. What lay before them was a modern version of a Roman amphitheatre.

It was curved in shape and consisted of three levels that seated no more than a hundred people. Its floor was of the sand variety, in accordance with the tradition of a combat arena. Gorilla doubted that it was original; it had probably been built specifically on Caravaggio's orders. In the centre of the circular floor Gorilla made out a glint of steel. His eyes took a moment to focus and then he recognised what they were: revolvers.

At the open end of the curve was a small, raised podium that was illuminated by two flaming torches. At the front of the podium, standing as if on guard, was the little assassin and torturer Chang, dressed in his usual black suit. But behind him was Eunice. She was standing, tied by the wrists to two poles which were embedded in the ground.

She was wearing an olive green mini dress with a rope belt and lace-up gladiator-style sandals. Her arms were up-stretched so that they made a 'V' shape. The flaming torches cast a red glow on her skin and made her hair look even more vibrant.

He glanced over at her. He thought she looked beautiful. "You okay?"

The withering look she gave him told him not to ask dumb-ass questions. Instead, she said, "I'm fine, Jack, just fine."

"We thought, given Miss Brown's skill-set, that it would be better for all concerned if she was restrained," said Caravaggio, gently stroking the side of her face and letting his fingers tenderly run down her cleavage.

She snapped at him and tried to bite his hand. Caravaggio pulled it away quickly. "How vicious, my dear."

"Try that again and you'll lose fingers," she warned.

Caravaggio scowled at the insolent woman and turned to more pressing matters. He turned and looked out at the darkness of the seats around the amphitheatre and said clearly, "Gentlemen, if you would join us?"

Gorilla looked around, confused. Then, glancing over his shoulder, he made out the dark shapes of two anonymous spectators making their way down to join them.

"Allow me to introduce two very special guests who will be joining us. Mr Devlin and Mr Nash," said Caravaggio. One man was tall and well-built and the other small and thin. Both were wearing dark suits and they looked alert and professional.

Caravaggio turned to Gorilla to explain. He motioned towards the small, thin man with the murderer's face.

"Mr Devlin is one of the finest Irish gunmen that I have ever come across. Over recent years, he has built up quite a kill-list on the streets of Northern Ireland for the IRA."

Next, he waved a hand over at the tall, heavy-set man. "Mr Nash works for several organised crime families along the East Coast of the United States, the La Cosa Nostra boys in Philly, Chicago and New

York. His speciality is, I believe, close quarter shooting with the Italian *lupara*."

Lastly, Caravaggio placed a comradely hand on Gorilla's shoulder. "Gentlemen, I would like to introduce to you the third member of our little contest this evening. Gorilla Grant, formerly of the British Secret Service. Gentlemen, I have seen Mr Grant's shooting prowess up close and I can assure you that he is not to be underestimated."

Both men nodded blank-faced in greeting.

"Excellent!" said Caravaggio, as he walked out into the middle of the arena and took centre stage. He turned to his captive audience.

"Gentlemen, we shall follow the rules of all duellists before us – the *code duello*. We will inspect our own weapons, then, when Chang calls, we shall turn our backs and walk to the edge of the killing ground, about ten yards. Then when Chang calls the second time, we turn let battle commence. The man who remains standing takes all. Any questions?"

Gorilla shrugged. "It sounds simple enough."

"Then please, let us collect our weapons and begin," said Caravaggio.

Gorilla took in the scene for a moment, to concentrate his mind: the arena of death, the hit men, Eunice Brown a prisoner, Caravaggio and his little throat-slitter Chang, who stood around like an executioner. He felt as if he were trapped in a sick game on an island solely populated by the insane.

He closed his eyes, took in a breath and nodded to Caravaggio. He looked the tall assassin dead in the eye and said, "Let's get on with it."

Each of the assassins started off slowly, cautiously, walking the perimeter of the amphitheatre, circling each other, each weighing the other up, alert in case of any tricks. When none seemed evident, they continued with their slow-paced walk, eyes locked, until they reached their respective positions at the centre of the circle where the revolvers had been placed.

They all individually bent down and hefted the large .44 Calibre revolvers in their hands, testing the weight of them. Gorilla recognised it as a Smith & Wesson Model 29 revolver with a 6" barrel. He flicked open the cylinder and inspected the six cartridges inside. Then, satisfied, he closed it back up and held it loosely at his left-hand side.

"Nice gun, Caravaggio," said Nash, his Brooklyn twang coming through. "I do like the old school wheel guns. Reliable."

"I prefer a semi-automatic meself," muttered Devlin.

"Ah, gentlemen, I chose these for a reason. Yes, they are reliable, as Mr Nash correctly states, but even more so, I wanted a limited amount of ammunition so that we can test ourselves to the extreme. I call it the law of the minimum. Six shots, that is all."

"And the money, the loot? When I've won, it will be ready for me?" said Nash, confident and cocky.

Caravaggio turned and stared the Irishman down. "I can assure you, Mr Nash, that the agreement will be met in full. *If* you win…"

"*ATTENTION!*" called Chang. They all gave each other one final glance and then stood back to back in the centre of the arena.

They pushed off from each other's backs, taking their first steps, and all the while Chang was calling out the paces. Gorilla felt the weight and slickness of the revolver in his left hand. This would not be like shooting the lighter ASP that he was used to. A .44 bullet was very unforgiving and he just hoped that his left hand was able to handle the jolt of the weapon when he fired.

"Five… four… three… two…" said Chang.

Chang called for the duellists to stop. Gorilla had decided what he would do, which was ignore the head shot and aim for the centre of mass. A .44 bullet at this range would knock the taller man off his feet. He could always finish Caravaggio off with a second shot.

"Ready… turn… *FIRE!*" called Chang.

Gorilla turned and was just in time to see the Irishman, Devlin, aim a shot at him, but it was high and wide. Gorilla ducked, feeling the whizz of the bullet as it passed him by. Out of the corner of his eye to the left, he saw Nash bringing up his own weapon and firing a single shot at the distracted Irishman. The bullet took him in the side of the head, making a gaping hole that poured blood.

Devlin dropped onto the sand, dead. One competitor down.

Gorilla fired a warning shot at Nash, but because of the angle it, too, missed. And then Nash was running for the concealment of the jungle.

Next, Gorilla pivoted in one perfectly executed move, his body crouched to make himself a smaller target. His revolver was up and already he was aligning the barrel on where he thought the main target, The Master, would be and he prepared to fire...

But Caravaggio had gone.

The Master ran fast, his body moving with the power and grace of a panther. He avoided the vines and tree limbs in the forest easily and pushed deeper into the heart of darkness.

When he had purchased the island more than a decade ago from the Mexican government, for a hefty fee, he had chosen it primarily for its hostile environment. He knew that inside the grounds of the villa there was relative safety and security, but that outside, it was a killing ground. The impenetrable coastline, jungle and swamps that made up the majority of the mile-long island, were enough to deter even the most determined of attackers.

Caravaggio himself had transported wild crocodiles, ocelots, grey wolves, snakes and a pair of jaguars to roam freely upon his island and more than one guest that had been invited to the island had ended up as fodder for the killers roaming the jungle.

He had spent many months familiarising himself with the terrain; he knew its dips, falls, and crevices. So in a sense, Caravaggio had an advantage. He knew the ambush points and, against his younger challengers, that would go a long way when gun was against gun.

He climbed further and further up the incline, eager to have the high ground. He dug the heels of his boots into the earth and pushed forward. Already, his shirt was saturated with moisture and clung to his body. Just as he reached the first crest of the hill, he heard a noise behind him, a rustling of the jungle floor that definitely wasn't animal.

He stopped and turned, aiming his weapon in a point-shooting technique. He instinctively dropped to one knee and waited. But he could see no figures moving in the darkness. It was an impenetrable wall of blackness. He knew that Gorilla Grant was down there somewhere, hunting for him.

My God, I feel alive, he thought. *I am hunting men to the death in a hostile environment.* He could feel his whole body, every nerve screaming at him. There was a rush of adrenaline coursing through him. And then, coming from the darkness, he heard gunfire.

Nash fired twice at what he thought was his enemy. He knew that shooting at an unconfirmed target was amateurish at best, but, with the intense blackness all around him, he doubted that he would ever get a clear shot. Nash had pissed himself twice. He was a city boy through and through, so this fucking about in the jungle with the bugs and heat was something that wasn't grooving with him.

Frederico Nash, half Italian, half Jewish, was a 'man of respect' and had made his bones for the Capo of the oldest Mafia family in New York when he was a teenager. So far in his career, he had been the button man on twenty-seven different executions and hits. He judged himself to be one of the best gunmen along the East Coast.

So when he had been approached by an intermediary of The Master six weeks ago, he had been intrigued. Nash didn't know much about espionage or spies; he knew about guns and killing people at close range. The intermediary, a lawyer from Manhattan, had whispered in his ear of a game, a mysterious benefactor and the chance to become the acknowledged assassin of his time.

Arrangements had been made and his journey south to Mexico had happened without problem. He had been looking forward to finding out if he was as good as he thought he was. Devlin had been no problem; it had been an easy shot. But that tough-looking Englishman had been an unknown quantity and as for his host, the mysterious Caravaggio, he scared the shit out of Nash. And Freddy Nash was not a man who scared easily.

Now, he wished he had stayed back in the USA. This fucking game was freaking him out.

He had no idea where he was. He thought at one point that he had seen a large cat and he had fired, killing it, he hoped. As for Caravaggio and that guy Gorilla? He had no clue where they were. He stopped once more, the sweat seeping through his shirt and staining his suit, and rested against the trunk of the nearest tree. He needed to think… rest… get his shit together.

He heard nothing from behind him, but, too late, he felt everything.

A long, strong arm wrapped itself around the truck of the tree from behind him. A hand clamped across his forehead, pinning him in place and then, almost instantaneously, he felt a sharp pain just behind his right ear. There was a blinding white light in his brain, excruciating pain in his head, and then his body began to judder and shake.

Then, almost as quickly, the pain was gone and the hands released him. He felt his legs give way and his body slither down to the base of the tree, snagging his suit on the way down. But by that time Nash didn't care. He was already dead.

Caravaggio stood back, wiped the blood off the stiletto knife that he had used on Nash, and admired his handiwork.

He did so enjoy the challenge of silent killing. Oh, he knew that the point of this particular game was to decide who was the best gunman, the best hit man, the best assassin. But… there was something just so addictive about stalking your quarry, getting in close and eliminating them with a knife. Just so… exquisite!

He knew it was against the rules that he had set out for this game. But then again, rules were meant to be broken, as Nash had just discovered. Even the most idiotic assassin knew that. There were no rules when you were carrying out a killing. Anything goes.

He folded away the knife and drew his revolver. He was happy. This was exactly how he would have wanted it – the two best gunmen going against each other. The Master and the Gorilla.

Really, Nash and Devlin had been brought in to make up the numbers; they were nothing more than cannon-fodder. No, what Caravaggio, the Master, wanted was for his perfect scenario to play out as he had envisioned. Two perfect spies, two perfect assassins, the old Master and the young pretender, facing off against each other to the death.

Gorilla had seen Caravaggio move fast in the distance and he had done well to catch up with the bigger man so soon, but jungle warfare was something that Gorilla knew little about. It was an alien environment to him. He was sure that there were a hundred different jungle warfare techniques that he should be using to help him track down Caravaggio, but Gorilla didn't know what he didn't know.

His natural environment was urban warfare, the streets, buildings, even vehicles. But this oppressive darkness, heat and noise was like an attack on his senses.

Up ahead in the distance, he could make out a glimmer of a light through the canopy. The moon. He moved forward cautiously, crouched, the revolver held out in front of him at waist height in what was known as the ¼ hip shooting position, ready to fire.

He moved slowly, aware of his own breathing. In the distance, no more than twenty feet away, he made out a shape against a tree. He brought his revolver up, aligning the barrel on the unmistakable shape of a body. His finger was resting against the trigger as he bent down at a safe distance to inspect it.

He could barely make out the face of Nash as his head was lolling at such an unnatural angle. His throat was covered in blood that shone black in the night. Gorilla could smell it, and so could the bugs and larger predators of the jungle. Soon. Nash's body would be to the focus of a feeding frenzy.

Gorilla stood up and did a scan of his surrounding environment. His survival senses told him something wasn't right. There was nothing around him, he could at least see that, but… it was something above the eye-line. He looked upwards, but in that decisive moment he knew he was already too late.

The large shadow dropped from behind him.

Gorilla's assessment of him had been right – 'cat-like' epitomised Caravaggio's movements precisely. The dark figure dropped onto all fours and then sprang up, lashing out a powerful karate kick to Gorilla's left side, disrupting his aim with the revolver. No sooner had he recovered than Caravaggio kicked out again and again with strong, powerful blows to the body, driving Gorilla further back.

Gorilla tried one last time to bring his gun up to the centre line, desperately trying to steady his aim at the dark figure, but was stopped by a spinning back foot that connected with Gorilla's shoulder, sending him crashing to the jungle floor.

On his back now, Gorilla brought the gun to his hip in a retention position and fired off two instinctive shots. The report of the weapon silenced the jungle… but the dark figure, the large, cat-like man, jumped to the side, the bullets missing him easily, and tucked himself into a forward roll and sprang off into the camouflage of the jungle.

Gorilla raised himself to a kneeling position, the revolver held out ready in case Caravaggio came back for another attack. *He's toying with me*, he thought. *He's showing off, showing off his skills and what he's capable of. Unarmed, knife skills, silent killing.*

Over to his right, he was aware of something running. Caravaggio. It had to be. The Master was trying to circle around him.

Gorilla flung himself against the nearest tree, partly for cover but also so that he could use the trunk to steady his aim. He pulled the gun up and aimed at the running shadow. He fired twice, aware of the shadow flinching and changing direction. Had he hit him? Damn, he didn't think so.

He was climbing up the incline, his free hand grabbing onto vines and trees to pull him up, when he became aware of something alive and breathing up ahead, no more than six feet away. He almost walked into a giant cat, its eyes shining in the darkness.

The jaguar hissed at him and lowered its back as if ready to pounce. Gorilla didn't even think about it.

He shot it once in the heart and the animal dropped dead.

Caravaggio turned in the direction of the gunshot. It sounded a good distance away.

He laughed to himself. Evidently the jungle environment had put Gorilla Grant on edge. Maybe he wasn't as tough as his reputation made out. Caravaggio knew that the jungle was a great leveller. In all the tournaments that he had held here on his private island, against gunmen, assassins, soldiers and mercenaries, only a handful, probably no more than three, had seemed at home in the jungle. Not that it mattered, he had won anyway. Caravaggio always won.

His original intention was to circle around his opponent and catch him unawares. He wanted Gorilla to think that he was behind him, when instead he would actually be in front of him. He was waiting for the Englishman to almost walk into his gun sights. Sadly, that was not to be the case. Gorilla Grant had obviously become aware of his ruse and fired off a couple of shots in the vain hope that they would hit.

But that was alright. The Master was nothing if not a tactician and he knew when to abandon one strategy in favour of a new one. Improvisation was the key, and The Master was an expert at taking a failed operation and turning it into a success.

He edged closer and closer, the moon in the background sending a smattering of light into the jungle.

Gorilla had everything in place.

It had been hard work and he had to move fast, but he was trusting that everything would work out, because he knew that he could not carry on the fight like this for much longer. He had to change his tactics if he wanted to survive.

He stood and offered himself up on the edge of the hill, the ambient light from the moon behind him creating a perfect silhouette of a figure standing still, his revolver held in his left hand.

For Caravaggio, it was an irresistible target and one that he couldn't resist. Gorilla could sense The Master moving closer and closer, taking his time, gauging the optimum time to fire the deadly kill shot.

Gorilla Grant was nearly fifty feet away, uphill, and it was at the extreme end of the heavy pistol's range. Caravaggio raised his weapon, centred it on his quarry's head and pulled the trigger. There was the sound of the shot followed by a scream of pain, and Caravaggio saw the head of Gorilla Grant's silhouette disintegrate.

The body spun once and fell over the side of the cliff into the swamp-like river that he knew was below. Anything that landed in there would not survive for very long. The wild crocodiles that lived in this part of the swamp would be brutal, strong and very, very hungry for human flesh. Even from this distance, Caravaggio could hear the desecration of Gorilla Grant in the swamp below and the thrashing of the crocodiles in the water as they feasted.

Caravaggio checked the rounds in the revolver and gave a satisfied smile. He considered it fortunate that Gorilla Grant had made the fatal mistake of pausing on the edge of the cliff. Coming down to a final round to take out an experienced gunman such as this, would have been a risk. He moved slowly up the hill, cautious in case it was a trap, but knowing that his enemy had already been taken. He made his way to the edge of the cliff where Grant had been stood and he looked down. He guessed it was a thirty foot drop at least.

Caravaggio let his eyes adjust in the night and was aware of movement in the murky darkness of the waters below. He could just about make out the elongated shapes of several crocodiles moving in the water, and then, there, he could see a flash of something... blue material, a shirt, and then one of the beasts rolled in the water and there was another flash of colour, the pale biscuit shade of the suit jacket that Grant had been wearing; except this time it was shredded, with only bits of torn flesh and entrails showing.

Then the crocodile completed his death roll once more and the remains of Gorilla Grant were pulled into the inky darkness of the swamp forever.

Caravaggio made his way back through the swamp and into the jungle. In the distance, he could see the lights of the villa.

He walked briskly. Now that he had vanquished his rival, Caravaggio felt a brief moment of elation. Elation that he still remained the best artist of his craft, having eliminated another man who had been a threat to his crown.

He was still *THE* Master. How many assassins had he lured to his island over the years? Fifteen, certainly, that he could remember, all of whom had come looking to remove him from the great game. All had been found wanting and had been fed to the sharks along the island's coastline.

He knew that his euphoria would be fleeting; it always was. He knew, too, that in time, there would be other challenges that could give him his 'fix'. Would they be as good an opponent as the man he had just killed? He did not know. Soon, the adrenaline dump would hit him and he would sink into the depths of boredom and depression. It was always the way.

Perhaps the woman, the redhead, could take his mind off it for a few days. She was prone to violence, for sure and he was certain that if she had the opportunity, she would try to kill him. But he still had some of the drug that he had spiked the drinks of the party guests with. He could make her more pliable with that and soothe his mind by getting lost in her body. Willingly or unwillingly on her part, he cared not. He would take what he wanted. He always had.

He took the main path out of the jungle and made his way to the Arena. When he arrived, Chang was still on guard in his position. When Eunice saw him step into the clearing, her face was aghast.

"Your man is dead, Miss Brown. If it is any consolation, he was the opponent that I expected him to be," said Caravaggio solemnly.

Eunice Brown's face turned from despair to anger. "Where is he? I want to see him one last time, you bastard!" she said, through gritted teeth.

Caravaggio shrugged. "The crocodiles have taken him down into the swamp. It is doubtful that we will ever find his remains. I'm sorry for your loss."

The screams that came from her were of pain, sorrow and anger. Caravaggio turned to his apprentice. "Chang, let Miss Brown recover here and then bring her up to the villa within the hour. I require some time for peaceful reflection and I do not wish to be disturbed by a wailing woman."

Chang nodded to his Master and then sharply slapped Eunice once across the face. The blow silenced her instantly. Caravaggio nodded to his apprentice and then strode out of the clearing, taking a circular route to avoid what was left of the orgy in his garden, and made his way up into the rear entrance of the villa and to peace.

Chang stood like a monolith. Silent, uncommitted to emotion, listening to the mewling and tears of the woman tied up behind him. He would give her another twenty minutes and then he would take her up for his Master's pleasure.

Chang reflected on his good *joss* to have been chosen to be the apprentice to such a man. He himself had never been with a woman or a man; such matters did not interest Chang. He cared not for the pleasures of the flesh, and certainly not with an ugly *gwaih lo* like this red-headed troll that had been sent to kidnap his Master.

Chang's only pleasures came from his teachings at the feet of Caravaggio; to revel in the art of the assassin, to serve his Master and, in the fullness of time, to achieve his own perfection as a professional assassin… and one day even be superior to Caravaggio himself.

He owed The Master everything.

He had been an eight-year-old street rat on the streets of Shanghai when Caravaggio had found him. His parents had abandoned him to the hell-hole of the streets in his sixth year and he had to endure the brutality of beatings, rape, starvation and violence. Chang had survived through stealing and pick-pocketing.

Then one day he had picked the wrong pocket. An iron hand had grabbed at his stick-thin wrist and he knew that he had been caught. Normally in such situations, he would expect a beating. But this time the fearsome Westerner had simply looked at him and said, in perfect Cantonese, "Are you hungry, boy? Let me feed you."

It had started with a simple meal of rice. Chang had never known such kindness. While he ate, the Westerner asked him about his life. Where was his family? How did he survive on the streets? Satisfied with the Chinese boy's answers, the tall Westerner simply nodded and beckoned him to carry on eating his rice.

The rest had been a frenzy of activity for Chang. He had been taken to the Westerner's house, fitted out with new clothes, and had then travelled through the streets in a vehicle to an airport and then away, never to return to that life on the streets of Shanghai. His Master had told him that he was now under his protection and that he would be expected, in exchange for a life and a future, to study and learn what he was taught.

"I expect great things from you, Chang. You will be my greatest and only student. You will be my apprentice," said The Master.

It seemed the most natural thing in the world to learn his master's skills. In The Master's dojo, they would train five days a week, studying the arts of Karate, Kung-Fu, and Judo and a host of weapons skills such as the knife, the garrotte, the sword, the flail, the metal fan, the staff and the stick.

"But Master," asked Chang once in his eighteenth year, "when shall I learn about *gwaih lo* guns and firearms?"

Caravaggio had scolded him for his insolence. "Never! There is no need for such bluntness. Guns are unsubtle and are for the stupid and the untrained."

"Then Master, what shall I be against an enemy with a gun?" Chang had asked, confused.

The Master had smiled. "You shall be a silent killer. They will not see you, they will not hear you, but you will snuff out their lives like a whisper snuffing out the flame of a candle."

After that, The Master had taught Chang about poisons, disguises, false passports, forgery and surveillance, all the skills that he would need to move stealthily from one country to the next and, on his twenty-first birthday, Chang travelled to Hong Kong under a false name to carry out and complete his first assassination for his Master. By his thirties, he had travelled to virtually every continent in the world as his Master's factotum, bodyguard and, when required, silent assassin.

Chang turned around to look at the woman, the one they called Nikita. She looked exhausted and it was only the restraints at her wrists that were holding her upright. Looking at her, Chang thought that he may have to carry her up to the villa. It was not a problem for him for, though he was only small-framed and frail-looking, he was remarkably strong.

He walked over to her and examined her like a chef examines a piece of meat – interested but detached. The woman seemed to have passed out, either due to the physical exhaustion of being tied up and suspended, or due to shock. He slapped her gently on the cheek, heard her moan, so he did it again, harder; again, the same pitiful moan.

These American women, they were all so brash and vulgar, thought Chang dismissively as he began to undo the special knots he had tied at her wrists. One arm flopped down and he caught the weight of her body as it sagged; then, with his free arm, he reached up and expertly undid the second restraint and felt the remaining arm flop free from its bonds.

But as he did so, he felt something that only a man of his level of training would be aware of – a slight stiffening of the woman's body – and, almost too late, he understood what was happening.

The red-headed woman was not unconscious. Her body said otherwise. She was very much alert and was arcing an elbow-strike down to Chang's right temple. He moved just in time and instead of taking the full force of the elbow-strike, it became a glancing blow, but one that still sent him reeling backwards.

Eunice watched as the little killer took the blow and rolled backwards. He was up on his feet instantly and sprang into a Shaolin Kung Fu fighting stance. Eunice rubbed her wrists and readied herself into a boxing stance, hands up, poised to guard and to punch.

Chang moved forward, ready to penetrate her defence and in response, she kicked out at him with a perfectly timed strike to the thigh. He felt the impact, winced and knew then that this woman wasn't to be played with and that her skill level in hand-to-hand combat was way above just boxing.

In fact, Eunice had spent one whole summer training under a world-renowned *Savate* instructor in Paris many years ago. The skills of *boxe française* were ones that complemented her physically and she knew how to use the techniques of pugilism and foot-fighting to devastating effect.

Chang moved forward with a lightning-fast hand strike that impacted on her arm and moved her back, allowing him to penetrate her defences with a low kick to the shin. But what Eunice lacked for in speed, compared to Chang's fast movement, she more than made up for in reach. Her right fist hit out with three successive jabs to his face and was followed up with a *Fouette* kick to the jaw that hit Chang like a baseball bat.

Chang rocked, unsteady, but still remained standing. The kick to his head had left a cut and blood was seeping down onto his face. He changed his fighting stance and approached her once more. Eunice threw out a combination of high and mid-line kicks which he either avoided, or took the impact on his bicep. He just needed her to come a little closer…

She attacked again, using a high-line boxing combination and then he threw himself forward into grappling range and he had her! Chang grabbed her around the body, his hands locking onto the material of her dress at the neck and elbow and completed a perfectly executed *Harai Goshi*, a judo sweeping hip throw.

Eunice felt the Chinese assassin grab her, lock onto her and then, with body strength that she wouldn't have given him credit for, he swept out her legs and threw her to the ground. The hard impact on the sand winded her, temporarily leaving her gasping for breath.

Chang was already in motion following the throw and was getting ready to hit her with downward boot kicks to pummel her into the earth. The first one took her in the thigh. She screamed, and then she was rolling away from the assault, trying to put distance between herself and her opponent.

She ran for the Podium as a means of escape, but Chang was too quick for her and managed to get a hand to her hair, pulling her back to him. She swung round a reverse hammer-fist blow which landed on his jaw, then an elbow, and then another hammer-fist – she knew that if the little assassin, Chang, got his arms around her throat, she would be finished. She could not allow that to happen.

She turned quickly towards Chang, whose fingers were already arcing towards her throat, and she thrust her head forward and delivered a full-force head-butt into his nose. It was enough. Chang momentarily let go and she was off! She reached the nearest brazier that held one of the flaming torches, lifted it out and swung it round like a club. It was a perfect shot.

The torch caught Chang full in the face, the fire burning his eyes and igniting his clothes. He screamed and fell to his knees, his upper body licked by the flames, his hands scrabbling desperately to put out the fire and stop the pain. Eunice took careful aim once more and threw a full-power Louisville Slugger-style whack to his head.

It was over. Eunice looked down at the unconscious body of Chang and said dismissively, "Men! They are such assholes."

Then she turned her attention to the lights of the villa up on the hill, and the man who had killed her lover and, for the first time in her career, Eunice Brown, bounty-hunter and tracker, was going into battle to kill a man in cold blood.

Caravaggio let himself in to the coolness of the open-plan lounge.

The air conditioning was set at just the right temperature and he already felt better. Now, he wanted nothing more than to sit and bask in the night's achievements. Soon, Chang and the woman would be here and he would deal with all of that, but for now, he desired tranquillity.

He poured himself a glass of tequila from the drinks cabinet, took an appreciative sip and then stood and stared out at the spectacle before him by the pool. The orgy had abated and the naked bodies were spent and exhausted, scattered around the gardens. In the distance, a firework display from the mainland was illuminating the sky. Caravaggio looked at his reflection in the glass, noting the aging around his eyes and the weariness in his face from the night's combat.

But he would recover, he always did. He had killed Gorilla Grant, a worthy opponent, and now he would go and fuck his woman.

He spent several minutes reflecting on the fortuitous nature of his life. He had it all. He was a man complete for now. He took one last sip of the tequila, closing his eyes as it slithered down his throat. He was still the best, he was still *The* Master.

Then he opened his eyes and stared into a face of horror that was reflected in the glass doors. Behind him was a beast covered in mud and dirt from the swamp. Its eyes were burning with a bright fury and its face was set in a furious rage. In its hands was a machete, similar to those the gardeners from the mainland used to hack back the foliage around the grounds of his villa.

Caravaggio's instincts took over and he spun, reaching out for the revolver that he had placed on the table to the side of him. He almost made it... almost, but just as he grabbed the handle, he felt the burning pain as the machete sheared his hand off at the wrist, leaving a neatly cut, bloody stump.

He clutched the injured arm to his chest, screaming in agony.

"I owe you that for Nice," growled the beast.

"You...? *YOU*? But... I saw you! You're... you're *dead*!" screamed Caravaggio, his mind a whirlwind of confusion, pain and failure. He had already dropped to his knees, his wrist spurting blood, and was crouched on the floor, preparing himself for the violence that was about to come.

"No, you're wrong," said Gorilla Grant, his voice deep and guttural. "I'm not dead. *You* are!" And with a scream of fury, he swung the machete downwards and hacked again and again and again...

The blood dripped onto the immaculate tiled floor in Caravaggio's private office. Gorilla was still in shock at what he had just done to another human being. Hacking a man to death took a bit of getting used to. He would deal with the horror and the nightmares later.

He quickly searched the villa and found nothing of use until he made his way up the staircase to Caravaggio's private sanctum. The office consisted of an ornate mahogany desk, a comfortable chaise lounge, a huge gun cabinet and several pieces of amateur art that were signed by Caravaggio himself. The pieces were portraits of tough-looking men in business suits.

The desk was bare, except for a heavily embossed envelope containing a handwritten note. Gorilla reached one hand forward and opened the flap. His fingerprints left bloody stains on the paper. He glanced down at the perfect handwriting. It read:

My Dear Mr Grant

If you are reading this, then you have bested me in single combat. I congratulate you. I hope I was a worthy opponent.

24-39-42

This is the combination to my private safe. It is hidden behind the portrait of Mr Vittelli behind my desk. Mr Vittelli wasn't as successful as you when he visited me here to play my little games. I always create a portrait of my late opponents in my death-games. It seems that you will never hang on my walls.

Inside the safe, you will either find wonders and riches beyond your wildest dreams… or you will find death. Do you dare risk it?

The Master

Gorilla crumpled the paper in one meaty fist and smiled to himself. Even in death, Caravaggio was playing mind games. He could open the safe and it could contain everything that he had been ordered to find by French Intelligence. Job done. Alternatively, he could open it only to find that it was rigged with explosives and he would be obliterated.

He stepped around the desk and pushed the leather office chair out of the way to give him more room. The portrait on the wall was that of a noble-looking gentleman of indeterminate age. He had Mafia hit man written all over him.

Gorilla ran his fingers around the edge of the large frame until he felt a small catch on the left side. He pressed it and heard a click. The frame swung towards him on a hinge. Hidden behind the painting and set in the wall was a standard metal wall safe with a generic combination lock.

Gorilla stood staring at it for more than a minute, trying to figure out the risks and the play that Caravaggio had instigated. He could see no wires, no scratch marks on the metal, nothing. It looked exactly what it was; a standard safe. He breathed once, twice, each time sucking in a full capacity breath to his lungs. What to do? In the end, it was the risk factor that motivated Gorilla. He had always been a risk-taker.

"Fuck it," he said out loud and he stepped forward and twirled the dial around to the registered numbers.

2… 4

3… 9

4… 2

Without a second thought, he pulled on the handle. If it was going to happen, it was going to happen now! But nothing did. Instead, the door to the safe gently swung open to reveal, in its gloomy interior, a large manila envelope that seemed to hold a cache of documents and a clear, sealed plastic bag that seemed to contain a large amount of currency.

The only other thing was another note in the same handwriting as the first. Once again, Gorilla opened up the sheet of paper and read:

Gorilla Grant

I am a man of my word. There is no more subterfuge here. You have your freedom. My files are inside the envelope that you have found. Do with them what you will. I no longer have any need for them. But be careful, that level of information comes with a heavy price, so use the intelligence wisely.

I have also provided a gift for you and the beautiful Miss Brown. Again, I hope that you will use it well for your future.

Your friend

Caravaggio

He had no idea how much cash there was. A million? Maybe two? Certainly enough to retire on for a while. He loaded the files and stacks of cash into a canvas rucksack that Caravaggio had helpfully supplied. What next? The gun cabinet. He would need weapons to get off the island. Despite what Caravaggio had said about him being free to leave, he didn't believe him for a minute. There was still a drugged-up mob of killers, terrorists and gangsters down there and they were between him and the ferryboat.

The gun cabinet was a large metal affair that was unlocked. He pulled back the door to find a treasure-trove of weaponry; pistols, handguns, automatic rifles, grenades and enough ammunition to start a small war. Gorilla looked over the arsenal with the appreciation of someone who is an expert in the tools of his trade. Really, there was only one choice.

He picked up the heavy, ugly weapon, attached a fully-loaded drum magazine and put the spare magazine into his rucksack, then hung it over his shoulder by the attached sling.

He wiped the sweat from his face and picked up the machete in case the little Chinese assassin was lurking nearby. He was ahead of the game; he had killed his target, he had the files, he had the money… all he needed now was to rescue the girl.

Eunice Brown had never needed rescuing in her life. There wasn't a situation created that she wasn't able to escape, talk her way out of or just downright fight tooth and nail to extricate herself from. Ever!

She had made it to the villa's grounds, ready to find Caravaggio and kill him. She didn't quite know how she was going to do that yet, but she would find a way soon. Eunice was a born improviser. She took in the half-naked mob around the pool and the grounds, most of them sated from their exertions. The problem was that they were between her and the villa. Dressed as she was, she would stick out and it wouldn't take much for them to pounce on her.

She was toying with the thought of stripping naked in order to blend in when, thankfully, she saw him at the top of the steps. His shoes were gone, as were his shirt and jacket, and he was wearing only the trousers from his suit. Over his shoulder there was a rucksack and a sling that held a semi-automatic rifle that was unrecognizable at this distance. He was covered in mud and sweat and the blood-stained machete that he held in his right hand told her that Caravaggio was dead. At least, she hoped he was.

Gorilla Grant looked like a monster that had emerged from the pit of hell. He stood staring down at them all, seemingly in a daze. Behind him, from inside the villa she could make out the orange lick of flames as a fire started. Then it was a blaze. Soon, she knew, it would be an inferno and the whole property would be razed to the ground. From inside, she could hear the popping and crackling as the fire began to spread.

Gorilla saw her and began to walk slowly down the steps towards her. Several of the guests from the orgy had roused themselves from their slumber and were watching the threatening figure that was approaching them. Most cowered and moved back, creating a pathway to let him through.

One tough-looking Italian man, naked, his body covered in scars, lifted himself up off the woman he had been molesting and began to walk towards Grant, his posture and body language aggressive. Gorilla flicked a glance at him.

"Hey, you... what da fuck?" said the man.

In one quick motion, Gorilla dropped the machete and in its place appeared an old but workable Thompson submachine gun with a drum magazine. Gorilla let out a short burst of 9mm rounds and the Italian dropped, riddled with bullets.

Several more of the males, and one tough-looking woman, made an effort to close Gorilla down. The Thompson fired quickly in lethal bursts, killing the advancing parties. The reaction from the rest of the crowd was instantaneous – screams from the women, naked vulnerability from the men. They scattered like ants, many of them running blindly towards the jungle and the swamp. The predators of the island would dine well that night. Gorilla fired a few more warning shots, but really, the fight had left the guests.

He came to Eunice, no longer aware of the violence of the night. He was spent. All that he saw was his woman. The red hair, the green eyes, her body. She put her arms around him and they embraced. Their kiss was long and slow, as was their way.

"Is it done?" she asked him, tears in her eyes.

He nodded. "It's done."

She kissed him again and looked into his eyes. "Then baby, let's go home."

He was back where he had started when he first arrived on the island.

The little ferryboat was there, ready and waiting. Once again, Caravaggio had planned everything perfectly. They climbed into the boat in a daze, started the engine and Eunice carefully guided it out of the swamp and into the tide. Gorilla sat on point, the Thompson ready in his hand, just in case.

"Here," he said handing her a file from the rucksack. "It's a gift from me to you and the CIA."

He had already found one for the SDECE that he would deliver back to Sassi.

"What about the rest of the files?" she asked.

"Gone. They'll be ash by now." The rest of the files, comprising the secrets of several dozen intelligence agencies, he had left to burn in the inferno of the villa. Caravaggio's secrets would be lost forever.

He saw her nod with satisfaction in the darkness as the boat began to pick up speed and head out towards the Mexican mainland. "That's the best outcome, Jack, for everyone. Caravaggio and his games have caused enough chaos. I'm glad he is dead."

Gorilla thought the same. He wondered if Caravaggio had secretly welcomed being eliminated... if it had come as a relief to him with those final few blows of the machete.

He turned one final time to look back at the raging inferno that had once been the villa. It was nothing more than an orange glow in the darkness. That night, the island burned brightly. To the locals on the mainland, it looked as if El Diablo had opened the gates of hell one last time.

It was the screaming that brought Chang back to consciousness; the terrified cries of people being hunted and devoured in the jungle.

He sat up and felt the pain across the side of his face and found that his vision on that side was gone. His fingers touched the burnt skin and he winced. Even with all his self-control, and Chang had become a master of self-control, he still felt the pain caused by the fire that had disfigured his face. He turned and became aware of the inferno in the distance. Even at this distance, he could feel the heat emanating from the blaze.

He stared at the scene of chaos around him. His Master would never have allowed this. Something must have gone drastically wrong. And it was in that moment that he knew that Caravaggio, his Master, was dead.

Chang took a moment to compose himself, said a silent prayer for his former mentor and began to walk up to the blazing villa. He would find his Master and bury his bones. It was about respect, and the passing of the mantle from master to apprentice. It was the natural order of things.

Mr Chang would rise like a phoenix from the ashes of the inferno and would at last become his own master. He had knowledge, he had skills, he had inherited the contacts from Caravaggio. He would take on the role of freelance assassin for whoever was rich enough to pay him. He would be a success.

And who knew how fate worked? Maybe one day, in the fullness of time, he would have the chance of revenge against the killers of his former Master – the Gorilla, the woman Nikita. One day.... Yes, one day.

Chapter Twenty-Four

The Mediterranean - two months later

You would have spotted them at some point if you had been a member of what the glossy magazines and gossip columnists of the social elite referred to as the 'Jet-Set'.

Regardless of their apparent wealth and ability to pop up in all the *en vogue* locations of the rich, they did rather stand out, for several reasons. Most notably, they were discreet, which wasn't a phrase used often about the rich. Second, they had a quiet containment about them. Even the most nonchalant concierge couldn't fail to notice that they always had a quiet, concentrated look about them, almost as if they were constantly on the lookout for danger. And who knew? Perhaps they were. They wouldn't be the first, or last, wealthy couple who were concerned about being separated from their money, jewellery, or even liberty, at the hands of the criminal class.

But the thing that attracted the eye to them most was their physicality, their appearance. They kept themselves to themselves, certainly.

They were always polite and tipped well. He was the well-dressed Englishman, obviously a self-made millionaire. He was short and trim, but with the close-cropped hair of the professional bank robber.

His lady, by comparison, was tall and elegant, her shock of red hair styled in the latest fashion to enhance her designer wardrobe. American, but still *terribly* nice despite her nationality. Not loud, like some of Americans, but more refined than most of her compatriots. However, despite their radically different appearance, they complemented each other perfectly. They felt easy with each other's company and skin. And, of course, they were obviously very much in love. That was self-evident, even a blind man could see that.

Occasionally, the man could be seen seated on his hotel balcony; white briefs, sunglasses on, letting the warm sun soak into his taut body and staring out at the sea in deep concentration, smoking a Cohiba cigar. He would usually be joined by his lady in a silk sarong. They would sit together, talk, laugh, drink and then disappear inside to their suite for the afternoon. Well, the rich had the time for afternoon lovemaking, didn't they?

Of an evening, when they dined in the best restaurants of their current favoured location, they would walk into the old town, hand in hand, lost in each other's words and senses. They glided through their adventures together, a universe of two stars.

And then, after they had exhausted themselves in their vacation destination, they would be gone, with no notice. They would disappear and fly out to the next exotic location… and the next… and the next.

Well, of course, the rich could afford to do that, couldn't they?

Following the hit on Caravaggio's island, Gorilla Grant and Eunice Brown had had enough.

They were both seasoned enough operators to recognise that they were burned out after their recent operations together, and both agreed that contracts, the spooks and the whole bloody lot of them could get lost for a month or two. They had decided to travel and get away from the stench of their working lives and enjoy each other, as new lovers do.

And they *were* lovers, lovers of a romantic grandeur and on an epic scale. Sardinia, Milan, Athens… they travelled far and wide, staying in the best hotels and making love all day in the best suites. They were insatiable.

"Can I ask you something?" she said, holding him as they lay entwined in another faceless hotel on a hot sunny day in Palma, Spain. They had been in bed all afternoon and probably wouldn't move until evening.

"Of course," he said, cupping one of her perfect breasts in his hand and playing softly with it.

"On the island. Caravaggio. How did you beat him? What happened in the jungle?"

He sighed, reached over and kissed her nipple and then thought back to that night of terror in the jungle. After a long while, he finally spoke.

"I knew that I wasn't able to beat him head-on. Remember, I had been tortured, half starved and disorientated. I was in no shape to take on a man with the skills of Caravaggio. I was almost out of bullets… and then I remembered something that the South African had said in Tenerife."

"What was that?"

"Remember, he said that if you wanted to beat The Master, then you would have to play to his ego. That it would be his downfall. So I was exhausted, low on ammo, in unfamiliar terrain… I was almost done. So then I reasoned, why not let him think he has won? Give him what he craves. After all, my mission was meant to be a redaction, not a fair fight duel. So I let him think that he had killed me.

"I draped the dead body of a jaguar that I had killed over my shoulders, so that I was carrying it on my back. I had already dressed it in my shirt and jacket. I held it in such a way that, at that distance, the head of jaguar would look like my head. Christ, that big cat weighed a ton!

But it was enough of a similarity in the darkness to make Caravaggio take the inevitable headshot, obviously thinking it was mine.

"I was lucky. He could have missed and hit me for real. I dropped both myself and the big cat and then kicked it down into the crocodile pit while I hid on a ledge out of sight. The most dangerous thing was hoping that Caravaggio wouldn't miss when he took a shot at me. Every assassin wants that fatal headshot. It played up to his sense of invincibility and false superiority. It caused him to relax and lower his guard. Once that was done, he was mine for the taking."

She lay silent against his chest for a long time, running over his words in her head. Finally, she said, "We are connected, Jack. You know that, don't you?"

"Connected how? Apart from the obvious," he said, staring down at their naked bodies, legs wrapped around each other, inside the bed.

She smiled that sad smile of hers and Grant thought she looked even more beautiful. "We can think like each other, we know when something is wrong with the other... we are compatible. We would make a hell of a team. I've never had that connection before with anyone," she said.

"In our line of work, it can be dangerous. Slows you down, weakens you, makes you vulnerable," he replied gruffly.

She shrugged. "Maybe. But not in our case. I don't think we would put ourselves in a position like that. I'd rather shoot myself in the head than take you down, Jack."

Grant had stared at her for a moment, etching her face on his memory, then he had kissed her and they had made slow love for the rest of the afternoon. When they had finished, Eunice always rose from the bed and brought him a drink. He liked that. No woman he had ever been with had ever done that after sex.

Over the coming weeks, Grant kept on returning to that conversation on a regular basis, running it around in his head... trying to decipher what she was telling him. That was Eunice's way. Every story had to have a hidden message and, dimwit that he was, sometimes he had to play catch-up to try to figure it all out. He got it, most of the time.

When they weren't being lovers or seeing the sights, they were eating and drinking at the best bars and restaurants in their current exotic location. They seemed determined to make a hole in the cash fund that they had recently inherited, which, even after their recent acquisitions, was still quite substantial, and enjoy themselves in the process. It was rare that they went off and did their own things separately, even for just a few hours.

But it did happen... occasionally.

On a whistle-stop tour to Lisbon, Eunice said that she would like to take a stroll down to the market at the far end of town. Grant had risen from his slumber and offered to come with her, but she had gently pushed him back down to sleep with a kiss.

"I'll just stretch my legs, I won't be long. Get some rest for... *later*. For when I get back," she said, in that suggestive drawl that drove him wild.

So Grant had slept and Eunice had gone off for an hour. There was nothing to it... and he had pushed it from his mind. She had returned looking distant and a little pensive, but only for a few moments and then her normal laid-back southern self had returned.

Several days later, just as they were getting ready to leave Lisbon, Grant did his usual routine of calling in to Sassi. It was standard procedure for a contract agent, at least every few weeks. He found a street telephone kiosk, made sure he wasn't being watched and then pumped in the necessary coins. He dialled the phone number and heard the clicks as the tracing tool was initiated somewhere in the bowels of the French Intelligence service, ready to record the conversation.

Then the voice that he knew came on the line. Sassi.

"*Allo?*"

"It's Gorilla."

"Ah... enjoying your vacation still, I see. Lisbon. Beautiful. I have not been there for many years."

"Actually, we are getting ready to leave and head over on the ferry to Tangier."

"Even better! Thank you for the recent parcel. Our superiors are very happy with the information that you recovered."

Gorilla nodded. As soon as they had made it back to the Mexican mainland following the hit on the island, Gorilla and Eunice had passed the American and French 'Caravaggio files' to their respective parent services, namely the CIA and SDECE Head of Stations in Mexico City.

"You are very welcome. I am glad to have been of help. Do you have something for me, Paul?"

"We do. A little job, just a little tidying up of loose ends."

"Okay, I'm listening. When?"

"Soon as you can… although I don't think you are going to like it."

"Why not?"

Then the French intelligence officer told him and Gorilla thought that his world had suddenly come crashing down around him in flames.

Chapter Twenty-Five

Casa Rouge Hotel, Tangier, North Africa

The suite was exquisite. It had a panoramic view of the city, en suite and silk sheets on the bed. Every amenity, even champagne on tap, could be arranged for an exorbitant fee. It was the finest that money could buy in North Africa. The Casa Rouge was the best hotel in the city.

It was also a hell of a place for a hit.

This was the final leg of their vacation. They both knew it, both felt it and thoughts of what was to come were hurting them both inside. The bell boy had carried their cases up the grand staircase from the main reception to their honeymoon suite on the top floor. It seemed that the Casa Rouge didn't do elevators. It was old school.

Gorilla had tipped the bellboy well and ushered him through the door, while Eunice had breezed around the rooms, inspecting and admiring their new home for the next day or so.

When she heard the hotel door close, she had stepped forward into her lover's arms and kissed him tenderly. They placed their cases down on opposite sides of the bed. There was a gentle click as each of them opened their respective suitcases.

There before each of them, nestled among the clothes, lay the weapons that had been provided for them for their respective contracts. They were both semi-automatics. Eunice's was a 9mm Walther, Gorilla's was his ASP. Getting the guns past the security checks on the ferry terminal had been laughably easy for both of them. They hadn't even had to bribe anyone. The wealthy-looking couple had been waved though without a second glance.

They both looked up from their cases and smiled. Sadness for both of them, longing tinged with regret. Even at this late stage of the game, both of them hoped that their love for each other would override what was expected of them, what they were being paid to do.

They both knew what was coming. After all, they were connected... they could, at times, think as one.

Gorilla thought she looked beautiful in the slim, above-the-knee cocktail dress, her red hair tied back in a simple pony-tail. For her part, Eunice took him in... shorter than her, slim, cropped white-blond hair, his new sunglasses and the suit and tie that she had picked out for him the previous day at a designer boutique. They looked like a couple who had 'made it' in life; wealthy, confident, respectable.

They fumbled with the items in their suitcases in an act of casual theatre and then, as if sensing a hidden signal, they moved simultaneously, both reaching quickly for their respective weapons. All attempts at deception were now gone, their training taking over.

A grasp and then the guns were up, Eunice's held in a two-handed grip and Gorilla using his single left hand, both steady and professional. Each weapon pointed at the other party. Their eyes locked. Sadness in hers, sorrow in his, tears in both.

"Don't do this, Jack. It doesn't have to end like this. We can figure it out," she said, a tremor in her voice.

They both stood stock still like statues, fingers on triggers, ready, with only the width of the bed separating them. They didn't need the 'why' and the 'how' about who had given the go-ahead for the kill orders. They had both been in this business long enough to know that it didn't matter. Their respective employers, the CIA and the SDECE, had each decided to remove the other team's contract agents, no loose ends allowed, and what better way than to have them take each other out?

But really, all that counted was the here and now and who would fire first.

They saw each other well.

"I know what they asked you to do to me," she said. "Take out the opposition, the loose ends. I know because the CIA asked me to do the same to you. But that's not me, Jack, you know that. I'd rather take myself out than have you be forced to do it. Baby, listen to me. Us, you and me, together, I meant every word I said."

They smiled. There was nothing more to be said.

Their fingers were poised on the triggers in that beautiful moment when they could either end it all completely, or risk it all and fight for each other against a combined enemy. In the end, it was Eunice who ended the stalemate; she was always the stronger of the two, the more confident. The look in her eyes said it all as she put her weapon away.

Gorilla did the same.

She looked at him with tears rolling down her cheeks and her voice was full of emotion when she said, "Baby, let's get out of here and not do this today. We are so much better than this."

"I love you, Eunice," he said, holding out his arms to her. She stepped forward and they embraced.

"I love you, Jack."

Chapter Twenty-Six

At first, there was nothing. No contact with their respective parent agencies. No sightings. No secure communication from either party. No confirmation that one contractor had taken out the other contractor. What's more, there were no dead bodies. The intelligence bureaucrats gave it a week, then maybe two more, just to be certain. But still nothing. No corpses meant no hit had taken place.

Then slowly, there was a hint of a rumour here and there. A sighting by an agent in Cyprus of a honeymoon couple; him short and tough, her tall, slender and red-headed. A watch was put on as many known associates as possible. So evidently they were not dead, not redacted... both very much still alive. And together! The spies soon came to the very annoying realisation that their two contract agents had decided to ignore direct orders; they had gone rogue.

The Kill order went out: **ROGUE WOLF STATUS/REDACTION IMPLEMENTATION**.

Telex machines, phones, dead drops and agent-to-agent meetings were hurriedly put in place with as many known contractors, hitters, and mercenaries as could be found and trusted. A Belgian hit man from the Congo was alerted; a Japanese Yakuza who occasionally did the odd throat-slitting for the intelligence services; a Corsican gunman who was handy with the odd contract killing; a former OSS agent who was not averse to taking on a temporary kill contract; and a dozen more of similar ilk.

All of them had their own skills and experience and, while even the agent runners recognised that none of them were in the league of Gorilla Grant and Nikita Brown, they felt sure that sooner or later, the errant pair would slip up and take a bullet in the back of the head.

Wouldn't they? I mean, it was only a matter of time and opportunity? Wasn't it? Well, they damned well hoped so.

So the spies set their tame killers loose and waited for the inevitable. They didn't have to wait long.

A week later, the body of a sixty-year-old former OSS agent, and now retired 'businessman' who did the odd job for the CIA, was found washed up on a beach on the Costa del Sol, Spain. The cause of death, two 9mm rounds to the chest and an execution round to the head. It was an inauspicious start to the CIA/SDECE Redaction operation.

Over the following weeks, the Yakuza contract killer was found shot to death in his favourite Sushi Bar. After that, the word soon got out that the kill contract really just wasn't worth the time or effort. 'Too risky' was the general consensus by the freelance community.

Exactly one week later, two letters were delivered to two intelligence officials on opposite sides of the Atlantic. The first was to Theodore Gibbs, Operations Director of a CIA front company named EXIS in Washington. The second was to Major Paul Sassi at the SDECE's Action Service station in Paris. They were in plain envelopes. The postmark indicated the origin as somewhere in Asia. A single typed sheet of paper was inside each.

Gibbs had just sat down at his desk when his secretary came in with the morning mail. It was the usual sealed packets from Langley, internal memos and the odd communiqué.

Several hours later, Major Paul Sassi would do the same thing.

The letters read:

We have destroyed the rest of the Caravaggio File. The risk to the networks is gone.

For the record, we quit.

We have decided that we are stronger together than we are apart.

Send more people after us and we will send them back to you in body bags.

It was the final warning from Eunice 'Nikita' Brown and Jack 'Gorilla' Grant.

THE END

Dear reader,

We hope you enjoyed reading *Rogue Wolves*. Please take a moment to leave a review in Amazon, even if it's a short one. Your opinion is important to us.

Discover more books by James Quinn at
https://www.nextchapter.pub/authors/james-quinn-british-espionage-thriller-author

Want to know when one of our books is free or discounted for Kindle? Join the newsletter at http://eepurl.com/bqqB3H

Best regards,

James Quinn and the Next Chapter Team

A Message from James Quinn

Rogue Wolves is my most personal book. It is personal in so many ways, some of which I am happy to tell you about and some that I can barely tell to myself, let alone my readers.

The theme of *Rogue Wolves* is that of obsession. For Caravaggio, it is the obsession to be the best in the business. For Eunice, it is the obsession to play by her own rules. For Gorilla, it is to hunt down a dangerous man whatever the cost. Out of all of them, I can associate with Gorilla's obsession the best.

I have spent most of my adult life tracking people. Some of these have been 'bad' people, some have been just misguided and in bad situations. Out of all of these jobs, one specifically stands out.

I once spent the best part of two years tracking a man down, trying to gather intelligence and information on him. This man was good at hiding, good at spreading false information. He was almost a ghost, a spectre.

Somewhere in that two years, it went from being a job that I had to do, to becoming (almost) an obsession to find him and discover who he was.

I tracked him across the globe over many different countries and, from each source, I got a different perspective on this person. When I finally discovered what I needed and found out who he was, the man (the 'target', in the terminology of our trade) was already long dead. It was a bittersweet moment. Good because I had closure to the operation, bad because I couldn't look him in the eye and say, "After every-thing – all the lies, the travel, the false leads, the buying of informants and sources… all of that – I found you."

That period of my life gave me the inspiration for the *Rogue Wolves* story and Gorilla's hunt for Caravaggio.

I also like to think of *Rogue Wolves* as my 'American book'. America without a doubt is a country of extremes, both good and bad. *Rogue Wolves* was born in the heart of the USA and my visits, and knowing the people of this great country, have had an influence on the characters and locations.

People always ask writers what other works of fiction inspire their stories. So let me tell you here, and with full disclosure, that if you are looking for the literary influence for *Rogue Wolves*, I can direct you towards Joseph Conrad's *Heart of Darkness*, mainly for its searching nature of a man being drawn towards his nemesis.

The other work is, of course, a Bond story. For someone of my generation, Ian Fleming's works had a deep-rooted effect and one of my favourite Bond books is the much underrated, and not universally loved, *The Man with the Golden Gun*. I love this book (incidentally, I have a very rare first edition copy – but that's another story). I have taken it all over the world with me and love the idea of two gunmen going up against each other.

So, if you are looking for reference points for *Rogue Wolves*, I would point you in the direction of both books.

Fundamentally though, *Rogue Wolves* is a fledgling love story between two lost people – Eunice Brown and Gorilla Grant - who just happen to be in the same profession. They are two sides of the same coin, who have gone through terror, hardship and overwhelming odds and, despite all of that, have still found love with each other.

They are, I believe, soulmates.

James Quinn
USA
2017

Acknowledgements

Life is, in my not so humble opinion, made up of a series of wonderful experiences and the people that add to those experiences and make them happen are just as important. That's what I truly believe. So, some thank-yous to some fantastic people who have helped with *Rogue Wolves*. They are, in no particular order:

Sgt Stephen Ertel, US Army, for letting me have the full Mustang experience in and around Fayetteville and Fort Bragg, North Carolina. I am forever in your debt Sir.

To my writer friends **Marnie Cate** and **Mike Stern**, who are always there with support and good advice. I would recommend that you check out their works. They are both fantastic authors and wonderful people.

The Creative team at **Next Chapter Publishing**, who always do a fantastic job.

To **Graham Blackhall**, who nudged me in the direction of Tenerife and the *Presa Canario* breed when I had hit a wall in the story. Graham and I have only ever met the one time (on that occasion we actually spent a day knife-fighting!!!). However, I think we should go for a second shot at a meeting and maybe have a beer or two? Knives are optional...

To **Steve** and **Dan** (my own personal "Q" Section), for pointing me in the direction of the ASP when Gorilla needed a new 'shooter'. I think it fits him perfectly. Thank you, guys.

To my beautiful **Lulu**, who as ever ALWAYS writes the last line of all my books, and to my little 'Gorilla' **Jack**, who inspires me in everything that he does. You are my world and I love you both completely
xxx

About the Author

James Quinn is the author of the Gorilla Grant spy novels. He works as a freelance security consultant, bodyguard and private investigator. He has spent nearly two decades in the secret world of covert surveillance, undercover operations and international security.

He is trained in hand-to-hand combat and in the use of a variety of weaponry including small-edged weapons. He is also a crack pistol shot for CQB (Close Quarter Battle) and many of his experiences he has incorporated into his works of fiction.

He lives in the United Kingdom and the USA.

You might also like:

Gorilla Warfare by James Quinn

To read first chapter for free, head to:
https://www.nextchapter.pub/books/gorilla-warfare

Manufactured by Amazon.ca
Bolton, ON

36764871R00143